THE GRIM PIG

BOOKS BY CHARLES GORDON

The Governor General's Bunny Hop
At the Cottage
How to Be Not Too Bad
The Canada Trip

THE GRIM PIG

Charles Gordon

National Library of Canada Cataloguing in Publication Data

Gordon, Charles, 1940-
The grim pig

"A Douglas Gibson book".
ISBN 0-7710-3397-4 (bound). – ISBN 0-7710-3399-0 (pbk.)

I. Title.

PS8563.O8354G74 2001   C813'.54   C00-933019-4
PR9199.3.G618G74 2001

We acknowledge the financial support of the Government of Canada through
the Book Publishing Industry Development Program for our publishing
activities. We further acknowledge the support of the Canada Council for the
Arts and the Ontario Arts Council for our publishing program.

This is a work of fiction. Characters, places, and events
are the creation of the author's imagination.

Typeset in Bembo by M&S, Toronto
Printed and bound in Canada

A Douglas Gibson Book

McClelland & Stewart Ltd.
The Canadian Publishers
481 University Avenue
Toronto, Ontario
M5G 2E9
www.mcclelland.com

1 2 3 4 5   06 05 04 03 02

For Lew Whitehead and Christopher Young
 – real newspapermen

THE GRIM PIG

Chapter 1

The first thing they told me at the treatment centre was stop being cynical. That would be a tough one, maybe even tougher than giving up the drink, although giving up the drink seemed pretty hard at that particular time. Give up the drink and give up being cynical.

Five years later and sober, I was sitting in a room full of newspaper guys and trying not to be cynical, when the new editor walked in to address the troops for the first time. Gladys Bushel from the lifestyles department actually stood up when the editor walked in, but the rest of us just sat there. Newspaper guys – anything could happen and we would just sit there. If Jesus arrived, we would just sit there. Some of us would criticize his clothes. Nobody wears sandals any more. We pride ourselves that we have seen it all.

The new editor had on sandals, in fact, and grey socks, grey slacks, a brown jacket, a green shirt that looked sort of Hawaiian, and a black tie, with a big knot. Actually, it's just as well I'm not cynical any more, because I'm not sure what a cynic would say about that, particularly the sandals. "Stylish," said my friend Davis, the business editor.

"Wait," I said.

"Sorry," she said, remembering negativity is not supposed to be good for me. She is very loyal to me, even though she knows I am bad for conversations at the big table in the cafeteria, which are snide and gossipy and cynical. At the big table, they try to be positive when I'm around, which makes the chatter sort of dry up. Sometimes Davis and I avoid that by going down the road to eat in the food court at the Grand Valley Mall. I like to think that makes people talk, but she says it doesn't.

The conference room of the *Grand Valley World-Beacon* is a big, squarish room, with windows. When announcements are made to the staff, which is hardly ever, they are made here. Otherwise, the room is made available free of charge for figure skating association annual meetings, rotisserie league drafts, and craft sales. Most of the big announcements, including Fred's appointment as the new editor, are made on the bulletin board in the newsroom. More and more frequently, they are made by e-mail.

Now here was Fred, shuffling to the front of the room, head down, hands in his pockets, preoccupied. He stopped at the easel with the giant pad of paper on it and pulled a grease pencil out of his brown jacket. He scribbled something on the pad that we couldn't see because he was blocking it. Then he whirled to face us.

"Destiny," he said, his eyes flashing, or at least his glasses.

"DESTINNY," said the paper.

There was a muffled laugh from the back of the room where the entertainment department people were sitting. Bad spelling could amuse them. Davis raised an eyebrow at me. I pretended not to notice.

For most of us "destiny" was the first word we'd heard from Fred. In a week here, he had spoken to none of us. He kept his office dark, the blinds drawn. Occasionally strangers could be seen coming out; no one was ever seen going in.

Fred stopped to let the word sink in. It was a high-pitched word, the way it came out, surprisingly so, given Fred's size and reputation.

"Destiny," he said again. "That's what our readers want. They want to be connected with their destiny. They need a sense of how their lives intersect with the final things in our existence, the spirits that will accompany them on their next journeys, as well as the sprites and demons they meet in their everyday comings and goings."

"I told you he was a genius," whispered Lawrie Andrews, the sportswriter, from behind us.

"Mmmm," said Davis.

Fred paced a few paces. Then stopped in front of the easel. He turned and tore off the DESTINNY piece of paper, laying it carefully on a table.

Then he wrote another word and stepped aside.

"HELL-O," it said.

Davis nudged me. "Hyphenated?" she whispered.

"Maybe now," I whispered back.

"Hello," Fred said.

"Hello," said Alexei Ponomarev, the *World-Beacon*'s Russian-born cartoonist, who was still finding his way around the language and didn't realize that Fred's hello was rhetorical, I think.

"Hello," said Dick Rivers, the Tri-Lakes Area's best-loved columnist.

Fred ignored them. "People sometimes tell me that I don't say hello enough," he went on. "I get caught up in my thoughts about making the human drama more compelling and forget to say hello. Please stop by my office, any of you, and say hello and I'll say hello to you. Being here for me, being able to give a new direction to this newspaper is really a . . ."

He paused, shook his head, paced, then stopped and looked out at us, as if waiting. I felt the first stirrings of a cynical thought.

For a moment, the room was silent, then Gladys Bushel, who always broke the silences in these meetings, raised her hand. Fred smiled at her. It wasn't quite a smile, but his teeth showed.

"Fred," she said, "when you were talking a minute ago about sprites and demons, that was a metaphor, wasn't it?"

Fred waved his hand and showed his teeth again, then walked back to the easel. He picked up the grease pencil, paused, then put it down. Then he picked it up again and underlined HELL-O. Then he put it down again and turned toward us.

"Instead of sprites and demons, we give our readers the clichéd agenda story. How does that help them — all these thousands of words about school boards and hospital boards and Parliament and hockey teams? Meetings, meetings, meetings," he said and picked up the grease pencil.

"MEETINGS," he wrote, spelling it correctly.

"Good one," somebody muttered from the general direction of the entertainment department. Davis nudged me again. I stared straight ahead.

"Where is the adventure of everyday life?" Fred asked, staring out the window at the employee parking lot. We all stared out the window. Although we were barely into April, the snow was gone, and one of the assistant managing editors, the one that nobody knew what he did, was going home early again.

"People are wanting the adventure of daily life and we are giving them meetings. This won't do. We must challenge our readers, take them with us into exciting worlds of travel and romance and fine cloth."

Another hand went up. Fred pointed and showed his teeth.

"Fred," asked Pete Lester, one of the rewrite people, "do you think they'll be adding to the size of the parking lot? Because if you work an afternoon shift, like I used to do, by the time you get to the office . . ."

Fred waved his hand again and Pete stopped.

"What is your name?" he asked.

"Pete Lester."

Fred walked to the board and picked up the grease pencil. We held our breath. He folded over the last piece of paper and underlined the word "HELL-O" again.

"Hello, Pete," he said.

Pete nodded gravely.

"Pete," Fred continued, "we're going to embark on a great crusade together. What do you cover, Pete?"

"I do rewrite," Pete said. Fred turned the page and found the word "MEETINGS" then turned another page. "RERIGHT," he wrote.

"Actually," said Pete, "I do a lot of accidents – you know, bus plunges, some fender-benders."

Fred brightened. "BUS PLUNGERS," he wrote.

"Now we're getting somewhere," he said. "Don't mind my spelling," he added, showing his teeth again. "There are so many more important things in life's daily adventure."

He paced again, staring at his sandals. "What do we think," he asked, looking up, "what do we think about when we think of bus plunges?"

There was a silence. The entertainment department was hushed. You could hear the squeak of the pen on Alexei Ponomarev's pad. Dick Rivers raised his hand but Fred ignored him.

"Buses," someone said at last.

"Good," said Fred. "What else."

"Plungers?" said Lawrie Andrews.

Fred turned over a new sheet, looked back at us and did that smilish thing with his teeth. "Words that sing," he said. "Words that sing. You all know the poet John Milton, I'm sure."

We all nodded and Fred wrote "JOHN MILTIN" on the next sheet of paper.

"You remember how he wrote '*He who of those delights can judge, and spare / To interpose them oft, is not unwise.*'"

We all nodded again, some of us a bit too quickly. Lawrie Andrews said: "How true." Davis made a muffled sound and I shook my head at her.

"That is what Milton was talking about – the bus plunges, great and small, that make up the adventure of our daily lives." He flipped back a sheet, underlined "BUS PLUNGERS," then walked out of the room.

There was silence as we all waited for a moment to see if he was coming back, then a buzz of conversation. Davis and I stood up.

"Soooo," she said.

"Interesting start," I said. "Notice how he just started right in, without saying 'good morning' or anything?"

"Yes," Davis said. "What does that mean?"

"I don't know. I think it means he won't be like the others."

"And is that good?"

"It's different. Nobody said different was bad, necessarily."

Chapter 2

The buzz carried down the hallway as we headed, past the publisher's office, past advertising and circulation, back to the newsroom.

"Did you hear something about cloth?"

"When was that?"

"It was after compelling human drama and just before avoiding the clichéd agenda story."

"I heard that, but I thought it was around the time of words that sing."

"No, words that sing was earlier, in the part about the adventure of everyday lives."

"I think he's a genius. Did you notice his eyes?"

"Never mind his eyes. What was that about cloth?"

"He didn't say cloth. He couldn't have said cloth. He must have said . . . what, sloth? Maybe it was avoiding sloth."

"Moth. Did he ever do stuff about moths when he was in Victoria?"

"No. There was a sixteen-part series about bats."

"This wasn't bats. It was cloth."

"Cloth? How could it be cloth? What's cloth got to do with newspaper stories?"

"His eyes were just flashing. Maybe we should do stories about cloth. Nobody's ever done stories about cloth. Maybe our readers need that and they haven't been telling us."

"It wasn't cloth. It couldn't have been. Broth?"

"Stories about soup. Didn't he win an award for that?"

"No, that was the thing on finger bowls."

"A sixteen-part series on finger bowls."

"Just twelve, I think."

"Goth."

"Froth."

"Moth."

"We already said that."

"Wrath."

"Huh?"

"Like the grapes of . . ."

"You don't pronounce it that way."

"I think he does. I hear we're going to have British spelling and put the Mr. and Mrs. back in the stories."

"Oh shit."

"We can't do that. Christ, we'll be running corrections every day about Ms. Jones is really Mrs. Jones and Mrs. Smith is really Miss Smith and the *World-Beacon* regrets the error."

"In Victoria, all the deskers had to learn the proper British titles for second reference."

"Great. The *World-Beacon* regrets that Sir Rodney is really Earl Rodney."

"Looks like we're getting British hyphenation too."

"Maybe it *was* cloth."

"Troth. That's it. The institution of marriage."

"I hear he's against marriage. There was a big campaign in the Lakehead. For weeks they ran articles about how marriage makes people more vulnerable to colds and gall bladder attacks."

"That's brilliant. See. We never do things like that. Just politics, politics, politics."

"Voth."

"What's Voth?"

"I don't know. I was just trying it. Woth. Yoth. Zoth. It has to be cloth."

"So we have a new editor who wants more news about cloth."

"Nothing wrong with fashion."

"I don't think that's what he meant."

C h a p t e r 3

The good thing about having new owners was that it made for a lot of farewell parties. We wouldn't have had any parties otherwise. That's what the newspaper business has come to: Everybody's older, nobody drinks after work, everybody has families and goes home to them.

You can get them out for a farewell party, however, and a lot of people had been leaving. Those of us left had been seeing quite a bit of each other socially. This was preferable, we all knew, to seeing people outside the business. We wouldn't know what to say to them. We spend all day every day in the newsroom with other journalists, except when we are in the outside world, where we are with other journalists. Contact with real people, civilians, is ritualized and severely limited, less than that experienced by bartenders or evangelists.

We keep in touch with the outside world through the wire services, which come in on computer. The databases are there for further research. So is the Internet. All-news channels play on newsroom television sets all day and all night. We sit there in the newsroom and watch the world. Going out would be a good idea, but parking is a problem.

As usual, a kind of black comedy had developed around the farewell parties. After the first two left, the first two being the editor and the managing editor, we began giving everybody the same cake, a two-layer thing made up to look like a computer screen. On the cake it said "GOOD LUCK, NAME GOES HERE," a reference to the way headlines are set up on our pagination system. The bakery could crank one out in half an hour.

Not having a family to delay my arrival, I arrived early for Lydia Byrd's going-away party, bearing the usual large plastic bottle of ginger ale for my personal consumption. There were already a few people there, drinking red wine out of plastic glasses and bitching half-heartedly about bad headlines and stupid assignments. The bitching would become more sincere later on as the wine kicked in and heightened everyone's sense of journalistic outrage.

I waved at Davis who was involved in what looked like a serious discussion with Tony Frusculla, the young business writer she had just hired. I found Lydia, who was wearing something slinky and black, and offered a light hug. She offered a heavy one in return.

"Parker MacVeigh," she said. "I'm really glad you're here. I was afraid you weren't going to make it."

That was odd. No one had said anything about me not making it. "I wouldn't miss it, Lydia," I said.

Lydia was probably forty-five, only a few years younger than me, and you could still see how cute she must have been when she started out. As she walked off to put my ginger ale in the fridge and get herself another glass of wine, I took a long look at her, something I hadn't really done up to now, but that hug had me thinking. What with one thing and another, it had been a long time. Divorced guy, single mom – this kind of thing probably happened all the time, although it hadn't been happening to me a whole lot. With the amount of concentration it took to not drink and the extra amount of concentration it took not to be cynical, there hadn't been a lot of concentration left over.

I started to follow Lydia into the kitchen but was stopped by Hugh Robbins, one of my colleagues on the news desk. "Hi Parker," he said. "Looks like the white stuff is history."

After years of processing the raw material of life into the cliché of newspaper headlines, Hugh talked like that. Snow was white stuff.

"Well," I said, "it sure makes the driving easier."

"That's true," he said, "but you know, I almost had a fender-bender on the way over here."

"No kidding," I said, looking past him to the kitchen door, from which Lydia was emerging, carrying a glass of red wine.

"It's true," he said. "This senior citizen in a late-model car came careering around the corner and a collision was narrowly averted."

I patted him on the shoulder. "Glad you didn't become a statistic, Hugh," I said, and walked past him into the kitchen for my first ginger ale of the evening.

As these things went, the party was quite well attended. Twenty or so people stood and sat around Jane Liu's apartment, watching Lydia get quietly drunk. Lydia had been at the *World-Beacon* for fifteen years, had worked in several departments of the newsroom, and had a lot of friends. They had watched her slowly work her way up, suffered with her when her marriage came apart, perhaps under the pressure of all the shift work she'd been forced to do.

Some of those friends were on the nightside and wouldn't arrive for a couple of hours. The usual routine was to hold off the cake and the presentations until they arrived, but it didn't look like that would work this time.

"What do you think about the cake?" Jane asked me, about 10:30.

"Is she planning to make a speech?"

"She told me she was," Jane said.

"Uh-oh," I said.

Davis saw us conferring and came over. "You thinking presentation now?" she asked.

"She really wants to make a speech," Jane said. "If we wait too long . . ." She shrugged.

"On the other hand," I said, "it could be a speech we'll always remember."

"We can't do that to her," Davis said.

"I know," I said.

"I'll get the cake," Jane said.

In a couple of minutes she brought it out, yelled for attention, and started the formal part of the evening, the one we had all got to know so well.

This one was more tense than usual, partly because most people knew Lydia had actually been fired and partly for the usual reason – that our group had come to contain a number of loyalists to the new regime, who did not find it amusing to hear it ridiculed and might, it was suspected, report back on those who had laughed the loudest.

The prime suspect, as always, was Lorne Marshall, an assistant city editor who was thriving under Fred, after an extremely uneventful career as a reporter. Davis, who worked near Fred's office, reported that Lorne made the journey into the office several times a day, often carrying an extra cup of coffee, and almost always emerged smiling.

On the day Lydia's resignation was announced, Lorne came out of Fred's office whistling.

But he wasn't the only one. There seemed to be more at each going-away party. I could see the signs – eyes averted when comic reference was made to Fred's spelling or his darkened office, a whispered and somewhat apologetic suggestion that the paper might be getting a little bit better under the new guys.

Well, far be it from me. I didn't much like how the *World-Beacon* was changing and I hated to see people like Lydia go, especially the way she was looking in that dress. She was a pretty good writer and she had struggled for years to get to the point where she was writing editorials, working regular hours at last, able to spend predictable hours with her children. It was shitty what happened to her. But office politics were not for me, not now.

Jane did her diplomatic best with the presentation. "Lydia," she said, when the party buzz had finally stopped and she had everyone's attention, "we all envy you and admire your decision to start a new career. We wish you luck in Toronto and we can't wait to read your novel and, just in case you need help, we've put together a couple of things that might help you."

She reached behind the chesterfield and brought up some packages which Lydia dutifully opened. There was a thesaurus, a John Grisham paperback, a few floppy disks stolen out of a newsroom supply cabinet, and a *World-Beacon* mouse pad. Finally, there was the mock page that was a staple of these occasions. This one was an editorial page, on which all the editorials were Lydia's, both the columns were Lydia's, all the letters to the editor were in praise of Lydia. All were on the same theme, Lydia's favourite theme, poverty. There was a big headline: LYDIA BYRD WINS NOBEL PRIZE. The editorial cartoon was about poverty too. Alexei Ponomarev had drawn the Grim Reaper, one of the first cartoon symbols he had learned since coming over from the former Soviet Union ten years ago. The Reaper was holding out an upturned baseball cap.

After the applause had stopped, Lydia held up the page and looked at it. "Well," she said, "this is fucking cheery."

Laughing seemed the best thing to do.

"I know you guys have always thought it was funny that I got sort of obsessed about poor people," Lydia continued. "But it's just the way I am. I'm sorry. My parents were poor and I wasn't exactly rich myself when that asshole took off and left me with three kids and a job on the night education beat."

We laughed again, as if this had been a witty thing to say, and to encourage her to say something light.

"So that's why I wrote about it all the time. And they hated it, this new crowd of idiots. They wanted me to write about new diseases and stuff on the Internet and getting rid of speed limits and why French wine costs too much. And I kept writing about poverty and they canned me."

There was a gasp from those few who hadn't known. Lydia nodded her head vigorously, picked up her wine glass and drank.

"They canned my ass and now I can get more familiar with poverty again. I'm going to miss all you guys, with a couple of exceptions, and thank you for having this party and . . ."

And then she just wandered out of the room and collapsed in one of the bedrooms. Davis followed her in. Jane hurried over to the CD player and turned up the music. The rest of us lined up for cake, as we always did at this time of night.

The party had thinned out considerably. Lydia's speech had somehow reminded a number of people of promises they had made to their babysitters to be back early. By 11:30, the living room was virtually empty. There were only three serious drinkers in the newsroom, Alexei Ponomarev, who always wound up with the drinkers, but didn't understand what they said very well, Charlie McPartland, the old desker, and Chet Edgemar, the TV critic. They were over in a corner having the same argument they always had no matter whose going-away party it was.

"I still say it's goaltending," Charlie said.

"Yeah, but that's not what I was talking about," Chet said.

"Life is shit," Alexei said.

"Fuck you, Alexei," Charlie said.

Lorne Marshall sidled up to me and said hello. We munched cake in silence for awhile. "It's a shame," he said finally.

"It is," I agreed.

"She was a nice person," he said.

"Still is," I said.

"Very talented too," he said.

"I know."

"It's a shame," he said.

"Yes."

"She could have done really well," he said.

"You mean if they hadn't fired her."

Lorne looked at me. "I don't think they had any choice. She was stubborn. She had a one-track mind. She couldn't get her mind out of the past."

"I guess that's one way of looking at it," I said, then took a sip of ginger ale. It was my third of the night.

"Seriously," Lorne said, "do you think they had any choice?"

How badly did I want to win this argument, I wondered. What would be gained if I did?

"I'm going to see if they need help cleaning up," I said.

I went into the kitchen. Davis and Jane were sipping on one of the many opened bottles of wine, wiping counters and throwing paper plates into the garbage. Lydia was sitting at the kitchen table, drinking coffee and smiling a little while Jane and Davis competed with stories about newspapers they had worked for that were worse than the *World-Beacon*.

"OK," said Jane, "listen to this. Berlin Wall comes down and the headline in the *Herald-Express* is 'NEW WAL-MART SLATED FOR AREA.'"

"That's nothing," said Davis. "Nothing! At the *Courier-Times*, they get the news on the wire about the wall coming down and they send me out to interview a local construction guy about whether it could be rebuilt."

Lydia laughed.

"You may not believe this," I said, "but I'm a little older."

"No-o-o-o!" Davis said, in mock astonishment.

I continued. "It's 1970, I'm a part-time copy kid at the *Advance-Gazette* when Trudeau invokes the War Measures Act. The city editor looks for the local angle and sends me over to the chamber of commerce to find out if they anticipate an increase in tourism because nobody wants to go to Quebec."

"You can't be that old," Lydia said, as I sat down with her at the table.

"I'm not really," I said. "But if you talk about 1970, there's nobody around to disagree with you."

"Except Charlie McPartland."

"Yeah, but he's talking about goaltending right now."

"Goaltending," said Lydia. "I didn't know it was that late."

"It's not," I said. "I think he got an early start."

"So did I," Lydia said. "Listen, I need to talk to someone."

"OK," I said. "Want to go sit in the living room?"

Chet, Alexei, and Charlie continued their argument over in the corner, not paying any attention to Lydia and me as we sat on the chesterfield and Lydia sat a lot closer to me, I thought, than was normal under the circumstances. "I thought you might understand," she began.

One of the realities of a life in journalism is that you're always standing off to one side of events, looking in, analysing, keeping your emotions out of it. One of the curses of a life in journalism is that sometimes you find yourself doing the same thing in your own life, standing off to one side of it, observing objectively.

So it was on this chesterfield, with Lydia, while the sounds of the Buena Vista Social Club wafted quietly from the CD player and the sounds of "it's goaltending, you asshole!" wafted over from the corner. She looks great, a voice said in my head. She's not that drunk any more. Besides that, the last time you can remember is when you couldn't remember. She likes you. Look how close she's sitting. She's leaving town soon.

But there was another voice, too, and I had to cover both sides of the story. The other voice, the objective observer, said: But I don't really feel that strongly about her. And it's been so long and maybe I've forgotten how to do all this and I'm tired and what if. . . .

The objective observer sometimes contributed news stories and headlines about my life. NEWSMAN CELEBRATES SOBRIETY BY WATCHING HOCKEY GAME ON TV was a fairly frequent one.

". . . the first time you handled one of my editorials," she was saying, "and you were so sensitive and the changes you suggested were so right."

It was true, I guess. They used to give me the editorial page to paginate and once I caught a factual error in one of her editorials and asked her about it. After that, she would check some of her stuff with me and I would occasionally say something about the writing. Sensitive wasn't how I thought about it. It was just more fun doing that than laying out travel pages.

"You were – I mean are – a good writer," I said.

I didn't mean that as a come-on, but sometimes it works, with writers. She reached over and touched my cheek.

"I need a ride home," she said. "I don't think I should be driving. Could you drop me off, if it's not out of your way?"

It was way out of my way. "Of course," I said.

We went into the kitchen and said our goodbyes. Davis raised an eyebrow at me and I shrugged as innocently as I could. Jane gave me a large plate to carry, with about half of an unsliced cake on it.

On the way to the car, Lydia walked unsteadily and took my arm for support. At the car, she leaned on me while I dug through my pockets for the keys. I listened for the objective observer and heard nothing.

I drove out to the bypass, an Ella tape playing "They Can't Take That Away from Me." Lydia hummed along and I didn't say anything. I wasn't sure what I wanted to happen, but either way, saying something would be sure to spoil it.

"It's the next block, left, just after the light," she said.

I needed a minute to think about this. There was a Tim Hortons on the right.

"What about a coffee?" I said.

She looked startled. "There's coffee at my place," she said.

"Well," I said, wheeling into the parking lot, "I wouldn't want to put you to the trouble, and since we're here anyway . . ."

I got out of the car but Lydia showed no signs of moving. "Are you coming in?" I asked.

"No, just bring me something. Cream no sugar."

When I returned with two coffees, she had regained her exuberance. "What a great idea," she said, taking the hot cardboard cup.

"Thanks," I said, accepting her congratulations and thinking, I've just stopped to buy a takeout coffee two minutes away from the house of a woman who wants to seduce me. How many men would have thought of that?

We started up and Lydia reminisced amusingly about her years with the *WB* – the time the assignments got mixed up and she interviewed an Olympic bronze medallist, thinking he was a spinal injury victim and made a big fuss over him for walking across the restaurant; the time the new publisher arrived and demanded that the previous day's editorial against the construction of a new harbourfront complex be rewritten to favour it. Lydia as a new editorial writer had been given that assignment. "New facts have come to light," she had written.

She was just finishing that story when we reached her house, a newish bungalow on a newish street. "This is where I live," she said.

It was now or never. "Lydia," I said, smoothly unbuckling my seatbelt and, in one motion, putting my arms around her.

"Oh shit!" she said, as her coffee spilled all over the front of her dress.

"Let me help you with that," I said, searching the Toyota for something like a Kleenex. Finally I found an old *WB* interoffice memo in my jacket pocket. It announced the policy against taking interoffice memos out of the building. I offered it to her and watched, sipping my coffee, as she tried to repair the damage.

"I'm sorry," I said. "I should have known that . . ."

"Yes," she said. "I mean no. You couldn't have known that . . ."

"Well," I said.

"Um," she said. "Would you like to come in for a coffee?"

"Oh," I said. "I'd better not. I've just had one."

"You sure?" she said.

"Yes."

"Well," she said, giving me a peck on the cheek, "thanks for the ride."

"No problem," I said. "If I don't see you, have fun in Toronto."

Chapter 4

I'm not too clear on all the history of the *World-Beacon*. To be truthful, there isn't the sense of reverence here about the institution that would make us all bone up on the *WB*'s glorious past. There was the *World* and there was the *Beacon*, we all know that. They competed with each other late in the nineteenth century. One was Liberal and one was Conservative. They wrote completely one-sided stories about what crooks and brigands were on the other side, editorials denouncing the other paper's editorials as damnable lies, then they merged, it being good business to do so, and that was that. Thereafter, the *World-Beacon* supported the Liberals in some elections and the Tories in others. Whichever was best for Grand Valley, was the way the *World-Beacon* looked at it.

New technology has come to the *World-Beacon*. The composing room, where they used to bang the hot lead around, is almost gone now, because of the computers. There are a couple of guys left and every day they paste on the page numbers and the photographs. The rest of the page is done electronically by people like me. We move the stories around on our screens, make them fit, take out most of the typographical errors and some of the bad writing. Then we push a button and a little message comes up on the screen, saying, in effect, "Are you sure you want to do this?" I always stop there for a minute, impressed by the fact that whatever blame falls from this page will fall only upon me. Then I hit the RETURN key, signifying YES, and a few minutes later the entire page comes out of a machine in the composing room and either Orville or Smokey puts the page number on it.

For most of the century, the *World-Beacon* was just a newspaper like any other newspaper. It covered the war and the World Series and the devaluation of the dollar and the hemlines going up and down. It ran all the comic strips that weren't wrapped up by the big papers. We still have "Henry" and "Mandrake the Magician." Locally, the *WB* covered – very positively – decisions that were made by the railways. Those that resulted in hirings would boost Grand Valley's economy. Those that resulted in layoffs would increase the company's efficiency. We covered the tourist boat disaster of '57, when the *Miss Grand Valley* was hit by a waterskier at night and two people drowned. The waterskier herself miraculously survived to become a regular speaker at the service clubs, giving thanks for her life and the community's support and urging new laws against night waterskiing. Later, she would become our mayor and, soon after that, our ex-mayor.

We covered the Great Bypass Debate of '76, when it was decided that the Trans-Canada Highway would no longer go through the town. We covered – very positively – the arrival of the first suburban shopping mall in 1972. A few years later, we covered the various proposals brought forward by a number of consultants to revive the downtown area. We covered the fire that took down the Prince of Wales Hotel with miraculously no loss of life while it was up for sale in 1996.

We chronicled the rise of crime in the Tri-Lakes Area, including the first marijuana busts at the university, the dermatologist at the clinic who turned out to be a minor league outfielder from Kansas, and the sex scandal involving the suburban man who attempted to live off the avails of prostituting his wife, although, admittedly, she was not aware of it at the time. But he was kind of thinking out loud about it in the George Drew Room at the Prince of Wales one night and the police got wind of it and then the *World-Beacon* did, too.

By and large, the Tri-Lakes Area has been a peaceful place, although the *World-Beacon* would have you believe otherwise. The chief of police has accused us of exaggerating crime to sell newspapers, which he helps us to do when the police budget is up for consideration.

The name "Tri-Lakes Area" has not been around too long. The argument about the name is one of the first stories I remember from my time here. Somebody from the chamber of commerce went to the States on one of those highways meetings in the mid eighties and came back full of the need to give Grand Valley more of a name than it had. Every area is a tri-something down there and it looks enticing on the billboards, the chamber of commerce guy said. He was a buddy of our editor, two editors before Fred, and soon the *World-Beacon* was in on the act, editorially and in news coverage too, with interviews just about every day with local dignitaries – doctors, funeral directors, the member of Parliament and the coach of the junior hockey team, all of them saying that Grand Valley had gone long enough without receiving the recognition that was emblematic of being part of a Tri-Lakes Area.

There were a couple of people who protested, but they were the usual crowd, the Unitarian minister, a woman to boot, and some professors from the university, UGV. The Unitarian minister said Grand Valley shouldn't even be called Grand Valley, since there wasn't really a valley here, just a couple of lakes on one side and the hint of a hill on the other. Everybody figured it was a bit late to begin worrying about that. The professors pointed out that there were really twenty-three lakes in the Tri-Lakes Area, twenty-four if you counted one that was often called a pond, but was really quite large. They also noted that one of the lakes claimed as one of our tri was included in the Land of Eleven

Lakes advertised by Small Portage, our rival city just fifty kilometres down the Trans-Canada.

I can remember the *WB*'s vigorous response because it ran the day after my first day at the paper and I was responsible for laying out the editorial page. The editor decided that the editorial, which he had written himself, deserved a special display and the task was given to me as someone who had worked at a big-city paper.

There would always be those timid and small-minded thinkers who quailed before visionary and courageous ideas, the editorial said. Such naysayers, not all of them Unitarians, the editorial scrupulously pointed out, sought refuge in technicalities, such as the alleged overlap in lakes between the Tri-Lakes Area and the adjacent Land of Eleven Lakes. The naysayers would quibble over the exact number of lakes in the area. But their real aim was to hold up the march of progress.

I decided to run this over four columns, instead of the usual two, illustrated by an aerial photograph of the three lakes. The library did have an aerial shot, but unfortunately there seemed to be nine lakes in it. I got some help in identifying the three relevant ones and it was not a difficult matter to crop out the others, which would have confused the issue if we had left them in.

Two problems remained. One was that there was a fourth lake right in the photo, in the midst of our three. Apparently the chamber of commerce could not figure out what to call an area with four lakes in it (Land of Four Lakes was clearly inadequate, given that there was a Land of Eleven next door) and Tri-Lakes just sounded better. Deciding which of the four not to include was simple enough; Wart Lake would not be a big tourist draw.

But there it was, right in the centre of the aerial photograph. To make matters worse, the aerial photograph, the only one in the *WB*'s library, had been taken during a time of heavy forest fires. I knew I would be getting off on the wrong foot if I ran, to illustrate the *WB*'s stirring advocacy of Tri-Lakes, a photograph of four lakes largely obscured by smoke. So I went to Charlie McPartland, the news editor. Charlie was an old-timer who had worked in Saint John, Montreal, Ottawa, Timmins, Winnipeg, Prince Albert, Winnipeg, Calgary, Vancouver, Victoria, and Brockville, never for very long at any one place. He had just come back from a late lunch at the Prince of Wales and was tidying up his desk in preparation for an early dinner at the Prince of Wales.

"There's lots of fuckin' lakes in the world," he said, then went back to his work.

That was true and it showed that he recognized in me a kindred spirit, a veteran newsman no longer unduly restrained by youthful idealism and thus unlikely to seek refuge in technicalities. I returned to the library and began digging through envelopes of photographs, each envelope labelled with the name of a country that might have lakes. Eventually I found what I was looking for in Switzerland – an aerial photograph of three shining lakes, surrounded by mountains. There were some goats in the middle, which wouldn't hurt, and a guy in short pants playing one of those long horns. The photo editor assured me that he could be manipulated in the photo department's computer and made to resemble grass.

The picture worked beautifully, enhancing the power of the editorial, and Grand Valley has been part of the Tri-Lakes Area ever since. My part in it was never overstated, which was fine with me, but it did help me develop a reputation in the *WB* newsroom as a real pro.

In my five years here, I've seen many major journalistic trends (all journalistic trends are called major, because they are reported by journalists). The trends started when television came and newspapers began to worry, for the first time, that there might not always be newspapers. So they tried various strategies, and called them philosophies.

One philosophy was to make newspapers more like television. Another was to make newspapers less like television. Given the way newspapers worked, it was never possible to tell whether a strategy was effective. At the same time as the intellectuals in the news department were making the newspaper less or more like television, the intellectuals in the promotion department were running a bingo in the paper for $5,000 and the intellectuals in the circulation department were raising the price of subscriptions. Even if we could tell what was happening, which was difficult, we could never tell why it was happening. So it made just as much sense to keep changing the paper.

When I arrived we were just on the tail end of entertaining people. All the stories were about celebrities and none of the stories was about political or social issues. There was lots of advice on what wines to drink and diagrams of the latest dance craze. Our reporters became celebrities and were photographed doing fun things, like whitewater rafting and playing trivia contests on machines in country music bars.

I was just getting comfortable with that, or at least resigned to it. In my fragile, newly sober state, I wasn't going to be the one to raise the possibility that we might be running a few more American starlet photos than was absolutely necessary for a Canadian town in which the railway was shutting down, lake-front property (even beside Wart Lake) was being snapped up by foreigners, and the provincial government was talking about shutting down our hospital and expanding the one in the Land of Eleven Lakes.

But I was getting used to it, when the chain that then owned the *WB* sent in a new publisher. The new publisher went to a cocktail party at the university and heard the dean of arts refer to the *World-Beacon* as the *Woeful Bacon*. The new publisher decided to make the *WB* less like television. That meant more serious. The trouble was that nobody, after all those years of covering the movie of the week, knew how to be serious. The senior editors went off for a weekend retreat to think about it, retreats just having come into fashion. After a weekend at the Prince of Wales, much of it spent in the George Drew Room, the senior editors decided to make the pictures smaller. The publisher hailed the retreat as an advance.

Chapter 5

Davis and I often got together to eat, both of us on our own, divorced, both of us secure in the knowledge that this was a friendship not a relationship. She thought she was too heavy to get back into the game. I thought I was too old and my hair was getting a little thin. My close encounter with Lydia Byrd hadn't inspired confidence either.

Davis and I both liked seafood and newspaper talk and there was a fairly quiet restaurant on Harbourfront Boulevard, with a good view of Watson Lake and no freshwater fish on the menu.

She walked in just after I arrived, a tall, big-boned woman, her face unlined, her light brown hair worn in a ponytail. When I stood up, we were the same height, although she had low heels on. "Nice hair," I said.

"Wish I could say the same," she answered.

We talked it over at dinner, how we were going to work this new editor thing. Davis had just turned forty-one and wanted to be an editor – a big editor, something bigger than business editor. And she wanted to do that without sucking up to anyone. As smart and talented as she was, there always seemed to be somebody moving ahead of her.

I – what did I want? I was pushing fifty and wanted to survive another ten years, maybe seven, and retire honourably, with enough money saved to buy a place beside a lake, where I could hang out in a canoe, play some golf, get a dog. I wanted to survive more or less peacefully, with minimum stress. I really didn't want to get mixed up in newspaper politics again. Every time I did that I got hurt. Once, in my drinking days, I accused the national editor of being way too friendly with a cabinet minister. There was a stir, a reprimand was issued and it wasn't the national editor who received it. Another time I got on the union executive and campaigned actively for a policy allowing us to withhold our bylines if we didn't like how our stories were edited. As a result, the editors withheld my byline frequently, especially when I didn't want it withheld.

These days all the union campaigned for was the company not firing us all without proper notice. And I hadn't campaigned for anything for years. But now Fred was here, and we could see that our lives were going to change. We could sit back and wait for them to change, which is what I was inclined to do; or we could try to get Fred thinking our way, on the assumption that it might be better for us than his way.

"You know what," said Davis, as she pondered the dessert menu. "You've got to meet with him. You've got to give him your idea."

"What's my idea?" I said. "I don't have an idea."

"If you don't have an idea, then you wind up with his idea."

"That's a point," I said.

"And his idea might be about destiny."

"That's another point," I said.

"I know you'd rather lie low," Davis said. "But you always lie low."

"Only for the last five years."

"OK. But five years is a long time in a newspaper. It's at least a generation. In this one it's three editors and four news philosophies."

"I thought it was only three philosophies."

"I know. You always forget about when we had the Good News front page."

"Right," I said. " 'Another crashless day at Tri-Lakes International Airport.' So what you say is that if I lie low he finds me anyway and sees that I'm old and comes up with a way to replace me with some kid who's been to the Harvard Business School and freelanced for *Shift* from Nepal."

"Yes," she said. "Whereas, if you make him notice you . . ."

"Stick my head above the trenches."

"Right. You stick your head above the trenches, make him notice what a good editor and writer you are and you'll wind up with something better."

"Like what? Like writing again? Like doing real stories about real people and real issues?"

"I know it sounds unlikely," she said. "But look at the alternative."

She was right. It was just hard to overcome this habit of not being noticed. Fortunately, I could read Fred. I could figure him out a bit.

I knew him, in fact, a point I wasn't prepared to discuss with anyone just yet. And he knew me, a point he didn't seem prepared to discuss with anyone either. We had worked together in Ottawa. We had been sort of friends once. Then we went in different directions and changed, in different ways. I hit bottom and worked my way up. Fred reached the top, then worked his way down. We both wound up at the *World-Beacon*.

I'd heard that he had weird eating habits, that he drank many herbal potions, that he had once been in a Swedish movie, that there was a child in the Yukon, that there was an ostrich farm in Alberta that he went back to whenever he could. Every newspaper there was, he had worked for it, if you believed what people said. Everybody had heard something about him. It was all different. And nobody ever got close enough to him to ask.

Wherever he had been, whatever he had done, we didn't

know each other now, only our journalistic tendencies. His was to mention, ever so subtly, something he wanted, and then reward the person who figured it out and delivered. When he was a parliamentary reporter in Ottawa, wore better shoes and was called C. Frederick instead of Fred, he looked for backbenchers and junior bureaucrats who would feed him material. The backbenchers who lunched with him at the Parliamentary Restaurant realized, if they were listening carefully, that he could get them onto the front page, which might lead to the front benches. The junior bureaucrats who listened carefully to him in government cafeterias recognized that he could get the knife into their superiors, thus increasing their chances of advancement.

Most of them didn't hear him at all.

Cloth. That was the key. That's what he wanted. I didn't ask why. Tomorrow it might be snakes. But today it was cloth. I could give it to him.

The way a newspaper works these days, a lot of pages have to be filled the day before. The good stuff – murders, resignations, floods, bus plunges, and hockey games – gets in at the last minute, although the last minute gets earlier every year. Because of technological advances, the last minute is now 11:45 at night in Grand Valley, much earlier than before. There are still twenty or thirty pages that have to be filled the morning and afternoon before. Guys like me, deskers, we are called, or sometimes rim pigs, scour the wires for stuff to put on those pages. Then we stick them on an electronic representation of a page, find some pictures to illustrate them, write the headlines and press the button. Bingo, a page.

The wires are from all over, the best papers and wire services in the world. Soft features – a new dance craze in Brazil – serious analysis – the effects on divorce rates of the new dance craze in Brazil – breaking news, columns, cricket scores, trends in volcano eruptions, recipes. And you would be surprised how much news there is about cloth, if you know where to find it.

And how to make it into news. The next Monday, working the inside World section pages, I found an Associated Press story about Edgar, a hurricane that might, but probably wouldn't, hit the coast of South Carolina. Half-hearted evacuation preparations were underway, a couple of merchants were nailing boards over their store windows, although they might have been doing it because they feared teenagers, not winds. A preacher in a suburban Unitarian church prayed publicly to the Supreme Being, If Any, for moderate winds. I looked up the encyclopaedia on-line and confirmed that they grow cotton in South Carolina, rewrote the first two paragraphs, stuck it at the top of page C12 with a "Special to the *World-Beacon*" credit and put a three-column headline on it: EDGAR THREATENS CLOTH PRODUCTION.

I was lucky, although South Carolina wasn't. Edgar grew in intensity, people packed their cars, and all the ministers started praying very hard. Every day, I produced headlines, bigger headlines, about how lives and cloth were at risk in the face of the deadly winds. By Thursday, the peril facing cloth was in the A section and so was I, recognized by the news editor as an expert on the subject.

It's true that the people of South Carolina were less aware of that specific danger, the threat to cloth, than the people of Grand Valley. The people of South Carolina were, according to the wire service accounts I edited, more concerned about trees falling on their cars, more worried about their houses flooding and their pets being carried away than they were about cloth.

But many other people were concerned, although they may not have known it in precisely that way. Using various newspaper databases and the Internet, I was able to track down fashion experts and industrialists who had spoken favourably about the fabrics manufactured out of the crops that could conceivably be flattened by the hurricane. Without actually saying, in so many words, that they were speaking about the hurricane, I managed to insert some of those comments into the wire service accounts.

Thus, a story headlined WORLD HOLDS BREATH WHILE CLOTH FUTURE HANGS IN BALANCE was illustrated by photographs of a leading fashion designer and two supermodels, all of whom were quoted in the story, perhaps thinking at the time that they were referring to something else.

"We'd be doomed without cotton," one supermodel said, high up in a story on A5, beside a photograph of her not wearing much of it.

When Edgar hit the A section, it was noted in the newsroom that Fred was showing a specific interest in the subject. He would come out of his office late in the afternoon and stand behind me, saying nothing, but looking intently at the words on my computer screen. That would have been the time for the national editor to pick up the hint, but he was all wound up in some parliamentary thing. Davis noticed, though, dispatching Tony Frusculla, her eager rookie reporter, to gather concerned quotes from concerned members of the business community and the industry minister.

Tony was a gangly kid just out of community college, but he had nerve and knew how the game worked. He got himself a trip to Ottawa. "Is Canada prepared to assist with the looming cloth crisis?" the reporter shouted out at the minister, as she was climbing a staircase outside the House of Commons chamber.

The minister did what ministers do when they haven't the foggiest idea what the question means.

"We're giving the matter careful consideration," she said.

OTTAWA CONSIDERING CLOTH CRISIS ACTION, said Saturday's story, bumped from the business front onto page one by Fred's intervention. The re-election of the Communists in Russia was moved inside.

The next Monday, there was a note in my mailbox from Fred's secretary. Fred would like to see me at 10:30.

Chapter 6

The blinds were drawn and it took a few seconds to find anything in the darkness. There was a glow off to one side, probably from a computer screen. And there were strange gurgling noises.

"Hello?" I said, and was greeted with a sound, which could have been, if I hadn't known better, the hoot of an owl. It's just that you're not used to hearing the hoot of an owl in a newspaper office.

"MacVeigh," said a voice. "Come in, sit down."

As my eyes became accustomed to the light, I saw a desk, over by the glow, and, seated at it, Fred Morgan.

"C. Frederick," I said. "I didn't get a chance to welcome you to Grand Valley."

There was a pause and a grunt that didn't sound like an owl.

"Nobody calls me C. Frederick any more," Fred said. "And I'd just as soon they didn't."

"OK," I said. "Nice office."

He brightened, and showed me around. The glow and the gurgling were from a fish tank over in the corner. There was a computer but it was turned off. I'd never seen that in a newspaper office. Above the fish tank, and just off to the side, was a large photograph of Fred with the noted American evangelist and fisherman, Uncle Bob. Uncle Bob, an extremely fat man, was holding a fish and wearing a baseball cap with a likeness of himself on it, in about the spot where a cardinal or blue jay would go; Fred wasn't holding anything, but he was showing his teeth.

Fred pointed out the small bookcase with a shelf devoted to books about cloth, a compact disc player and some trophies. The walls were dark green, the desktop black, the couch dark blue, and as I sank down on it I thought I heard a harp and then I thought I heard a bullfrog.

"Do you hear something funny?" I asked Fred.

Fred made a noise and showed his teeth. He might have been laughing. "That's my soothing music," he said. "*Wilderness Serenade.* It helps me concentrate and I like to hear the animals."

Above his head was an expensive-looking painting of what looked like the solar system.

"I was in a gift shop last weekend," I said, "and I think I might have heard it. Is there also one about *Desert Winds*?"

"Yes. Would you like me to put that one on?"

"That's OK," I said and waited for him to ask me a question. He asked me nothing, just stared into the fish tank beside him.

"So," I said, "how come you don't like C. Frederick any more?"

"It was a wasted period of my life," Fred said. "I don't want to be frequently reminded of it."

"I don't understand," I said. "You win two National Newspaper Awards, blow the lid off that golf course scandal, get a daily column. How can that be a waste? You were on TV all the time."

Fred tapped the fish tank with a fingernail. "Meaningless," he said. "Trivial. Compared with what's presently going on now."

"I guess," I said. "But I sort of miss Ottawa."

It was a cue for him to ask what I'd been up to the last five years, but he missed it. He tapped on the fish tank again and stared some more. It was a cue for me to ask why he'd summoned me in here. I chose to miss it.

"What happened to that great-looking woman," I asked, "the researcher in the Speaker's office, the one you were –"

Fred stopped tapping and raised his hand for silence. A loon called.

"What we were then is not what we are now," he said.

"And what are we now?" I asked.

"I want you to meet someone," Fred said. "It's very important."

He picked up his phone. "Send the professor immediately in right away," he said.

The professor and the intern held forth for half an hour, while Fred nodded appreciatively and showed his teeth three times. The professor, a chubby, prematurely greying man about my age, was called Professor Blanchard. I never learned what his first name was. It might have been "Professor." The other one I'd seen around the newsroom, one of those kids you're always bumping into in this age of freelancers and part-timers – maybe she was a summer student, maybe she was an intern from Harvard, maybe she was the niece of one of the vice-presidents. They came and went and occasionally you were forced to notice one, when she became your boss.

She was attractive, which she hid behind serious thick-rimmed glasses, and she let the professor do most of the talking, while she referred occasionally to a sheaf of handwritten notes in the file folder she carried. Most of the talking, which was very fast, was about dangers to the planet and the Tri-Lakes area and its water and how the left-wing media had been hushing them up.

"My researches confirm that, by the way," said the intern, who was called Juanita Eldridge, looking at me as if I might somehow have been harbouring lingering doubts. She had an ethnic look, but I couldn't figure what kind of ethnic it was. There was a scarf-like thing she wore.

The situation had been allowed to worsen, the professor said, owing to the negligence of the government that might be the result of – well, you know . . .

I'd been trying to find a pause in the professor's torrent of words in which to interject a question. None seemed available until the professor suddenly came to a complete stop and looked at me for confirmation of what the negligence of the government might be the result of. I had no idea. "Well," I said, "I'd be interested in hearing your take on it."

The professor glanced warily over his shoulder. Over his shoulder was the fish tank. He glanced warily over his other shoulder.

"It is very hard to keep track of exactly who gets hired in government," he said. "New people, from all over, join every day, different departments, different agencies. Who knows where they come from or what they believe, these people."

Juanita nodded. "I know a little about that," she said. I waited for her to say a little about what she knew a little about, but nothing happened. What was it with this gang? I glanced over at Fred. He seemed at ease.

"You were at Harvard?" I asked.

"Princeton," Juanita answered, with some irritation.

"And you studied this stuff?"

"I studied film."

"So . . ."

"I attended many meetings," she said, glancing at the professor, who glanced again at the fish tank. A seal barked.

I turned to the professor. "And you teach . . .?"

"Latin, a language now called dead, although, it was not long ago that –"

He nodded at me significantly, then nodded at me significantly again and let it hang and once again I knew that I should have been able to complete the sentence with him. Fred nodded too. Sentences didn't have to be completed here.

I thought it would help if I stared at the fish tank. Before I could do it justice, however, Fred stood up. "We've taken up too much of your essential time, Professor," he said. "You'll be hearing from my capable colleagues very soon and I think we can all look forward to some revelatory journalism."

"I hope so," said the professor. "I hope it's not too late."

"It's never too late," I said, for something to say, as I shook the professor's hand.

"I hope so," said Juanita, clutching her file folder as she stood. She and the professor left the room, but Fred motioned for me to stay behind.

Pine branches sighed in the wind. I stared at the fish tank. There didn't seem to be branches in there. "You can see why I called you," Fred said.

I couldn't. "Up to a point," I said. "But why me?"

"You have some experience," Fred said. "You have travelled globally. You have expert news judgement. You understood the cloth aspect. You can be helpful with the professor." Fred leaned forward. "Just between you and me, he can occasionally be excitable. You can be a restraining influence."

Out in the newsroom, they would be watching the office door, those who were in range of it. Those who couldn't would have someone nearby delegated to keep watch. In the old days, you could see in, through the glass. You could see people getting fired or getting a surreptitious gift of hockey tickets for work well done that the editor didn't want to note in your file just in case he wanted to fire you later on. Now the office was so dark that from outside, you could only see the fish tank when it was lit. I'd been in the office almost an hour, which was too long to get fired, and way too long to get hockey tickets. What could have happened to me? I was mentally composing my story for the big table in the cafeteria. I was also looking for one of the smaller yellow fish that I hadn't seen for about ten minutes. I was going to be a restraining influence on the professor. That's what I knew so far.

"And Juanita?"

"Juanita is extremely well educated and she knows everybody. That's what everybody tells me. She is very good on the Internet. She has found many possibly vital documents on Web sites in Finland and many other places. She has an excellent style sense. You probably notice that she wears scarf-like things."

"You're fucking her, aren't you?" I said, before I had a chance to think about it.

A brook babbled.

"I won't dignify that rude interjection with a sincere response," Fred said. "She went to Harvard."

"Princeton."

"We don't hire people all the way from Harvard just so we can —"

"I'm sorry I said it," I said, and I was. "It was sort of an old-style comment to make."

"No offence taken at all," said Fred. "You see, her news sense needs to sharpen up a bit. And her typing."

"She doesn't type?"

"She said that there were always people to do that sort of thing for her. Once you get on the story and there are all the fascinating interviews to transcribe and so forth, her typing will develop quickly, I know."

There was a story to get on, and her typing to sharpen up and the professor to restrain. That much was clear.

"The actual story . . ." I began, as if could finish my own sentence.

"Listen," Fred said. "How you do it is up to you. The task force approach has always been methodologically good. The professor's research will be of extreme significance. Juanita's contacts will come in usefully handy. Put them together with your wonderful savvy and splendid acumen and I think we'll all have a story we'll be proud of."

"In terms of . . ."

"Take all the time you want," Fred said. "I can see a twenty-part series, but if you think it will take more, just give the high sign. There's an empty office just behind the place where that man with the strange hair sits."

"The entertainment department."

"Right, the entertainment department. That office will be for your task force meetings and documents. You will have the only key, I think, and it goes forcefully without saying that the door will be firmly locked when the office is not in use." Fred stood up. "Any questions?"

It was going to be a task force on something, a twenty-part series, and I was going to be heading it up.

"In terms of the subject . . ." I began.

"The Saturnians," Fred said. "Don't worry. I'm sure they don't know you're onto it yet. They are pretty smart, as you know. But we can show them a thing or two, can't we?"

"We can," I said. It would have been wrong to say we couldn't.

"They haven't taken over everything yet," Fred said. He shook my hand and I walked out into the newsroom, squinting into the glare.

Chapter 7

I t might have seemed odd to see me sitting in the cafeteria by myself, trying not to spill the chicken and rice soup over Volume 10 of the encyclopaedia, RETI to SOLOVETS.

Odd wasn't the half of it. "You're almost fifty years old and you're sitting in the cafeteria of a daily newspaper, reading about Saturn in an encyclopaedia," the little voice, the one that sounded like mine, said to me.

"Well," I answered, without moving my lips. "It's for a story."

"You're doing a story on Saturn?" the voice asked. "And by the way, how come you're not using the Internet? That's the space-age way to do these things."

"Listen," I answered. "Why shouldn't I be interested in Saturn? It's an important planet. As for the Internet, when I punch in 'Saturn' I get Web pages about Saturnalia and naked Saturnalian teenage sluts in heat."

The voice went away as Davis approached my table carrying a tray. "I don't think you want me to sit down," she said.

"I do," I said. "But I've got to read some stuff."

"I thought so. I'm not offended," she said. "I know you wouldn't be reading the encyclopaedia for fun. Have you tried the Internet?"

I showed her one of my fingers and she wandered off, laughing, and sat down with Tony Frusculla.

When C. Frederick and I were reporters in Ottawa in the eighties, it looked like we were going all the way. He knew all the deputy ministers. The politicians returned his phone calls. He could feed political gossip to the publisher when the publisher came into town for dinner with the bureau. He had no bad habits, not even ambition. People liked him. Everybody knew that C. Frederick would be called back one day to Toronto and become national editor, then managing editor, then editor.

Then something happened. He left the *Globe* soon after the 1993 election and went out west. He did carpentry on Vancouver Island, one report said. Or painting on the Queen Charlottes. Some said he was painting pictures. Others said he was painting houses. Another report had him buying a farm. Still another had him living on a reserve and becoming a practitioner of native medicine.

No one would ever know if it was true because no one would ever ask him. There was something about him that forbade you to ask. So it could all have been true, or none of it.

And anyway, he was hard to find. In 1996, *Maclean's* decided to do a where-are-they-now? story on him and was forced to abandon it when it couldn't find out where he was then.

The first rumours began around 1995 when he turned up as the editor of a small daily in the B.C. interior. Maybe it was Kamloops. Some reports said it wasn't the interior, it was the coast – Victoria, maybe. A year after that he was the editor of a larger daily in Alberta. Then another and another, as he moved east, each paper doing bold new work and making money.

Fred, as he was known by then, would show up at journalism conferences and give talks that no one could understand. As a result, he would be invited to give more talks at journalism conferences. His reputation grew. Eventually he showed up at our place, appointed by the new owners. No one knew why he had left journalism. No one knew why he had come back.

But he was back and now I had to learn about Saturn. Saturn, according to the *World-Beacon*'s encyclopaedia, has at least nine satellites. It's an old encyclopaedia and there might be more by now. Saturn has rings around it, which is what astronomers find so interesting. Galileo discovered those rings, or at least some of them, somewhere between 1564 and 1642, which was the period he was alive. Probably he didn't discover them until at least 1580, say, after he got out of high school.

There wasn't much in this encyclopaedia about whether or not there were Saturnians and whether they might be inclined to visit other planets, such as our own, and do stuff to the water.

I kept the soup off it pretty well and enjoyed reading the part about Saturnalia, when they outlawed wars, closed the courts, traded girls, and allowed slaves to eat at the same tables as their masters. All of this was in honour of Saturn, the Roman god of harvests, husband of Ops and father of Jupiter, Juno, and Neptune. I'd never read any of this in any newspaper, a fact that probably would confirm some of the professor's worst suspicions. Maybe somebody was preventing us from reading it in the newspaper.

Saturnalia happened on December 17, and lasted a few more days after that if it got going well. I wondered if December 17 had any special significance for Fred and made a mental note to watch the paper when it came around again. There might be a sign in our pages, hidden back with the warnings about unsafe holly and hazardous pudding.

I made another mental note, that this was crazy, then went on reading. Saturn had an atmosphere. That was good, or bad. Good for the Saturnians who wouldn't have much of a life without an atmosphere. Not so good for us, if the existence of Saturnians was as bad as the professor thought it was. But there wasn't anything else about the atmosphere, other than the fact that there was one. So, was it enough to have an atmosphere, or did it have to be a good atmosphere?

In Ottawa, when Fred and I were working against each other, we weren't close, but we weren't rivals, either. We were just too different. C. Frederick moved in the right circles. His stock in trade was being connected. When he wrote, all of Ottawa and a lot of Toronto (and especially his publisher) knew that he was speaking almost for the government, or maybe people who were even smarter than the government. If he said the government was going to do something, the government would, or the government had better.

I was just a day-to-day reporter, a hack, a grunt, filing for the *Winnipeg Free Press* and some other papers. While C. Frederick was up in the front of the campaign plane, talking to the leader's top strategist and getting the insider's perspective that he could exclusively reveal to *Globe* readers, I was in the back drinking with the other reporters, having already filed my nine paragraphs on what people in the crowd said about the leader's speech, plus a short sidebar on a goofy fringe candidate who wanted to criminalize chewing gum.

The next day I would do the same thing again, following the leader around, doing two or three stories while C. Frederick did a lengthy analysis piece for the Saturday paper and appeared on a CBC panel about the necessity of electoral reform while I was settling into my fourth beer.

We did talk from time to time. He tried to be helpful during my divorce, which was taking place during the '84 election. I was very sad, when I was sober enough, which was every day before filing my three stories. There was something about getting off a plane and onto a bus and checking into a hotel and then getting back on the bus and standing behind a rope to listen to the leader speak and then getting back onto the bus and then back onto the plane that didn't seem fulfilling to me. It made me want to go home, actually, which was when I remembered that there was no home to go home to. One day I remember in particular. It was the closest Fred ever got to discussing any personal details with me.

"How's it going personally?" he asked, in that way he had, after dropping into the seat beside me on the Mulroney plane.

"Shitty," I said.

"I heard about your unfortunate divorce," he said. "Is it true that your wife became romantically involved with someone from Finance?"

"That shithead," I said.

"A senior official?" C. Frederick asked.

"ADM."

I could see C. Frederick mulling that one over, wanting to comfort me yet fighting off intriguing thoughts about the rank of public servants and their hobbies.

"He has a rear-view mirror on his fucking bicycle helmet," I said.

"When I was growing up, there was a divorced couple two doors down," C. Frederick said.

I recognized this for an intimacy. C. Frederick had never before talked about growing up. Even through my grief and anger and thoughts of ripping the mirror off the bicycle helmet, I knew I had to seize the opportunity. Any good journalist would.

"Where was that?" I asked.

"Two doors down," he said.

"No, I mean what town."

A pause, during which C. Frederick might have been wondering what dangerous chain of events he had set in motion.

"Guelph," he said finally.

"Ah, Guelph," I said and decided to let the matter drop.

"You know," C. Frederick said, "many famous statesmen have lived through the terrible agonies of divorce and gone on to have storied triumphs."

He then listed them – Adlai Stevenson, I think one of the Ataturks, Ronald Reagan, Frank Sinatra – while I half-listened. I thought I heard a bottlecap snap a few rows ahead where the radio guys were. At the same time, I was touched at the way C. Frederick was reaching out. I tuned back in.

". . . afflicts many people at the highest levels of our public service, even more senior than assistant deputy minister. The PSC commissioned a task force report on the subject, which I have seen, although it was never released. I'd be extremely glad to lend you my copy, if you think it would be of particular comfort to you."

"Thanks, C. Frederick," I said. "I appreciate it. Maybe when the campaign's over and I have some time to read."

"Speaking of reading," he said, "I have to reread yesterday's speech. I have a nagging feeling that there were some nuances I missed."

He stood and, caught up in the emotion of the moment, tapped me on the shoulder, before returning to his seat. I sat there for a minute, then headed off in the general direction of that bottlecap noise. The next I remember, it was Baie Comeau, a week later, and I was filing the victory speech story. I must have filed other stories in the intervening week, because nobody on the desk said anything. I wondered what those stories were like and made a mental note to look them up some day. Some day I still might.

C. Frederick was helpful again a few years later when I was working on a book about the Kim Campbell government and the three months it lasted. I had sort of pulled myself together, cutting back on drinking and more or less behaving myself for three or four years. Because I had been around Parliament Hill for a decade and knew which was the East Block, I was now expected to do solemn analytical articles giving meaning to the chaotic events of the day. These pieces could be really long and didn't have to quote real people, unless absolutely necessary. They would recount what government insiders and veteran parliamentary observers had to say about such issues as the prime minister's apparently cavalier attitude to the unemployment problem.

" 'It is an apparently cavalier attitude,' one veteran parliamentary observer reflected as the Hill buzzed over the new prime
minister's seeming gaffe."

I wrote that and many others like it, without going out of the
office, since I always knew where to find a veteran parliamentary
observer, being one myself. So good at it did I become that
reporters for other news outlets, bumping into me at scrums
outside Question Period, would seek out my opinion on the
current happening.

"This sort of thing hasn't been seen here in years," I would
say. "It is more or less without precedent."

Or, I would say: "This sort of thing happens all the time. It
happened with Bennett, it happened with Diefenbaker. I don't
know what everybody's getting so excited about."

Either way, it would turn up in somebody's story, quite frequently on television, attributed to a veteran parliamentary
observer. Sometimes, if my view was particularly astute, I would
be identified plurally as "veteran parliamentary observers," which
always made me proud.

Inevitably, a publisher came calling with a book contract.
Political books were all the rage in those days. Nine out of ten
didn't stay on the shelves past their first Christmas, and very few
of them even got into paperback. But occasionally one would hit
it big – Sawatsky's book on Mulroney, Chrétien's book on
Chrétien – and that gave publishers reason to hope that the next
one would be the big score.

They scoured the talent pool, the anchors, the young turks,
the TV academics, the pollsters, the professors. No one much
wanted to do the Campbell book. By the time the publisher got
around to me she knew she had to sweeten the pot a bit. Being a
Canadian publisher, she wasn't going to do that with money; all
she could offer was immortality.

Which is what she offered me over a long lunch, along with
quite a short skirt. "Don't think of it as a book on Kim Campbell,"

she said, two-thirds of the way through the first bottle of wine. "Think of it as a book on Canada at the denouement of the second millennium; think of it as whither our country."

Two-thirds of the way through the second bottle of wine, I was half in love with the idea and completely in love with the publisher. Money, immortality, the short skirt – there was no shortage of compelling reasons to write a book about the brief, yet symbolically crucial prime ministership of Kim Campbell.

When I went back to the office after lunch, I drank some coffee, tried to work for a couple of hours on an advance story about the budget. What would happen to the deficit and what did the usual organizations in my Rolodex think about that? About five paragraphs in, when I had lost enough giddy exhilaration to be able to think straight, I sat back to analyse the situation.

Something was making me discontented, otherwise I wouldn't have fallen in love with the publisher. I knew myself well enough by now to know what falling in love meant. It meant that there was something wrong with my life. I wasn't married any more, so I couldn't be discontented with marriage. Nor was I involved with anyone I could be discontented with. I didn't have children, although it might have been nice to have some to be discontented with. I was content with my car, a fairly new Corolla. I was content with my golf game, having given it up five years ago after some dis-content with my nine iron, which sank where it landed after I threw it. I was content with my apartment, the furniture in it, the elevator up to it, the parking garage below. My health was all right, although I was mildly discontented about not being able to quit smoking.

But did I fall in love with the publisher, even briefly, because I couldn't quit smoking? That didn't seem plausible. So what was left? What was left was the only other thing I had to be discon-tented with – my job. A job reporting on life on Parliament Hill after the premature departure of Kim Campbell. I was discon-tented as hell with that.

So there was a way out. I could quit the job, or at least leave it for a while. The book would give me the chance to do that. I'd take a leave of absence of half a year, and do the book. Maybe the book would be a great success, the definitive work on Kim Campbell, and I would become rich and famous. Maybe I'd stop being discontented. At the very least I'd get to hang out with the publisher.

I called her hotel, before the mood left me, and said I'd do it and was she free for dinner? She said she was delighted I would do it and was tied up for dinner. I said I assumed there would be an advance and she named a figure. I fought back a slight discontent and said that would be fine. Could I produce the book in six months? she asked. Of course, I said. Although books were a lot longer than newspaper articles, six months seemed like enough time to do just about anything.

"I'm very excited," she said.

I had an impure thought. "So am I," I said.

"What are you going to call it?"

"Huh?"

"Have you thought of a title?"

I had, in fact, been thinking about a title just before I called. A catchy title, with my name in only slightly larger letters just above it.

"What about this?" I said. "*The Campbell Interlude.*"

"That's very nice," she said. "I like it. Although I think it could be improved just a little."

"How would you improve it?"

"Well, it needs a subtitle."

This was all new to me. "Why does it need a subtitle?"

She was patient with me, which I liked almost as much as her skirt. "In Canada, every non-fiction book absolutely must have a subtitle. This is so people will know what the book is about."

"Won't the title tell what it's about?"

"Definitely not. The title's there to be catchy and intriguing and to use certain words that have been proven by market research to be attractive to book buyers."

It was interesting learning about the book business. "I can see that we would want to do that," I said. "But if we have a title like *The Campbell Interlude* and a picture of Kim Campbell on the cover, why would we need a subtitle?"

"Point one," she said. "There won't be a picture of Kim Campbell on the cover. People didn't vote for her; they won't spend $29.95 to buy something with her picture on it."

"They bought Brian Mulroney's picture a few times," I said, annoyed enough to stop having impure thoughts.

"Absolutely. But they hated him. They don't hate Campbell enough. And by the way, that's why we can't have her name in the title."

"I get it," I said. "We have to have certain words that have been proven by market researchers. What are some of those?"

"Just a second," she said. She put down the phone and when she picked it up I could hear the clicking of computer keys. "Power," she said, at last. "I was just double-checking."

"Power."

"Absolutely. That was point two. We need to have 'power' in the title. All of the big-selling political books in Canada and the U.S. and British markets have had 'power' in them. *Discipline of Power. Absence of Power. The Power and the Glory. The Power and the Tories. Renegade in Power.*"

So it was that, six months later, I handed in the manuscript of *The Power of the Power: Kim Campbell and Canada at the Denouement of the Second Millennium.* Six months after that, the book, without Kim Campbell's picture on it, hit the pre-Christmas bookshelves. There was a launch at the National Press Club. The publisher spoke glowingly of our literary collaboration which had, in fact, turned out only to have been a literary collaboration. My friends, including a couple of politicians who saw their names in the index, lined up for me to sign their copies, while I sat at a table trying to keep my wine consumption to sips and trying to think up something better than "Best wishes" to write in the books of people I had known for decades.

Across the room my colleagues and competitors chatted amongst themselves, occasionally glancing my way. Having been over there on other such occasions, I knew what they were saying. It was about how they turned down huge advances to write exactly this book, except that it would have been better researched or better written if they had done it. When I was over there, I could never bring myself to line up to buy a book and line up again to get it signed by someone clearly inferior to myself.

Except for C. Frederick. He was there, he got the book, lined up to have me sign it and wished me good luck. "For C. Frederick," I wrote. "I couldn't have done this without your help." Then, because I had taken a bit too much wine and couldn't help myself, I added: "Hang loose."

The rest is history, not that you'd remember it. *The Power of the Power* sank like a stone after a two-week season in which it was scorned by academics in the book review sections and condescended to by journalists in the book review sections that couldn't afford an academic. I was interviewed once on the CBC, paired up with the author of a book on curry powder. On private radio I was asked "Why did you write this book?" so often that I forgot. My book tour was two (nearby) cities in two days, which should have been a sign. During it, I fell in love with two publicists and one bookstore owner, which should have been another sign. Authorship wasn't going to be any help.

Still, there was always the public. The reviewers might withhold their praise, the book chains might choose not to erect pyramids of *The Power of the Power*, taking out full-page ads to invite the public in. But the public might hear, one at a time, of the worth of my book. In small groups, they might file into bookstores just before Christmas, clutching their $29.95 or multiples thereof. After all, millions of them had voted for the woman. In January I might get a call from the publisher that the The Power had sprouted wings and, now that it had wings, had legs, and would be reprinted in great numbers. Would I be able to embark on a ten-week, fifteen-city tour to meet eager readers in some of the places I had missed, the tour starting with dinner at her place?

January passed without such a call. So did several months after that. In May, the publisher's revenue statement arrived. It was surprising, to look dispassionately at it, how few Canadians were actually interested in Canada at the denouement of the second millennium.

Still, I had endured worse (or probably had: I hadn't actually sat down to run over the list) and I still had my health. The world didn't know, and didn't have to know, how badly my book had done, although the world might suspect, seeing me journey through it in the same car and wearing the same clothes as my pre-publication self.

I was not that difficult to console. Thoughts of a second book, to capitalize on the lessons I had learned doing the first, drove me to the IKEA store. A better desk would help, and maybe one of those modernistic metal desk lamps. I could picture myself, looking authorly and maybe smoking a pipe, illuminated by such a lamp, late at night, the computer screen casting a glow on my authorly face. I walked among the desks and sofas, looked at the imitation computers and VCRs sitting on the furniture, the fake television sets fashioned out of plastic, the bookcases lined with . . .

Well, the bookcases were lined with _The Power of the Power: Kim Campbell and Canada at the Denouement of the Second Millennium_, by Parker MacVeigh. There were twelve bookcases in the room and each of them had at least five copies. One had sixteen. Without understanding everything about the publishing industry, without knowing where the IKEA store went when it had bookcases it needed to fill cheap, I knew this wasn't a good place to find my book. I sat down on a chesterfield named after some Scandinavian child – Öland, I think it was – and tried to think of a way to take something positive from this experience. I decided I could think about it better in a tavern.

I'm told now that I did a lot of thinking in many taverns over quite a lengthy period of time. It didn't take too long, or so it seems in blurred retrospect, before I was in Grand Valley, broke, sober, and working on the rim.

Chapter 8

From my new office, I could look out at most of the newsroom and see most of the newsroom looking in at me. No
wonder. Yesterday I was a rim pig and today I was in an office,
with my feet up on the desk, milking the moment just a bit. For
the time being, there wasn't any particular need to let anyone
know that the office belonged to the STF (as I was beginning to
think of the Saturn Task Force) and not to me exclusively.
Because of the need for absolute secrecy, Fred hadn't put a note
up on the bulletin board about why I was in the office, but he had
whispered something useful to the office manager, who let me
have the key.

Once inside, I arranged some paper clips and checked out the
drawers, on the off chance that some of the previous occupant's
ghoul collection was still there. Chet Edgemar, the TV critic, was
an old-timer whose collection of grisly wirephotos went back to
Jayne Mansfield's fatal car accident and he had them all. Every
newsroom has someone like that and he is usually tolerated, as
long as he washes, unless, as in Chet's case, he is inspecting his collection just as an elementary school tour goes by his open door.

Ordered to leave the office and work at home, the TV critic pleaded that his knowledge of the subject went back to the days of *Don Messer's Jubilee*, which was true, and that he needed the office for thinking, which was not. Rather than risk a union grievance, Fred arranged for a thirty-six-inch television set to be delivered to Chet's home. Reluctantly, but with a sense of anticipation born of never having had anything bigger than twenty-one inches, the critic packed up his photographic collection, his framed and autographed portrait of Raymond Burr, and headed for home.

Pacing the dimensions of my temporary home, I watched, first Lorne Marshall, the assistant city editor, and Dick Rivers, the columnist, approach the office manager and speak earnestly, pointing occasionally in my direction. An office would make all the difference to them, which said something not terribly flattering. Fred knew it, though, and the fact that he had kept it empty showed he could play bureaucratic games better than he let on. The way to that office was by pleasing him, and everybody was aware of it. Occasionally, while the office stood empty, he would have the business manager open it and put something in or take something out, just as a handy reminder.

There was some space art I had found in a head shop downtown and I hung it up. I put Mars on one wall, Venus on another, and Mercury on the door. I couldn't hang Saturn, because that would give everything away. But I thought we could at least get in the mood, me and the Latin prof and the intern, while we pondered our next move.

Fred didn't want Saturnians knowing we were on their trail and I could sympathize with that. We were under instructions to discuss the task force with no one, which I strictly obeyed, apart from telling Davis as soon as I emerged from Fred's office. Aware that people might be watching, I made gestures as if I were disgusted while I told her the good news.

It was all she could do to keep from jumping up and down. "That's so neat!" she said, only barely keeping a straight face.

"What's neat about it?" I asked. "I get to hang out for maybe years with a deranged professor of a dead language and a snobby girl from Yale."

"She's cute."

"Only until she talks. So what's neat?"

"It's history," Davis said. "It's journalistic history. No newspaper has ever done this, set up a task force to investigate visitors from Mars."

"Saturn."

"Saturn, and you get a front-row seat. You can watch it, and be a witness to it, and even if you don't get the story —"

"Even if? You're not saying there's going to be a story!"

She hesitated. "Well, I remember how you always get the story. Sometimes even when the story wasn't there, you got it."

"Oh no," I said. "Not this time. There's no way I'm going to do that. No way I'm going to invent something or spin something. If you listened to these people you'd know that it's wrong to encourage them."

"So what are you going to do?"

"Stall," I said. "The research will take quite a long time. It won't be any good and we won't have to print anything."

"I think you're underestimating Fred," Davis said. "He might think some of that research is fabulously great."

That was factually true. I hadn't thought of it. C. Frederick had been tough to impress, but it didn't appear that Fred was. And I worried that Juanita Eldridge would be able to sway him with the evidence she found on the Internet. I had heard you could find anything there.

I had one hope. "The thing is," I said. "The research is still going to take a long time. And by then, Fred may be on to something else."

"There's a chance of that," Davis said. "Last month, we were in the middle of a ten-part series on eavestroughs when he took the entire team off it to look for the Holy Grail."

"I'd forgotten about that. Where was it?"

"They never found it. But they were looking in Lake Huron, mostly in shallow water."

"And what about the eavestroughs?"

"Nothing."

I sat there with my feet up on the desk, pondering eavestroughs and wondering if I could work them into the Saturn story. It would make me a double hero. Then the telephone warbled quietly. That would be the Latin prof at the front desk. "Task force," I said into the receiver, feeling a slight thrill at the words.

"Yes," said a woman's voice. "What gives you the right to say such things?"

"Such things as what?"

"You said that *Don Messer's Jubilee* was better than Ed Sullivan. Don't you remember Topo Gigio, the little Italian mouse? Did you miss Elvis Presley and the Red Army choir? What gives you the right?"

"Who is this?"

"That's my private business, Mr. TV Know-it-all."

Of course. Calls for the TV critic had probably been coming in to this office for two months, quietly warbling. The office was closed and nobody knew. Now I would get them, I and the Latin prof and the intern from Princeton. Calling the switchboard and complaining about getting the TV writer's calls might work. But the calls could come in handy, actually, adding to the confusion, taking up some of the task force's valuable time. Also I liked the idea of Chet Edgemar never getting any calls at home. How long before he noticed? How long before he cared?

The phone warbled again and I picked up the receiver. "This isn't television," I said.

"Good," said the voice at the other end of the line.

"I beg your pardon?"

"I like how you answered the phone." It was Professor Blanchard's voice. "Keep them guessing."

"Thank you. I've been giving it some thought. Are you at security?"

"I am."

"Wait there," I said.

Leaving the office, I closed and locked the door, then walked slowly past the news desk, dangling the keychain from my finger. Dick Rivers averted his eyes. Lorne Marshall, holding a container of fish food in one hand, was watching the door of Fred's office. I nodded significantly in the direction of Juanita Eldridge, then turned left, down the corridor past Fred's office and a meeting room, from which I thought I heard the word "eavestrough," past the test kitchen where the night deskers used to keep their booze, past the community relations office, where they were working on the next in-paper bingo, and past the publisher's office, where they kept the secret circulation numbers.

Professor Blanchard was holding a large paper bag, which I knew had to be his research. It was an old journalistic axiom: the weirder the theory, the more likely it was to be carried in a paper bag. I opened the door for him and he shook my hand, after first looking over his shoulder. "Is he . . . OK?" he asked, shooting a glance at the security guard. The security guard used to work in the composing room, before the machines took his job. There was nothing Saturnian about him, as far as I could tell.

"He's OK," I said.

"Fine," said the professor. "Is there a secret way to the office?"

"Of course," I said, trying to think of one. I walked him down a long corridor past camera-plate, out a door into the mailroom, then into the garage, back through the mailroom, out the same door we came in, then into the newsroom library, by way of a side door.

"Wait here," I said, while the librarians looked puzzled. I started out of the library, then thought of something and returned.

"The microfilm is over there," I said, pointing to a dark corner. The professor nodded gravely. Actually, the microfilm *was* over there, but there was nothing on it except back copies of the *World-Beacon*.

I stepped into the newsroom, took a long look around, then came back to the library.

"It's all right," I said. "Follow me."

We walked quickly across the back of the newsroom. I unlocked the office, the professor stepped in, after looking over his shoulder, followed closely by Juanita, who had scurried over from her desk. I closed the door behind us. That would drive them crazy in the newsroom, looking at a closed door, with people behind it and a painting of Mercury on it. Nobody worked behind closed doors.

The professor shook hands solemnly with Juanita, and then with me, although we had shaken hands just moments ago. We sat and I asked, because I wanted to get it over with, what the professor had in the paper bag. The professor looked over his shoulder, where the wall was, and the picture of Venus. Then, ignoring me completely, he spoke to Juanita.

"Mr. MacVeigh has an ingenious way of answering the telephone and I think we should all adopt it. He says: 'This isn't television.' If we all do that, it will confuse our enemies."

"It might confuse us, too," I said.

"No, no," the professor said, "not if we know what to reply. All we need to do," he said, and glanced significantly at us.

Juanita looked into her purse for something and didn't find it. "What, exactly, did you mean by 'This isn't television'?" she asked.

Explaining would do no good. I could see that. "Well," I said, "in cases such as this," and gave a significant glance at the professor.

It seemed to work. They both nodded. "So," I said, "what's in the bag?"

"The jaguar missed the bus," the professor said.

"In the bag?"

"'The Jaguar missed the bus,'" the professor said. "That's what we should reply to 'This isn't television.'"

"Shouldn't we be getting on with it?" I asked.

"Don't be silly," the professor said. "Everything could be lost if we don't know what to reply."

Apparently, something along those lines had been said at Princeton too, but while Juanita agreed on the need for a code phrase, she didn't like jaguars in the phrase, being a vegetarian. She offered a sentence she had learned at Princeton, but I had trouble pronouncing two of the words.

We talked about code phrases for twenty minutes. After a while, I realized I was enjoying it. Talking about code phrases not only was fun, it postponed talking about Saturnians. It also postponed the beginning of the research and postponing the beginning of the research postponed the writing of the story. So it was fine with me. I even offered a couple of my favourites, such as: "There is a teapot in my tree house," just to keep the discussion flowing, and when Juanita and the professor seemed to be in agreement on "The camera always lies," I pretended to be hurt, saying that my father had been a wedding photographer. That kept it going.

There are an infinite number of possible code phrases in the world, the sources ranging from the Bible, to hockey telecasts, to cartoons, and I wasn't prepared for how emotional people could be about them. The professor was in the middle of an angry defence of "Cheese is best before noon," when the phone warbled.

The professor stopped talking, Juanita stopped interrupting and they both stared at me, while I stared at the phone. Finally, I picked it up.

"This isn't television," I said.

"Goddamn right it isn't," said Davis. "What on earth is going on in there? Who is that creepy-looking guy?"

I looked at the professor. "A friend and a trusted colleague," I said.

Davis laughed and hung up.

I replaced the receiver and looked at the professor again.

"It was one of them, wasn't it?" he asked.

"Don't worry," I said. "I'll get the number changed."

"But how would they know?" Juanita asked.

I raised my eyebrows knowingly at the professor. "How wouldn't they, eh?" I said. The professor nodded, then glanced over his shoulder and muttered something in Latin. It sounded pharmacological.

Then he reached into the paper bag. Realizing that we were in danger of injecting actual content into the discussion, I steered discussion back to the password, which Juanita happily seized upon, dipping into her favourite authors, who included J. R. R. Tolkien, Ayn Rand, and as many Brontë sisters as there were, and maybe a brother too. The professor, with his love of wild animals, sulked at the intern's insistence upon plant names.

"Couldn't we even have a fish?" he asked at one point. "Listen to this: 'This isn't television.' 'But the coho knows something new.' What about that?"

"No fish," Juanita said. "I'd vomit."

The professor began staring at her in a peculiar way, as if it had suddenly occurred to him that she might, just possibly –

The phone warbled again.

"This isn't television," I said.

"What are you going to do about that garbage on Channel 11?" asked a man's voice. "Hold it. Did you say this isn't television."

"No," I said. "I mean, yes, it's not."

"Oh sorry," said the voice.

I hung up the receiver very gently and looked at the professor. "It was, wasn't it?" he said.

"We can't be sure," I said, "but it appears that way."

Juanita stood up. "I had no idea," she said, adjusting the brightly coloured wrap that had fallen off one shoulder. "Look, I'll agree to the fish. There's some urgency here."

"That's wonderful," the professor said. "It ties in with our concern about the water."

The water? What was it about the water?

"But maybe not the coho," Juanita said. "Could we have something smaller, like a perch?"

Then I figured it out. Water levels were down. This would be an explanation.

"Good," the professor said. "This isn't television."

"But the perch knows something new," Juanita answered. They shook hands solemnly.

It seemed a good note to end on. "Well," I said, standing, "we've made some great progress today. Perhaps we should adjourn for now."

Professor Blanchard was not happy. "But what about . . ." he said, holding out the paper bag full of documents.

I knew how to handle that. I reached for the bag, saying, "If you wanted to leave it with me overnight —"

The professor shook his head and clutched the paper bag to his chest as he stood up and waited for me to open the door. We entered the newsroom, with people pretending not to look at us. I pointed the way to the secret exit route we would follow as soon as I could make it up. The professor looked over his shoulder. As we began to walk away, I could hear the task force phone ringing.

Chapter 9

This was a strange double life I was leading, on the one hand carrying on like a normal person – or at least a normal desker – and on the other hand having this new-found awareness of the Saturnian dimension. As much as I reminded myself that we were in fact Alone on Earth, I kept noticing things that lacked a normal explanation. Button-down collar shirts had disappeared, for example. All of a sudden. Everywhere I looked, there weren't any. When I asked salespeople about it, they didn't look at all surprised. "No, we don't stock them now," they'd say, declining further elaboration. Tunes on the radio weren't tunes, all of a sudden. They were just beats. A song would begin with some beats and I'd wait for the tune to begin, but it never would. On television, I'd see kids dancing to these, not seeming to miss the idea of melody.

I was listening to one of these non-tunes the next morning at nine when I attempted to turn into the *WB* parking lot and found yellow police tape blocking the entrance and no one there to explain why. I drove a block down the street to the Grand Valley Mall, where they hated us to park, and parked where I figured it would look most like someone with a *WB* sticker in the windshield was shopping, instead of parking for the entire day. In the old days that would be the liquor store. Now it was at Mister Vitamin, the new health food superstore. Several other *WB* staffers had the same idea and we walked back to the plant together.

It was a warm May morning and it felt like you could smell the new growth on the trees, although there wasn't a tree in sight, except for some plastic ones in planters beside where the shopping carts were stored.

"Christ, another frigging indignity," said Jane Liu, the most cynical of the entertainment department staffers.

"What do you think's going on?" I asked.

"Who cares?" Jane said. "I have to go to a frigging garden show at eleven and that means coming all the way back over here, all because some management idiot wants to play games with the parking lot."

Jane was the theatre critic and she doubled as the garden writer. She hated flowers and trees, but she liked the freelance money she was getting for the column, which she wrote under the name of B. K. Yard, the obviousness of the name being her little dig at a paper dumb enough to print it. The paper thought the name was very clever.

Jane also wrote recipes, restaurant reviews, an outdoors column and a stamp column, each under a name she took pride in making as stupid as possible.

We neared the yellow tape. "Maybe they're expanding the parking lot," said Pete Lester, the day rewrite guy. "That would be good. Most days if I get here only a little after nine, there's no spaces left, except maybe in February when everybody goes to Florida. Mind you –"

Talking parking lot with Pete was something all of us had done at one time or another and I wasn't anxious to continue.

Neither was Jane. "Maybe somebody got murdered," she said, brightening.

We chatted for a while about the people most likely to be murdered.

"That computer guy," Jane said, "the one who asks how the ladies are doing this morning."

"I like him," Pete said. "He helped me put a sound card on my computer at home."

"He could be dead," I said. "Or what about Norwood's secretary, always jumping in front of you in the cafeteria to get him his tea?"

"There's this icky guy in advertising, who has the big garden store accounts," Jane said. "He's always suggesting features on different kinds of bulbs and he wears those glasses that get darker in the light."

Talk turned to the possible perpetrators. We all knew who they were; every department had one. "A quiet guy," his neighbours would say when the reporters came. "Never said much. You wouldn't notice him. Kept pretty much to himself."

Jane and I were laughing about this until we remembered that Pete used to be the number-one newsroom suspect. He was a quiet guy, nerdish, his hair short, but not stylishly so. People didn't notice him. We could see Pete, hauling the machine gun out of the violin case under his desk. "I've always hated you," he would yell, as he sprayed the newsroom, shredding the display of candy bars on top of the filing cabinet beside the news editor's desk, the candy bars being in aid of sending his daughter to ballet camp, and only by the grace of God avoiding wiping out the sports department, which worked nights. Pete had been dethroned as machine-gunner in recent years by an even shorter, even quieter and unusually muscular editorial writer, Rand Barry, who spent his lunch hours at his desk, reading hunting magazines and listening to Céline Dion on headphones.

Pete, for whom machine-gunning was a completely new concept, was trying to figure out a way in to the conversation and we were trying to figure a way out of it when we were met by a beefy and quite ugly man at the main entrance. He wore a black suit, carried a clipboard, and looked like a killer.

"Do you have business here?" he asked.

"Yes," Jane said and began walking by him.

He shifted and blocked her path.

"Excuse me," she said. "I work here."

"And your name is?"

She gave it, with some exasperation, and he looked at his clipboard for a long time. Then she spelled it and he made a pencil stroke.

"I need some I.D.," he said.

"Who the fuck are you?" she asked.

He stared at her, the words striking him strangely, perhaps, and stayed in her path. Pete Lester cleared his throat and when the black suit looked at him, produced both his name and his driver's licence. The black suit stepped aside and let him enter, then stepped back into Jane's path.

I tried to mediate. "Can you tell us what this is about?" I asked.

"Orders," he said, in a way that seemed somehow Saturnian.

"Oh," I said. I had to pee. The closest bathroom was inside. The alternative was the long walk back to Mister Vitamin, where they might try to engage me in lengthy conversations about herbal alternatives to the use of the washroom.

"Jane, let's go in," I said. "We can't find out what's happening if we stay out here."

"This guy reminds me of a tree," she said, but produced a press card, which he carefully examined, glancing up at her several times. I went through the same procedure and we got inside.

"Have a nice day," the black suit said.

"Have another doughnut," Jane replied.

Inside everyone was buzzing, but then, somebody was always buzzing over something. You could ask, but most of the time it would turn out to be a cold coffee somebody bought from the cafeteria, a change in the approved spelling of the word "analyse," or a photograph of somebody's new puppy. If it mattered, it would be on the bulletin board or the company e-mail. Nobody was standing in front of the bulletin board, so e-mail would have it, if there was anything to be had.

What it had was a message from the publisher, a rare occurrence:

> From: Publisher <publisher@world-beacon.ca>
> To: Staff (Grand Valley)
> Subject: Our Eagerly Greeted Visitor
> Date: Monday, 8 May 2000 08:48:05
>
> The World-Beacon is today proud to welcome a visit by Our New Owner, Dr. Thelma Baxter. Dr. Baxter, along with her protective staff, will be touring our WB facilities and I know that everyone will make her feel most welcome, if they are spoken to.
>
> I would like to take the opportunity to apologize for the inconvenience anyone may have experienced in the parking lot this morning. This was because of security considerations and could not have been announced in advance.
>
> We at the World-Beacon are proud of our offices and desks and chairs and will endeavour today, as on all days, to keep them neat and free of any decorations that might be misunderstood, by 10 a.m. this morning when the tour officially begins.
>
> Dr. Baxter and I look forward to passing among you.

It was now 9:45. That gave me fifteen minutes to read the wires and remove from my wall any decorations that might be misunderstood. Perhaps that included the photo I had clipped out of a Toronto newspaper, showing Mrs. Baxter laughing with a Latin American dictator at a banquet at a rich person's mansion in the Caribbean. From the angle of the picture, she appears to have her right hand on his ass. Some people thought I had tacked the photo up because I admired Mrs. Baxter, which was all right.

Others suggested funny captions for it, which I resisted. The picture really was misunderstood, and I kept it there for that reason.

I decided to leave it up. The *WB* had an open-concept office and I would be able to see from my desk the spot where Our Eagerly Greeted Visitor entered the newsroom and would have lots of time to take down the offending photograph if the entourage turned in my direction. Davis's desk near Fred's office across the room would give her a front-row seat. I phoned her extension and watched her look with exasperation at the phone before picking it up.

"Do you have any idea what's going on?" I asked. "What would she be coming here for?"

Davis answered in a lowered voice. "I see some stirring down the hall. I think they're on the way. You still got the photo of her hand on the generalissimo's ass?"

"I'm leaving it up as a matter of principle," I said. "Lorne has already asked me to take it down."

"Was he carrying fish food?"

"No, a magazine about guppies."

"Be careful," Davis said. "The task force is depending on you."

"Well," I said, "if it looks like she's coming close I may take it down. Tell me what this is about. What do you hear?"

"I'm not sure. Some people say we're not making enough money for her. Others say she wants to congratulate us on a job well done."

"I didn't know she was a doctor."

"Honorary, from the university of wherever the generalissimo is. Gotta go."

She hung up and within seconds, a large man in a black suit came into view near her as I watched from across the room. The black suit was followed by a hairdo, which was Mrs. Baxter's, followed by a smaller man in a blue suit, followed by the publisher, followed by Fred, who was wearing something green, probably that blazer he had that made him look like he won the Masters.

Behind him was another large man in a black suit, the one who gave us trouble at the front door. They stopped, the publisher pointed, and they all looked generally in our direction, all of us suddenly clicking away at our keyboards. A moment later, they turned and went into Fred's office.

They were in there for an unusually long time, we all thought, as we gathered in twos and threes at various points in the newsroom, each with a clear view of Fred's darkened office and the blinds hiding the occupants. Jane Liu thought something was up.

"Why would they be in there so long?" she said. "There's nothing to talk about. We produce the numbers showing that our circulation drop is really a gain when you measure Monday to Wednesday penetration as compared with the same period in 1987. She says keep up the good work and they go to lunch, walking around the outside of the newsroom, carefully avoiding contact with any of us. Except that they've been in there an hour. They must be selling it."

"Or closing it," I said, just to see what the reaction was.

"That's not what I hear," said Lorne Marshall. "I'm told that there will be a big circulation drive, and a total makeover to pitch the paper at the new generation."

"What new generation is it this time?" asked Jane.

"Well," said Lorne, "I'm not supposed to tell anybody this, but they've got a pollster working on that right now. Probably in a matter of weeks we'll know."

"What the new generation is?"

"Yes."

"That's fascinating," I said. "Do you know if the new generation is going to be younger or older than the one that reads the paper now?"

"I can't tell you any more," Lorne said. He walked away, quickly, as he always did, carrying a piece of paper, as he always did, stopping by his desk to pick up the guppy magazine.

"Has he ever been right about anything?" Jane asked.

"I don't think so," I said. "Although there was a time when he had advance copies of the cafeteria menu."

"What do you think they're doing?" she asked.

"They're looking at the fish, maybe, or admiring the picture of Fred and Uncle Bob. Maybe they're in there laughing at all the speculating we're doing out here."

My phone rang and I jumped to answer it. "I have some preliminary information," Davis said.

"Go."

"The two big guys are bodyguards and one of them carries her purse."

"That's cute."

"He has carried it into something like seventy-five newsrooms in nine countries."

"Must be getting good at it. Who's the small guy?"

"I had to make a call on that. It's Warren Eldridge."

"Sounds familiar . . ."

"Parker, you're so out of touch, no kidding. You know, from head office, travels with her everywhere, pinches pennies."

"Counts the chairs in the newsroom. Yeah, I've got it. Nice to have him pass among us."

"That still doesn't tell me what they're doing, though."

"We may never know. Or something will happen and we'll look back at this and think we should have known. It's not time for lunch, is it?"

"It's 11:15. Get back to your work."

I did that for a while, scanning the wires, routing the stories here and there. Business leaders wanted tax cuts, the opposition parties were still mad about what the prime minister said in the Middle East, some of our animals were in danger of disappearing, Europe was debating something about cheese. The different editors would look at these stories and decide whether to use them. Or they might decide to localize them, get someone from

Grand Valley to comment on cheese or the Middle East or salmon. Worse yet, Fred might see one of those stories and become interested in it. Everybody dreaded that. He would get one of his favourite reporters assigned to do the complete history of cheese, which had to be ready for tomorrow's paper. Somebody from the news desk would hound the library to come up with an appropriate cheese-related illustration, preferably illustrating a movie star in a bikini. That would be page one tomorrow and as I routed the cheese story off to the foreign desk I had a pang of regret.

On the other hand, it might take his mind off Saturn.

Out of force of habit I looked for cloth-related stories, but didn't see any. Nor was there anything about Saturn, or even space. It was odd, but what I really wanted to work on was the Saturn story. The story had entered that place in the back of my mind where ideas tended to stick, and the fact that they were bad ideas didn't make them any less sticky.

I had to put this stickiness to good use somehow. If I worked too hard on Saturn, the story would get done, and I didn't want that. The trick was to work on Saturn in a way that would send Juanita and the professor off on twisted trails that would slow their work. The phone rang again.

"Look out," Davis said.

I looked up and saw the procession heading in my direction. A few feet away, they paused and Fred said something to the group, speaking in a low voice. He had a red plaid tie, maybe a MacGregor tartan, to go with his green blazer. He pointed in what I took to be the direction of the STF office, then glanced at my desk. They all nodded. Then they walked slowly past my desk.

I was congratulating myself for having a story about low water levels on my screen when I remembered that Thelma and the generalissimo were still on my desk wall.

"This is the news desk," Fred was saying, "where they process the news and prepare it for publication."

I tried to appear as if I were processing the news as they reached my desk, in a wave of cologne that appeared to come from one of the bodyguards. "Good morning," Mrs. Baxter said. I turned. She was amazingly short and her hairdo really did shine, just like on the news.

"Good morning," I said.

"This is the man I've been telling you about," Fred said. He looked at my desk, at Mrs. Baxter and the dictator and then back at Mrs. Baxter. "Of course, under the circumstances it is necessary that he."

"I understand," Mrs. Baxter said. "Carry on."

They walked on, Warren Eldridge making notations in a pad.

My phone rang almost immediately. "What was that?" Davis asked.

"They know my work," I said.

"No, really."

"I think Fred informed them of my mighty mission."

"Yikes. It means you're actually going to have to do it."

"Yes, or open up that hardware store I just remembered I always wanted to open."

At lunch that day, we were joined by Lorne Marshall, a rare event. He would not normally allow himself to be seen sitting down with rowdies and ne'er-do-wells. Like all who had sworn allegiance to the new regime, he would eat at his desk and make sure that people saw him doing so. If he was joining us, it could mean only that he wanted to know what we were thinking or wanted us to know what he was thinking.

As he put down his tray, there was a sudden halt in the flood of caustic comments about Mrs. Baxter, her hairspray, her purse, her tailored suits, her lack of height, her plummy accent and her entourage.

"Hello, Lorne," said Jane Liu. "Heard anything more about the big makeover?"

"Makeover of what?" asked Lawrie Andrews.

"The newspaper, for God's sake," Jane said.

"Oh," said Lawrie. For the five years he had been in sports, he had one goal in mind, to get to Indianapolis to cover the 500. Every change in the management and content of the paper was examined with that in mind. Would it get him closer to Indianapolis?

"What makeover?" Davis asked.

"Oh, nothing," Lorne said. "Just a rumour."

"But you were telling us all about it," I said, "how we were going after the new generation and so on."

"Well, nothing's definite," Lorne said. "A lot will depend on what comes out of this visit." He turned to me. "I think Fred wants to see you."

"What visit?" Davis asked, innocently.

"Dr. Baxter's, of course."

"Oh, her," Jane said. "How often do you think she's had her eyes done?"

"Oh, not at all, I don't think," Lorne answered. "Did you know that we're from the same hometown?"

So that was it.

"I didn't know you were from England," Davis said.

"I'm not," said Lorne. "I'm from Timmins."

"But she's from England, some really fancy part of it, too," Jane said.

"Nope. She's from Timmins. But doesn't she speak beautifully?"

"Where did she learn that?" I asked.

"Her parents sent her away for a couple of years in junior high school. They owned the radio station."

"School in England?"

"No, in Toronto."

"That's really something," Davis said, "to be able to speak like that and grow up in Timmins. Was she popular there?"

"Oh, I imagine so. She was quite a bit ahead of me. I was in Grade 7 when she was graduating. Did you see her car?"

Jane was not giving up on this history lesson, even as Lorne recognized that vital information was in danger of falling into the wrong hands.

"Was she a cheerleader or anything?" she asked.

"Well, I didn't, um, go to many of the games, so I don't know, actually."

This had to be bullshit. Imagine being a boy in Grade 7, thirteen years old, and not knowing who the cheerleaders were. I still knew who the cheerleaders were in Kingston Collegiate and Vocational Institute.

"Not a cheerleader," Jane said.

"I didn't say that."

"Even if she wasn't a cheerleader," Davis asked, "was she popular with boys? Was she good-looking?"

Lorne shrugged and turned to me. "How's that project going, you know, in the unused office?"

He didn't know what it was. Maybe that was why he was here – that, or bragging about growing up with Mrs. Baxter, which wasn't going exactly as he had hoped.

"First, answer Davis's question, Lorne," I said. "Was she good-looking? Was she popular with boys?"

"Yes, she was very popular with boys," Lorne said. "She was, I don't know, I wouldn't say unattractive . . ."

"She was a dog," Jane said.

"No, she just . . ."

"But she was very popular with boys," I said.

"Yes."

"Interesting," I said. "Drop down to my office some time and we can talk more about this."

"Right," Lorne said, and got up hurriedly from the table.

"Nice chatting with you," Jane said, as he retreated.

"Yes," Davis said. "How interesting that you grew up with Mrs. Baxter."

"Dr. Baxter," Lorne said. "I didn't exactly grow up with her," he added, before he went out the door.

"So she wasn't very attractive," Davis said.

"But she was very popular with boys," Jane said. "I wonder how she did that."

I walked through the newsroom to Fred's office. Normality was returning. People were putting things back up on their walls. I saw solitaire games and hockey Web sites on some computer screens. Smithers, the managing editor, was looking over the shoulder of the news editor at his screen, upon which were displayed several photographs of Mrs. Baxter's visit. One of them would be on page one tomorrow.

Fred didn't say anything at first, just motioned me to a chair. He would do that sometimes, fail to speak. Usually it helped with the mystique. Today it just made him look overwrought, or at least, wrought.

"I just wanted a bit of an updating," he said.

"On the," I said.

"Yes."

"Have they gone?"

"Yes," he said. "They've gone."

"But they know."

"Yes, they know, in a general sense."

"Not about Saturn?"

"No, but about the water and the general outlines of the significant crisis facing our treasured society."

"And they like the idea of the story?" I asked.

Fred looked at the fish, then back at me. "They . . . think it's very important for the country," he said, "and the newspaper."

"In that order?"

"Not necessarily in that order."

There was a waterfall sound, then a slapping noise. I waited.

"There was a thought, which I share," Fred quickly added, "that the investigation would need to be somewhat broadened."

"To include what?"

"Perhaps some activist groups, some tennis players . . ."

"Tennis players," I said.

"Yes. You know how some of them . . ."

"I guess we'll find out," I said.

"Good," Fred said. "How are you enjoying Professor Blanchard?"

I thought for a minute. Leaves rustled and a bullfrog croaked.

"He's a very interesting man," I said. "You'll be glad to know that the professor is going to be showing me some of his research next week."

"Excellent. Couldn't you make it sooner, because of the express urgency?"

"He needs time," I said. "You can't rush this kind of research."

Fred turned to his computer, which was on, and typed something. "I suppose you're right," he said. "It's just that time is marching on at the speed of light."

"Is that what you wanted to see me about?" I asked.

"No," Fred said. "It was about . . ." and he consulted what looked like the note he had just typed for himself. "It was about moving you to nights. I'd like to do that, just to make your endeavours less publicly prominent."

Nights. When I first started out in Peterborough it had taken me three years to get off nights. Now, twenty-five years later, I was going back. But I remembered Davis and her enthusiasm about the story and my chance to be a part of it.

"Will I still . . . ?"

"I'd expect you to do a bit of a stint on the desk, just to keep up appearances, but I want you to spend as much time in the office as you can, working on the Saturn project."

I agreed. I would have the days free. Maybe I could take up golf again. Fred shook my hand. Everybody in this business seemed to want to shake hands.

Maybe there was a secret handshake I was supposed to know. Maybe I was doing it.

Chapter 10

For the next week, the professor dropped out of sight. I couldn't figure out why, but I assumed I was being tested. There were a couple of suspicious hang-ups on my phone in the STF office. Sometimes, while I sat on the night rim, the phone would ring, about two in the morning. I would pick it up, say "MacVeigh," and the line would go dead.

I bumped into Juanita Eldridge in the cafeteria one night and asked her how her research was going. She said her researches were going well. One research would be insufficient. I asked her if she knew how the professor's researches were going. She said there had been discussions and. She glanced at me significantly.

"Of course," I said.

As a Princeton graduate – or was she a graduate? No one had asked to see her degree – Juanita was taking her time with her researches. For most newspaper people I knew, the word "research" meant making more than one phone call and maybe going to the encyclopaedia. More recently, using the Internet was research. If you spent fifteen minutes on any of them, that was research. Doing research meant you turned your story in tomorrow instead of today.

For Juanita, doing research meant she wouldn't even think about writing anything for two weeks. Appalled as I was, I liked the idea. Every two weeks would help.

"Take your time," I said in the cafeteria. "Don't rush it."

She thanked me and said maybe she'd have something for me in three weeks. There were things at city hall that were interesting. There was a restaurant in the suburbs. There was a tennis club just off the bypass. There was an interesting irregularity at the Grand Valley Mall. All of that needed looking into, particularly with respect to the Belgian model.

"Of course, the Belgian model wouldn't . . ." I said and stopped right there, which was a good thing because Juanita couldn't wait to explain and, although I understood very little of it, I did pick up that the Belgian model was not a model, in the sense of strutting down the runway. It was more of a concept.

"Concepts take time," I said. Across the room, Alexei Ponomarev was sketching. I wondered if it was the Grim Pig, his trademark garbling of the two leading political cartoon symbols of the eighties. When he arrived in this country in 1990, just after the breakup of international Communism, everyone was drawing pigs, to represent patronage under Mulroney. Somehow Alexei got it confused with the Grim Reaper, which everyone was drawing to represent everything that wasn't patronage. The Grim Pig offended our publisher, who loved animals and Conservatives, and Alexei had been cautioned against drawing it. But in times of stress, it sometimes reappeared. The owner's visit might have brought it out.

"The best ones do," Juanita agreed.

I stopped looking at Alexei. "The best what?"

"Concepts," she said. "The Belgian model, remember?"

This was beginning to make me feel as if I was speaking fluent Saturnian, which would make it easier to report to Fred, when he called me into his office for a progress report. He'd like the interesting developments at city hall, the irregularity at the mall, whatever it was at the tennis club, and a couple of other things that have the possibility of. The trouble was it would make him eager to see some of the products of our researches.

I repaired to the task force office to think about it. This time I closed the door, to add to the intrigue, then went straight to the filing cabinet, unlocked it and took out the golf magazine I'd been reading since my switch to nights. At the bottom of the filing cabinet, behind a file folder filled with photocopies from the encyclopaedia, was my golf ball, a Bank of Montreal 4, that I'd found on one of my walks that coincided with the annual Grand Valley Chamber of Commerce Tournament.

I dropped the ball on the floor, opened the magazine to the article on new theories about where your chin should be pointed. I was reading about how the chin had been neglected by many of the older-style theorists, who worried too much about where the eyes were, vis à vis the ball. Later, of course, there was the whole movement toward establishing the centrality of the nose at the moment of address.

I think it had something to do with needing a new obsession. Being obsessed with not drinking was OK, as far as it went, but it lacked a little in the area of fun. Being obsessed with work was dangerous. Being obsessed with a little white ball looked as harmless as anything else.

At least it seemed harmless now. In the old days, my club-throwing days, a bad golf game was prelude to a long evening at the 19th hole. But then, so was a good golf game. Even now, I wasn't sure I could handle it.

The professor played golf. He and I were going to discuss the chin theory next time we met, although he didn't know it yet. Half an hour of chinning about chin theory would help us to bond and then we could really make some progress on this Saturnian thing and I could keep the pace of progress under control.

The phone rang and I quickly picked up the golf ball and put it into my pocket, so that the phone could not see it. More and more the Saturnians were getting to me, although I had yet to meet my first one.

Probably.

"This isn't television," I said.

"But the perch knows something new," said the professor.

"Hello, Professor," I said, realizing all at once that there should be another code phrase. It was a let-down just to say "hello" after all that.

"Are you alone?" he asked.

"Just me and my golf ball," I answered.

"Ha ha," he said. "That was a good one."

"Thank you."

"We must talk," he said.

"I agree," I said, "because of some newly emerging."

He waited, and I looked at the phone significantly.

"The mall, at seventeen hundred hours," he said.

"Check. Where in the mall?"

"Beside the lottery desk."

"Fine," I said, then something occurred to me. "Is there a way we are supposed to say 'goodbye'?"

"I do not believe so," he said. "Goodbye."

The next day I got to the mall early, to get the drop on the professor, and it's a good thing I did. When I walked in, people were running around screaming, security guards were talking on their phones, and men in coveralls were running up and down the corridors carrying green garbage bags and large sticks.

Naturally, I assumed it was one of the festivals Grand Valley has all the time. The Tri-Lakes Area Large Stick Festival, for example. But after a while it seemed odd that there would be so much screaming and I went to check it out. Then I went to a pay phone and called the city desk.

Pete Lester answered. "Pete," I said, "listen to me carefully. There're snakes all over the Grand Valley Mall."

"I know," he replied. "It's Grand Valley Mall Wildlife Week. We did a story last week on the wild animals exhibit over there."

"Well, some of the wild animals are loose. The anaconda got away and went around to the Duck Club booth. Now it's got two duck-shaped bulges in its tummy. The Duck Club's lawyers are already here. The crocodile was heading in the direction of the bunny rabbits last time I looked and a couple of the smaller snakes are in the bingo game."

"My God," said Pete. "What's happening there?"

"Nothing," I said. "The people refuse to stop playing. You better get somebody over here, especially a photographer. They're still trying to round up the animals and people are just going berserk. There's not even a lineup at the lottery booth."

"Hold on a sec," Pete said and I was put on hold. I listened to the on-hold music and realized that it was exactly the same music as the mall music. I pondered how that could happen, while I fingered my button-down collar and watched people jumping up on tables in the food court. The guys with the sticks and the bags were still running around, only now lawyers were chasing them.

Pete came back on. "Uh, Parker?" he said.

"Yep."

"Could you do, like, a brief on it for tomorrow?"

"What, you're not sending anybody over?"

"I talked to them and they said we just did an animal story last week."

"That's crazy," I said. In desperation, I lied, but only a little. "An iguana is attacking Ronald McDonald!" I said.

"I'm sorry," Pete said. "Is there a cloth angle of any kind?"

I hung up and walked over to the lottery booth. The professor was there, pretending to be having difficulty choosing among the many lucrative lottery options available to him. As I approached, he turned his back on me. I turned my back on him and we chatted, as if to other people. It might have looked a little odd, because there were no other people in the immediate vicinity.

"Isn't this crazy?" I said, "Snakes and crocodiles all over the place."

"I expected as much," the professor replied. I was struck suddenly with admiration. This man had a theory that was so all-embracing that it could encompass reptiles on the loose in a shopping mall.

He handed me the paper bag, which he had been clutching. "Be very careful of it," he said. "It's my only copy."

"You have it on disk, though," I said.

The professor looked over his shoulder, where there happened to be a large and foreign-looking frog on the lottery counter.

"To have it on disk would be . . ." he said, shaking his head, then glanced significantly at the paper bag, then walked away.

Of course, I thought, and then thought, of course what?

It was too early to go in to work. The trick now was to find a quiet place to have a sandwich and read the contents of the paper bag, a place where I wouldn't run into anyone from the office. A bar would be right. No one in newspapers drank any more, except white wine, and rarely in public.

I could safely go to a bar, then, and, as a bonus, indulge my sense of sober superiority. Ever since I discovered, a couple of years ago, that I could sit in a bar and not be tempted to order anything other than ginger ale, I did it whenever I could. As it turned out, I probably spent more time in bars than any of the people on staff who actually drank. Every once in a while, when this began to puzzle me too much, I'd drop in at an AA meeting.

Score's, the place where I usually went not to drink, was just down Michener Road from the mall in what was called the new part of town. The parking lot was full of minivans and the bar was full of women. As usual, curling was on all twenty-three television screens. I'd never heard of sports bars for women curlers before I came to Grand Valley, but I guess every town has them now.

I grabbed a booth, ordered a ham sandwich and a ginger ale with a slice of lemon, and watched curling for a while. It was soothing and took my mind off snakes. When the sandwich arrived, I opened the paper bag and carefully withdrew the professor's theory. A dozen rubber bands held the pages together. A dozen paper clips did too. Yellow Post-It notes stuck out, perhaps twenty of them. There was a title page, attached to the back page by Scotch Tape.

The whole thing was entitled "Report to the STF: The Unseen Enemy Secretly Walking Among Us Without Anyone Knowing About It." It was marked "Confidential" and "Copyright, 2000: Prof. Blanchard." Turning the title page over to begin learning about the unseen enemy, I got a little mustard on it.

The first page stunned me, even before I read it. I had never seen such an assortment of fonts, type sizes, and colours. The first paragraph was justified left and right. The second was centred. The third was flush left, the fourth flush right, the fifth underlined, the sixth a combination of all of these.

Once, before I went to Ottawa, I worked in the West for a paper that was so small that handling letters to the editor was a part-time job. I combined it with being the news editor. Every day after I finished putting out the final edition, I would look at the letters and see if any of them were publishable. Sometimes three or four would arrive in a day, sometimes none.

It was there that I developed what I called the Typographical Indices of Paranoia. Under my theory, the more types of emphasis a letter contained, the more likely it was to be written by someone who believed that forces, of one sort or another, were out to get him.

Capital letters were a sign. Underlining was another. Letters written all in caps *and* underlined were very likely to be by a total loony. Often, the letter would be turned on its side, so that more thoughts could be scrawled in the margins. An added bonus was the use of different-coloured inks, or, in the case of the more technologically advanced, different-coloured typewriter ribbons. Once you had a basic grasp of the theory, all you had to do was take the letter out of the envelope to know what thoughts were in it.

A letter written all in caps, underlined in red, sometimes with words circled and decorated with little stars, would talk about the coming of the Communists, or the United Nations, or the sodomites or the French. Advance notice of the invasion would have been broadcast on a toaster, directly into the reluctant brain of the correspondent. Further signs would be contained in cloud patterns. Those who disputed the truth of the hypothesis were either innocent dupes or had already been taken over by the invaders. And by the way, those editors who refused to publish the warnings were clearly playing for the other team.

The advance of technology, particularly the home computer, had, for a time, a stifling effect on the design of these letters. Composed with an up-to-date word processing system, coming off a high-speed printer, the loony letters came to resemble everybody else's. They looked fine – legible, neat, well-ordered, and you actually had to read the contents to recognize what they were. But now, with the professor, a breakthrough had been made. He had recognized what his fellow believers should have seen all along, that the computer had wondrous ways of creating an impact on the printed page.

You could make letters bigger or smaller. You could print them in italic or boldface. You could make the boldface green and the italics red. You could double space, indent. You could change from Helvetica to Corona. You could change from nine-point to twenty-four-point.

And you would *want* to. With an important message, one that the government is hushing up, that the media is keeping the public from knowing, you would use every means at your disposal, including Post-It Notes, to give your message the maximum impact.

I looked around Score's. People were laughing and arguing at the bar. At the nearest table there was an argument about in-turns and out-turns. One was better than the other, but there was some difficulty establishing which. Nobody was paying any attention to me, as I opened up the professor's report. The report was about an inch thick. I flipped through the Post-It Notes, past the one labelled NO WATER ON SATURN and found one labelled SPORTS and opened the report there, turning the pages until I came to a section on curling.

CURLING: A NOT–SO–INNOCENT PASTIME, it was headed.

It is no coincidence that teen-age pregnancies are high where so-called "curling" flourishes. Although commentators attempt to conceal it, with their references to the "four-foot" and the "rings," the target area in a curling rink clearly, and not UNDELIBERATELY, resembles female genitalia, specifically the breast area, with the so-called "button" standing in for the nipple.

Scientific studies show, further, that the path of the rock down the curling ice represents the journey of the sperm, a clear attempt to subvert the youth of curling-infested areas and influence them into lives of promiscuity and free-thinking.

Defenders of so-called curling, confronted with this scientific evidence, often attempt to deflect it by saying: "Well, what about the sweepers? How do the sweepers fit in to your theory about sperm coming down the ice?" And indeed, this is a difficult question to answer. Nothing in our family-life education, either from our parents or from Bible study, makes any reference to sweeping, as it relates to intimate moments in our lives.

However, the issue is more easily understood when we make reference to the CUNNING and UNSCRUPULOUS nature of our opponents. OF COURSE, they would insert sweeping into this activity, PRECISELY to draw attention from its essentially corrupting and sexual nature. It is not wise to underestimate these people, if indeed people they are.

This brings up another point worth considering. These are not people, in the sense that we understand them. Remember, they are from Saturn, where curling originated. We have not yet compiled adequate data on the various forms of ACTIVITY that they engage in there, but it is not outside the realm of POSSIBILITY that Saturnian sexual practices do involve brooms of some type. Indeed, it is not outside the realm of possibility that curling IS a form of Saturnian sexual activity.

The frequent sliding, the practice of wearing "rubbers," and other such . . .

A shadow fell over the page. I looked up and saw, through the haze, a large person standing beside my table. The large person was wearing a Disney World T-shirt, upon which a large mouse was swaying. Looking up from this large, swaying mouse, I saw a familiar face, except that I couldn't remember where it was familiar from.

It was a fat face, a cruel face, a face that —

A face that was at the paper last week, checking I.D., a face that had arms attached to it that carried Our New Owner's purse.

The face was considerably drunker than it was then.

He stopped swaying for a moment and squinted at me. "We are acquainted," he said.

"I don't think so," I answered.

He resumed swaying for a moment, then stopped and squinted again.

"Are you in the midst of reading something?"

Damn! Here I was, surrounded by curlers, and he could be one of them, for all I knew. Hastily, I attempted to stuff the report back into the paper bag. As I did so, I knocked over my ginger ale and some of it spilled onto the pages and a puddle headed rapidly in my direction. I jumped to my feet to avoid getting soaked.

An odd thing happened then. As I stood up, he flinched, jumped back, and nearly fell over.

That led to an equally odd thing, which was me apologizing to this man, 280 pounds and, I would guess, 6'4", whom I had just terrified.

"Sorry," I said. "My ginger ale spilled."

"No harm has been done," he said. "I've just been a trifle lately jumpy, jumply latey . . . jumpy lately."

He sat down beside me in the booth. "I seem to be in need of a seat," he said. "Would it inconvenience you if I sat down?" he asked.

"Of course," I said, meaning "of course not." I moved the

report over to my side of the booth and put it on the seat away from him. He squinted at me all the while.

"You work at the *Beacon* publication," he said.

"That's right. And you were there the other day."

A look of desolation came over his face. "It ranks among the worst days of my life," he said. "She left her frigging – excuse me – purse on a counter somewhere, when she was obliged to go powder her nose and spray her hair and what have you. When she inquired after it, I was unable to locate it immediately. I had to retrace my steps and locate it, which I did successfully, but she terminated me as soon as we vacated the premises."

"I'm sorry," I said.

"Best position I ever had. All I had to do was carry her purse around and stand in doorways looking malevolent."

"You were good at that," I said.

"Thank you," he said. "Now I am uncertain as to my immediate course of action."

"What about the *WB*?" I said. "They could use someone who looks mean, I bet."

"The *WB*?"

"The paper. The *World-Beacon*. You look mean enough to work the security desk. And they'd really love to have you around in case of a lockout."

"I *look* mean," he said. "Anyway, what's the point of working there?"

"The point?"

"Yes. It has limited prospects."

"We're making money."

"On the contrary, it's hemorrhaging like a stuck pig."

"C'mon, where do you get this stuff?"

"Don't forget. I carried her purse."

Chapter 11

By Brian Blezard

Grand Valley community leaders today overwhelilimingly welcomed the announcement of an upcoming visit by the reknowned American evangelist and fisherman, known affectionately the world over as Uncle Bob.

Dr. Uncle Bob will attend this year's annual Grand Valley Foshing Derby, to be held June 30–July 2.

A spokesman for Dr. Uncle Bob, reached at his headquarters in Cary, N.C. said that the world-acclaimed preacher had decided to combine his passion for moral values and his passion for fishing and hold a crusade in Grand Valley to coincide with the the Dreby.

"We are going to call it the Mass for Bass," the spokesperson said.

Grand Valley Mayor Martin Havelock, interviewed by telephone from a fact-finding tour in Euope, expressed delight with the announcement.

"This is just what our community needs," Mayor Havelock said.

Chamber of Commerce President James Norwood, publisher of the *World-Beacon*, said the visit would be good for the local economoy.

"This will put Grand Valley on the map as a world-class fishing and religion centre," Mr. Norwood said.

Members of the local clergy, while unavailable for comment, were said to be pleased.

I become aware of something beside my screen and looked up, to see Hamilton Thistle, the night news editor, rubbing his hands on his tweed jacket. Newsroom veterans knew what this meant: he had been into the jelly doughnuts again.

"Great news, wot?" he said.

"Is that our style on second reference, to call him Dr. Uncle Bob?"

"I think so," he said.

"Who is Brian Blezard?" I asked.

"Freelance bloke. Used to work with Fred and me in Alberta. Just came to town. Fine writer."

"He can't spell," I said, grouchy enough to blame him for the *WB*'s usual assortment of typographical errors. "And what's this about the local clergy being unavailable for comment? The ones I know, the only way they're unavailable for comment is if they're dead."

Although Hamilton was not yet forty, he tried to look older. This involved wearing the complete Brit uniform, consisting of brown tweed jacket worn over green sweater, the same one every day, worn over a tie from some old school. Both jacket and sweater were covered with several weeks' accumulation of powdered sugar.

"Actually," Hamilton said, "it didn't seem wise at this point to be putting in comments from them. They tend to be rather negative about some of Dr. Bob's methodology."

"Is he a doctor?"

"He must be."

"Putting in negative comments would piss off the chamber of commerce, and maybe even the publisher."

"That's not an exceedingly helpful way of putting it. I thought it was rather clever of Blezard to put in those words about them not being available for comment."

"And what about the words about them being said to be pleased."

"That was clever, too."

It was Fred himself who suggested contacting the mayor on his fact-finding tour of Europe. The mayor, in fact, was fact-finding at Lakewood, the drying-out centre for the Tri-Lakes Area, where he did fact-finding every couple of years, and would have been unavailable for comment. But Fred thought he would not object to being quoted as welcoming Uncle Bob's visit, and Brian Blezard, like a good soldier, put the quote in.

This was a lot to happen to me in one day, what with snakes and the bodyguard and learning about the unholy origins of curling. I wondered if this would be a good place to draw the line. I could refuse to handle the story; I could challenge this roving band of Brits and freelancers. But Fred had gone home and I was tired. I ran the spell-check on the story, changed "spokesman" to "spokesperson" in the third paragraph and then, just to be consistent, changed "spokesperson" to "spokesman" in the fourth. I put a headline on it, FISH DERBY MENU: FILET OF SOUL, and sent it on to the night news editor, who would change it to CITY EAGERLY AWAITS NOTED EVANGELIST.

After that, I did my usual newsroom rounds to find out how this particular story had come into being. These days, the origins of the story were often more interesting than the story itself. This one had begun as a press release to the agriculture reporter, who doubled as religion editor. He, being a Unitarian, if anything, didn't see it as a religion story and passed it over to the sports department.

Like the religion editor, the sports editor was from the old school. He thought sports was baseball and hockey and didn't see why anyone would want to read about fishing. The sports editor also failed to recognize the important role religion played in today's newspaper and failed to remember seeing Uncle Bob's photograph on Fred's wall. He said he didn't have the staff to cover a fishing derby and passed it over to the city desk.

But Lorne Marshall knew what pictures were on Fred's wall. When the press release landed on the city desk, he took it to the managing editor, who took it to Fred, who called a meeting on how the story would be covered, what the follows would be, who would be called for comment. The news desk was given the responsibility of finding photographs of some of the great religious leaders of the past – Jesus, Martin Luther, Mahatma Gandhi, Mohammed – to run with the big feature on Uncle Bob, which was planned for the weekend ahead. When the news desk reported that no photographs were available, except for Charlton Heston, it was decided to use paintings instead, which were scanned from the encyclopaedia.

The city editor, who didn't understand Fred, made a half-hearted attempt to assign the story, but all of the reporters claimed to be busy. Brian Blezard happened to be in Fred's office, paying a visit, when the word about the shortage of staff was received. He was introduced to the city editor and, according to sources near the city desk, informed him that he didn't have time to make any calls but had a list of the quotes needed in the story.

By the time the story was completed, late in the afternoon, the day shift had gone home, the night shift had arrived, and the story was slotted for an inside page by a desker who was not aware of the meetings that had taken place. The matter was rectified after the desker laying out page one asked why his desk was covered with photos of popes. Someone put two and two together, a call was made to Fred's home, and the story found its proper home, its spelling vastly improved. It would run on page one, accompanied by pictures of Uncle Bob, Charlton Heston, Gandhi, and Julie Andrews dressed as a nun.

On the surface, it was just another in a long and growing line of *WB* tales. They would be great to tell over a long dinner in five years, when all these people were long gone and another journalistic era, weird in an entirely new way, had begun.

One look at the sked of upcoming Uncle Bob stories convinced me that once again I was present at the creation; another magical moment in Canadian journalism was about to begin. I was in the catbird seat, as they would say in Cary, North Carolina, where Uncle Bob made his headquarters.

The sked was dropped on my desk by a puzzled Lorne Marshall. "Fred wanted you to have this," he said. The words "God knows why" hung in the air, although they were not actually spoken.

The list of stories was intensely detailed, a Marshall trademark.

- Business would do a story on the economic impact of Uncle Bob's visit.
- Editorial would provide 300 words of welcome.
- Sports would do the history of fishing.
- City would collect stories of people whose lives had been changed by Uncle Bob or, if that was not possible, were about to be changed by Uncle Bob.
- Editorial would find a university professor to write about the positive link between fishing and religion.
- Business would send a reporter to Cary to describe the headquarters of Uncle Bob's organization, the Worldwide World of Uncle Bob.
- City would collect testimonials from all over the world from leaders whose lives had been enriched by Uncle Bob.
- Photo would prepare pages of pictures of Uncle Bob with world leaders and common people alike, including Fred and Mrs. Baxter.
- Entertainment would do a retrospective on the movie *The Big Fisherman*.
- Lifestyles would print some of Uncle Bob's favourite recipes.
- The assistant managing editor that no one knew what he did would make an attempt to acquire the rights to reprint several pages from Uncle Bob's latest fishing memoir, *The Holy Creel*.
- City would prepare a chronology of Uncle Bob's life.
- A freelancer was working on the cloth angle.

For one quick meeting, that was a pretty impressive list and there would be lots more. I should have been excited about it. So much to mock. I should have been anxious to pick up the phone and share all this with Davis. Even better, there was the definite possibility that in the excitement over Uncle Bob, Saturn would slide to the bottom of Fred's mental priority list.

But I didn't feel good. Somehow Saturn beckoned. I edited a few more stories, wrote some boring headlines, then wandered into the STF office, closed the door and took out my golf ball.

After rolling it along the top of my desk for only twenty minutes, I firmly established that the desk was not quite level. It broke down and a bit toward the advertising department. There was some pondering involved in this activity, a weighing of choices. On the one hand was a story about Saturnians trying to take over the world, or at least the Tri-Lakes Area. On the other hand was a story about an American evangelist and fisherman bringing joy and prosperity. Being involved in the Saturn project meant I didn't have to be involved in the Uncle Bob project. That was good, I concluded.

I wondered if Professor Blanchard's paper might have some things to say about fishing, religion, or even Uncle Bob Himself. Establishing some sort of relationship would keep up Fred's interest and keep me on Saturn for a while. It was strange to think that I was suddenly trying to keep Fred interested in Saturn, but the alternative was worse, not to mention far less interesting.

There was a third choice, finding a job on the rim of some other newspaper. I pondered that too, as the golf ball rolled back and forth. The thing was, I was more or less at peace in the Tri-Lakes Area. I liked many of its people and all four of its lakes.

Chapter 12

There is something about coming home from work to an empty apartment at four in the morning. Long ago I decided I would make it be something good – good to be by myself, to be the only one in the world up and about. It would be good to have the apartment empty and creaking, good to have nothing on television but half-hour commercials for anti-aging products, good to be too wide awake, good not to be able to have a couple of beers to put me to sleep.

The blessings could really add up, when you counted them.

The apartment, second floor of an old brick house with a view of Watson Lake, wasn't so bad. Determined to avoid the stigma of the pathetic slobby divorced guy, I kept it clean and neat. Not that anybody but me ever saw it. But you never knew. And it made coming home alone at four in the morning easier when you didn't have to walk over pizza boxes, compact disc cases, and old newspapers.

There was a bedroom and a big living room with a small kitchen off it. There was a TV and a chesterfield facing it that wasn't too old, and in front of it a coffee table with some golf magazines, a John le Carré novel, and yesterday's newspaper. On the wall to the right was a bookcase, also containing a CD player and turn-table. There was an assortment of CDs and LPs, a wide range, the main feature being a lot of stuff by Ella Fitzgerald. The walls featured some Canadian art, landscapes by people nobody ever heard of. In a corner of the living room, by the big window facing the lake, was my desk with an old Macintosh on it, a dictionary and the professor's research paper, still in its original paper bag. Over the desk were a couple of framed front pages. One was a Montreal _Gazette_ from election night, 1988, the picture showing Brian and Mila Mulroney waving to the crowd. In that crowd, just below the platform and discernible only to me, is me. The thing that makes the picture so extraordinary is that I don't remember being there. I never know what exactly to think when I look at it, but I need to look at it occasionally.

The usual routine was to fill up the kettle, plug it in, take a spin around the place checking for leaks, burglars, short circuits, mice, or whatever was concerning me at the time, such as Saturnians, then drink some tea and read the paper I'd grabbed out of the mailroom on my way out. That was another good thing about being awake in an empty apartment at four in the morning: I got to see, before all the sleeping people, what was happening in the world and the Tri-Lakes Area.

EDITORIAL

A visit to Cherish

In less than one (1) month, residents of the Tri-Lakes Area will have one of the opportunities of their lifetime – to meet and learn from one of the most prominent and revered personages ever to grace the Tri-Lakes Area, prominent evangelist and fisherperson, Uncle Bob.

People the world over, including Canadians from coast to coast, have benefitted from their exposure to the thoughts and words of this man, his emphasis on spirituality and people lifting oneself up by their bootstraps. His philosophy is tailor maid for our difficult times, in which so many are seeking so much so often from so few.

Dr. Bob says "No!" to handouts and spiritual decline and we say "Yes!" to that.

How often have we, in the Tri-Lakes Area, heard the words: "Yes, I would like to participate in the spiritual development and economic growth of our fine community, but it is simply too darned hard to find the time to do so?"

This is the challenge that the celebrated evangelist and fisherperson, Dr. Bob, poses to us in his long-awaited visit. Can we take the time from our busy days and, in some cases, nights, to capture the essence of the message that will be sent to us, along with a rollicking good time catching fish and getting them weighed for valuable prizes?

It is to be hoped that the legendary hospitality of the Tri-Lakes Area will shine on Uncle Bob and his capable staff as they make their way among us, pausing to offer wise counsel and catch fish, then release them. In the words of the immortal John Keats, a British writer, now deceased:

"He who of those delights can judge, and spare
"To interpose them oft, is not unwise."

Over the editorial was Alexei Ponomarev's cartoon of a smiling Uncle Bob, which I recognized as drawn from the photograph in Fred's office, only with Fred taken out of it. In his place were three smiling children, one white, one Asian, one black. Uncle Bob appeared to be holding the Statue of Liberty's torch in one hand and a fishing rod in the other. Alexei's command of the North American cartoonist's vernacular was improving. In his early days here, every cartoon he drew featured breadlines. Very occasionally it worked: the odds were that it would from time to time. People did line up, even in North America. But most of the time it was just puzzling. His drawing of Bill Clinton and Monica Lewinsky in a breadline was so puzzling that it won a National Newspaper Award.

I worked my way through the rest of the paper. Usually in the

WB, the best news wasn't on page one. The president of Algeria had proclaimed Canada to be the best country in the world, even including Algeria. Canada and Japan were considering free trade. National parks were threatened with global warming. The death rate from cancer was way down. A Commons committee proposed a ban on lawn pesticides. An Ontario cabinet minister blamed nature for pollution. Four were killed in riots on the West Bank. Nigerian peacekeepers threatened British peacekeepers in Sierra Leone. Those stories weren't on page one. Prince Edward wanting to start a family was on page one, although with a headline far more modest than that greeting Uncle Bob. Uncle Bob also got a sidebar and a locator map showing Cary, North Carolina. There was a story and picture about the opening of a cloth museum in Tennessee, a story about people not eating enough vegetables, and a feature about Britney Spears's nose, which made me walk to a mirror to check my own nose. I occasionally looked at it to see if it would suddenly turn into one of those booze noses. It was still all right.

As always, reading the paper tired me out. I wondered what it did for ordinary people. The effect was probably less severe than we in the business feared or hoped. The majority of them would not see the editorial. They would check the weather and compare it with what they saw outside, then check the weather again. They would look at the TV listings. They would look at box scores. Then they would put the *World-Beacon* down, intending to pick it up again. When they got home from work the paper would be there and they would pick it up to see what was on TV and notice an article they would want to read later. After watching TV they would go to bed. The next morning they would find the *World-Beacon* on the couch and forget why they had left it out and throw it in the recycle box.

I went to bed thinking I would dream of Saturn. Instead I dreamt of a breadline. I was just getting to the front when I was awakened, hungry, by the phone.

"Don't you know it's three in the afternoon!" I barked.

"Don't you know how funny that sounds?" Davis said.

"Sorry. You know how nights is."

"OK. Listen, Parker, do you think you could wander over to Score's. I've got a friend with a hot story."

Chapter 13

Generosity, serenity radiate from HQ of Uncle Bob empire

By Anthony Frusculla

with files from Brian Blezard

A small group of cheerful people stand contentedly on the "front porch" of Sunbeam House, the international headquarters of the much-honoured charitable organization, the Worldwide World of Uncle Bob.

In the group are all races, mingling happily, talking of fishing, the weather and, of course, Uncle Bob.

The acclaimed evangelist and statesman will be paying an eagerly awaited visit to the Tri-Lakes Area next month. The visit has been enthusiastically welcomed by civic leaders.

"Uncle Bob saved my life," says Thomas Washington, 23, a well-dressed African-American from Winchester, MA, as the others nod in agreement.

"I was awash in materialism and video games and all that," Washington says. "But Uncle Bob showed me the way and I know that he will show the way to all the residents of the Tri-Lakes Area too."

Sunbeam House, located in the centre of the fabled North Carolina Research Triangle, is a three-storey structure of pink glass that blends into the rolling hills and green trees that surround it. But at the front of the building is an actual front porch, constructed of materials carefully chosen to resemble wood.

"It's just like my front porch at home," said Sandy Yamagata, 19, of Los Gatos, CA, "although I never actually had a home until Uncle Bob gave me one.

"The residents of the Tri-Lakes area are so fortunate that –"

Tony Frusculla grabbed the newspaper out of my hand and tore it into small pieces, the bits of paper floating onto the table and several landing in my ginger ale and Davis's beer.

"Nice story," I said, not knowing what else to say.

"Fuck," Tony replied.

"Tony's miffed a bit," Davis said.

"Is that why you called me here, to say that Tony's miffed a bit? Not that I'm sorry you called me here."

"The thing is," Davis said, "that Tony didn't write that story."

"Assholes," Tony said.

"It's got your byline," I said.

"Pricks," Tony said.

"You didn't write it?"

"Shitheads."

I turned to Davis, who was pretending to be interested in the Norwegian bonspiel that was showing on one of the bar's big screens. She had jeans on and a University of Manitoba sweatshirt, the sleeves pushed up to the elbow.

"Your man isn't making much sense," I said.

"If they had completely rewritten your story on Sunbeam House and left your byline on it, you wouldn't be making sense either," she said.

"C'mon," I said. "Stories get rewritten all the time."

"Pissers," Tony said.

"Pissers?"

"I'm running out of bad words," he said.

"Anyway," I said, "I'm sorry that your story got rewritten. What was it like, travelling with Brian Blezard?"

"How would I know? He never got near Sunbeam House," Tony said. "I went down there by myself, to North Carolina. I wrote a pretty good story, I thought, and they got him to rewrite the whole thing about how nice it was on the front porch and they stuck his name on it below mine. Shit."

"What was different? There was a front porch, right?"

"Oh sure. It was made out of, like, aluminum siding, and full of racks with pledge forms and brochures."

"What about the happy interracial group of young people on the porch?"

"There was a white woman. That was all. She was Uncle Bob's PR person. She showed me around and I never saw anything, except banks of computers through partly opened doors."

"Did you meet Uncle Bob?"

"No, there was a spiritual emergency that he had to attend."

A shadow fell over the table, a familiar one. I looked up and saw the huge, mean security guard.

"Good afternoon," he said. "Is everything to your satisfaction?"

"Fine," I said. "Every time I'm here, I see you."

"I was able to locate a position here," he said, "as an exit consultant."

Davis looked confused.

"A bouncer," I said. "Great. I'd like to introduce my friends, Shirley Davis and Tony Frusculla."

"Pleased to make your acquaintance," he said. "Rodney Sullivan."

"Rodney used to work for Mrs. Baxter," I told Davis and Tony. "Now he's in a more honest line of work."

"You get a lot of action here, Rodney?" Tony asked.

"Action?"

"Fights at closing time, that sort of thing?"

"Occasionally," Rodney said. "Perforce, the women enter into acrimonious discussions concerning the roaring game, and it can be a trifle combative."

"But in the afternoons, like now?"

"Naw. They just like me to perambulate around the room and interact harmoniously with the customers."

"You're doing a good job of that," Davis said.

"Just let me know if you are in need of anything, or if anybody is being vexatious," Rodney said and lumbered off. We watched.

"A broken man," I said.

"He seems nice," Davis said, "although awfully big."

It took Tony a while to fight through his rage and get to the part of the story that caused Davis to summon me to a sports bar in the middle of a sunny May afternoon.

As a young business reporter with investigative urges, Tony had jumped at the chance to travel to North Carolina for the set-up piece on Uncle Bob's headquarters. He knew that nothing remotely critical was either expected or wanted, but he harboured a faint hope that he could come up with a story so compelling that even the *World-Beacon* could not turn it down.

In five days in the Research Triangle, Tony had come up with nothing compelling, learned nothing of any consequence about Uncle Bob, aside from what he needed to write the kind of puff piece Fred wanted. The organizational flack steered him expertly through the tour, through the discussion of the finances, the organizational hierarchy, the links to worthy causes, the testimonials from world leaders. Tony saw the award-winning fitness centre and daycare facilities at Sunbeam House. He saw the plaques, the framed and laminated sermons, the smiles of Sunbeam House staffers, and he had nothing to write, except about the plaques, the framed and laminated sermons, and the smiles of Sunbeam House staffers.

In desperation, Tony wandered into the Sunbeam House gift shop, where the usual wares – T-shirts, coffee mugs, wall hangings, key chains and calendars – were on display. He noticed that one entire wall was devoted to fishing lures, notably, the Uncle Bob Holy Bass Basher, which came in a variety of colours and sizes. He bought one and asked where it was made. Right on the premises he was told, in the Uncle Bob Fishing Workshop. When he asked if he could visit it, he was informed that only authorized personnel were allowed into the workshop.

He put that into his story, the workshop being a closely guarded secret, but the story was otherwise non-controversial. It concentrated on how large and smoothly running was the World-wide World of Uncle Bob.

He sent in the story, and thought nothing of it until it appeared in the paper, with another writer's name on it and no resemblance to the story he had written.

"Well, I'm sorry," I said. "If it had gone through me I might have asked some questions. But then, I might not have known to ask some questions. Anyway, it's over. Now you know how a big-time newspaper operates."

This was making me feel sad again, which I didn't need.

"There's more to it, Parker," Davis said.

"Yeah," Tony said. "After I filed the story, I got curious about the Bass Basher and the workshop. So I went to some sporting goods stores around town and asked about it. They all said they didn't sell it, but it seemed to work really well. Uncle Bob has won lots of fishing derbies. Finally at one place they gave me the name of the guy who is supposed to have invented the Bass Basher and I tracked him down."

"Wait," I said. "Let me guess. He was a total rundown drunk living in a rooming house and living on cat food."

"No, he was the vice-president of a software company, living in a nice house in Chapel Hill and driving a Lexus."

"I don't get it."

"They bought him out, he invested in some high-tech stocks, made some dough and learned the game."

"So no story."

"No, but he referred me to a total rundown drunk living in a rooming house and living on cat food."

"Now we're getting somewhere."

"And this guy used to go on fishing trips with Uncle Bob."

"What was it," I asked, "hard liquor and fast women?"

"No, nothing like that," Tony said. "Uncle Bob is pretty straight. Sometimes he would bring along some licorice allsorts."

Davis looked at her watch. "Parker has to be at work pretty soon, Tony," she said. "And I have to be somewhere too."

"OK, OK," Tony said. "He says, the drunk, that the reason Uncle Bob wins all the fishing tournaments has nothing to do with the Bass Basher. It's because he pre-fishes and stashes away the catch."

"Huh?"

"Bob has some favourite lakes where the bass are big. He goes to one of those, catches a prize-winner, then keeps it alive in a special pool in his private jet, flies to wherever the tournament is and arranges to 'catch' the fish he has already caught."

"Was your source angry about this?" Davis asked. "Is that what drove him to drink?"

"No, he said it was having to stay sober on the fishing trips and eat licorice allsorts that drove him to drink. He actually didn't mind the cheating all that much. He figured that Uncle Bob did good work, and winning the tournaments helped him to keep his reputation up so he could do more good work."

"Why did he tell you all this?" I asked.

"I bought him a drink," Tony said. "A few drinks," he added.

"I don't get it. How come nobody else knows this story?"

"Nobody else bought him a few drinks, I guess."

"It would be a great story," Davis said, looking at me imploringly. "If only we could find a way to get it into the paper."

"Not in this paper," I said. "Not at this time."

A thought occurred to me that had nothing to do with fishing, or even journalism. What did it mean that Davis had to be somewhere?

Chapter 14

Tony had calmed down a little by the time he left. Now Davis and I were alone, which made me suddenly uncomfortable. It was that line about her having to be somewhere. She had a date, I bet. A vaguely familiar feeling of discontent descended upon me. What was it?

We sat in silence for a minute or so. She stared into her beer. I stared into my ginger ale with a slice of lemon and caught myself wishing it was a beer. Uh-oh. That almost never happened. To break the silence, I asked her about Tony.

"He's a city kid," she said. "Right out of school. He won some awards there, got offers from the *Star* and the *Globe* and the *Post*."

"How'd he wind up here?"

"He heard Fred speak at a CAJ convention. He was dazzled."

"Fred did 'destiny'?"

"All of it. Tony went up to talk to him afterwards. Such nerve. He was carrying his resumé with him and he handed it to Fred. When Fred got here, he called and offered him a job."

"Now he's finding out about real life," I said.

Maybe it was a kind of anticipated guilt about the tale Tony had told us. I wasn't going to have the guts to help him. I knew that. Maybe that was what was making me discontented. And of course, Saturn was never far from my mind.

"I hate to see him disillusioned," Davis said.

"He'll be OK," I said. "He finds this out now, it will toughen him up. He looks like he's going to be a good reporter."

"Yeah," Davis said, and went back staring into her beer. I went back to staring into my ginger ale. The lemon stared back. It suddenly occurred to me that I wanted to know where it was she had to be tonight.

"Davis," I began, and looked her right in the eye, as I figured I should. There were tears in her eye. And there were tears in her other eye.

Wait a second, I thought. I haven't said anything yet.

"What's wrong?" I asked.

"This stupid place," she said.

"There's worse bars," I said, trying to be reassuring.

"You know what I mean. This stupid newspaper."

"Yeah," I said, wondering which aspect of it was upsetting her most.

"Here's a really good story staring us in the face and there's no way we're going to be able to put it in the paper because the owner is a globe-trotting snob, the publisher is president of the chamber of commerce, and the editor is the subject's best friend."

"Plus," I said, "he's more worried about developments on Saturn. But that's no reason to cry."

Actually it was, but it turned out she had other things to cry about.

"Look," she said. "I'm forty-one years old. I'm smart, I'm experienced, I can write and edit and I understand things."

I was useless in the face of this. "And?" I said.

"How do you think I feel when I go to some business editors' seminar and we're talking about our papers and how we do our work, comparing notes and all that and I tell them that I have a cloth reporter on my staff. A cloth reporter!"

"They're not envious, I guess."

"Shit. Every day I stay at this place hurts my reputation. Every page I put out, all the booster bullshit, the Tri-Lakes Area on the move, the cloth angle on everything – everything I do makes my reputation worse. People used to think I was going places in this business. Now . . ."

It was true. Davis was a good reporter in Brandon and then Winnipeg. She did an excellent job at the legislature and was just moving into editing, looking like she had a shot at city editor, when her husband was transferred to Grand Valley. Even after he walked out, life didn't seem so bad for a while. She didn't like him much any more and her professional life was looking promising. The *WB* was looking for women to train as managers. Davis was perfect. She did a brief stint as a business reporter, a briefer stint on the desk, and was named business editor a year after she arrived, which was about the same time I showed up.

The first time I talked to her for any length of time it was at a farewell party. She was happy. The business editor appointment was still fresh and she was moving up. "You'll like it here," she said. "It's a good place." I remember her saying that, but I can't remember what she was wearing, or who was leaving.

That was two years ago and a lot had changed. "Now look at me," she said. "I want to be editor, or at least managing editor."

"You'd be good," I said.

"I don't want to live my whole life as the business editor for this crappy rag. But what're the chances of anything good happening for me with this gang?"

"You could leave," I said. "But I'd be sad if you did."

I hadn't known I would say that. Why did I? At any rate, she ignored it, distracted by a shadow crossing the table. It took me a minute to recognize that it was a real shadow, not a reflection of our mutual mood.

"Is everything to your satisfaction?" Rodney Sullivan asked.

"Fine," we both said.

"My profuse apologies for interrupting," he said. "I was merely endeavouring to ascertain the degree of your contentment, as I do with all the customers."

"We're content," I lied, and he walked away.

"What's going on with him?" Davis asked.

"I think he just likes me," I said. "He's had a hard time and he needs a friend."

"What if he's a spy?"

"A spy?"

"He hasn't really been fired by Mrs. Baxter at all. He hangs around and listens to what the staffers are saying, looking for subversive thoughts. Then he reports them to the management."

"I don't think so," I said. "He doesn't even look Saturnian."

Davis gave me a funny look. I liked it, though.

"I'm sorry," I said. "Saturn's on my mind."

I was blithering. "Other things are too," I added. "I was thinking that that beer looked pretty good."

"We'd better get you out of here," she said.

It was then that I realized what was wrong. I was in love with Davis. Damn! I hadn't known I was that discontented. We walked to the parking lot. If we were in Scandinavia or some environmentally conscious place we would have carpooled and one of us would have needed a ride. Then I could have said what was on my mind. But this was North America. I had my car and she had hers. She was going home and I had to go to the office.

This new relationship wasn't getting off to a good start, especially since not everybody in the new relationship was aware of it. The parking lot outside Score's wasn't an ideal location to explain it to Shirley – I had begun just this minute to think of her as Shirley. What a nice name.

Something had to be done so I did the only thing I could think of, which puzzled her a bit. We didn't usually shake hands.

She stared at me as I walked to my car, waving to Rodney Sullivan before I drove off.

For me, falling in love always went with being miserable. It didn't *make* me miserable. It just meant that I was. Whenever there was something drastically wrong with my life, I would fall in love, and rather quickly too. A couple of times, once with the mayor of a small Prairie city, I made the mistake of assuming that falling in love actually meant that I was falling in love, and followed up on it. With the mayor it meant having to fit romantic interludes around committee meetings and ribbon cuttings, and there was also a bit of a conflict of interest problem, given the fact that I was covering city hall at the time.

It being a small town, the only way I could disguise what was going on was to pursue a policy of tough, investigative coverage of the mayor's office. As a result, no one ever learned that the mayor and I were carrying on a romance. As another result, the romance didn't survive the second edition on the day the first products of my research appeared in the newspaper. And that was only because she hadn't seen the first edition.

"What the fuck was that?" said Her Worship, when she phoned.

"What, the story?"

"Yes, the story. I thought you liked me."

"I do like you. That's just journalism. It doesn't mean anything. It's a story, that's all. That's the way stories go. Somebody charges, somebody replies. Tomorrow, there's another story."

"There certainly fucking is," Her Worship said, and hung up. I knew what she meant: she meant, there's no other story for us. The funny thing was, it didn't bother me as much as I thought it should. That may have been the first time I realized that falling in love, for me, didn't have all that much to do with falling in love. It had to do with not being happy with what I was doing. What I had been doing, up to the point that I became better friends with the mayor, was writing routine stories, with no effort, no commitment. When I wrote the story that ended the dance with the mayor, I lost the mayor, but I loved the story. And that got me excited about writing again and as soon as that happened, I stopped loving the mayor – not that she would have had anything more to do with me anyway.

As soon as I stopped loving her, I started covering her more gently. Eventually we became friends again.

But this was different. I was sure it was. It's true I was pretty discontented about the prospect of spending my fiftieth birthday with the Saturn Task Force. And it's true that the spectacle of my newspaper rolling over for Uncle Bob did not give me great pride in a life spent in newsrooms.

All that was true. But there was something about Shirley. Part of it was the fact that she didn't seem aware that there was something about her. She was smart. She was talented. She knew how to laugh. And the times when she didn't know how to laugh were the right times. Like now.

Besides, maybe I had changed. I hadn't been in love since 1994. Maybe there was more to it than being miserable this time.

Chapter 15

When I got to the office, I glanced at the news editor's screen on my way by. Usually I can find out what's going to be on page one by looking at it. This time it was a very large bug, or a picture of a very large bug. Several editors were standing around looking at it. Fred was two desks away, conferring with someone.

"What's that?" I asked.

"I think it should be looking left," Hamilton Thistle said. "It won't do to have it looking off the page."

"It's a fucking bug, Hamilton," said Charlie McPartland, who was handling the page and, I knew, counting the days to his retirement. "Who cares where it's looking?" But he punched some keys anyway and the image of the bug flopped.

"What's the story, Charlie?" I asked.

He nodded his head in Fred's direction. "Mr. Spock over there finds this boll weevil's picture on the Internet. He wants it on page one because he likes the picture. The thing is, there's no story about a fucking boll weevil. And there's no boll weevil within a thousand miles as far as I can tell. But Mr. Spock wants it on page one anyway. I just do my job."

When Charlie was the news editor, at the time I arrived, we never had bug pictures on page one, unless by accident – if one were on, say, the Hon. Winston Booker, MP, without his knowing it.

I left Charlie to his troubles and took mine over to my desk where I found an e-mail from Fred. Brian Blezard would be doing a page-one story on a possible new threat to the cloth sector. Would I keep an eye open for related stories that could be tied in?

Would I? I ran my usual search of the wires, using the word "cloth," and turned up nothing. There was nothing recent in the database either. I tried "fashion" then, and did better, coming up with a photograph of a supermodel dressed in the tiniest little bit of cotton, the kind of thing a boll weevil would definitely have his or her eye on. I printed the picture out and took it over to Charlie.

"Here," I said. "Your turn to be a hero."

He looked at the picture, cursed and thanked me. When I got back to my desk, Brian Blezard was waiting for me, one foot on my chair. The foot had a sandal on it.

"Chief says you're the cloth expert," he said.

"We haven't met, have we?" I said.

Perhaps I sounded as if that was not one of the great sorrows of my life, because he forged on without offering either his name or a handshake.

"The way I see it, what we did in Orillia, we get this rat, this big rat, and we trace its life back to where it grew up and how it got here and how it developed its vicious outlook on life. Then we run the picture really big, we interview all the local health officials, they say there's no problem, we quote some people accusing them of cover-up and there's the story."

"But this isn't a rat," I said. "It's a bug. And it's not even here."

"Not yet," Brian Blezard said. "Bug, rat, they all have the same story."

"How did you get that?" I asked.

"Get what?"

"The story of how the big rat got here and developed its vicious outlook on life."

"Well, it's a, a technique. I guess it hasn't reached this town yet. But, you know, the big papers do it. You just have to know what you're looking for."

"And then the reaction more or less looks after itself."

"Right," he said. "People are going to be outraged when they see this cockroach."

"Boll weevil."

"Whatever. And then, these small-town bureaucrats and politicians. All they want to do is cover up. Next thing you know, it's a big story."

"Without even one weevil setting foot in town."

"Thanks to us."

Hamilton Thistle arrived, out of breath from the news meeting. How he could be out of breath was a puzzle. It wasn't from talking. All he ever said in the news meeting was "Good idea, Fred."

"OK," he said. "It's boll weevil played big. Under the picture, we run the historical perspective, all the bad things that boll weevils have done in the past. Across the top of the page is the cover-up story. You've got that, Brian?"

"Just about done. One more phone call."

Hamilton looked at me. "You find any related material?"

"There's a picture of a potential victim, scantily clad. I turned it over to Charlie."

"Great. Anything else?"

I thought for a second. What could I possibly contribute to this dialogue. "There's a song, 'Bo Weevil,' by Theresa Brewer, came out about 1956."

"I don't know," Hamilton said. "Fred hates music. But I'll get the library to look up the lyrics. Now we need someone to do the expert reaction story."

I saw Tony across the room. He didn't work nights, but he

had a hard time leaving the place. I wanted to talk to him anyway. "There's a kid from business here. I'll talk to him," I said.

"Good," said Hamilton. "This will be big. We've even got an editorial on it. Rand Barry has written an analysis piece blaming socialists and big-spenders for the boll weevil infestation."

"What are we doing for follows tomorrow?" I asked.

Hamilton stared at me. "Follows?" he said. "The story's over tomorrow. On to the next, I say."

"I'll go talk to Tony."

He was standing in front of the bulletin board, hands in his pockets, reading the stuff that had been there for months – retirements, postings for permanent part-time deskers, and temporary full-time reporters, union diatribes on air circulation and repetitive strain injury, notices of free tickets for last October's home opener of the Grand Valley Valleyers, our junior hockey team. Aside from the union stuff, the bulletin board was mostly the product of the assistant managing editor that nobody knew what he did.

"You're off shift, aren't you?" I said.

"Yup."

"Feel like doing a story anyway?"

"OK."

Reporters like Tony, the driven ones, would sooner do a story than anything, and it didn't matter much what kind of story it was. It beat going home. I explained the story to him and his eyebrows went up.

"I know, I know," I said. "But look at it this way. You do the story and you show Fred you've got the right stuff. Then the desk gets off your case, plus you're a step closer to being able to do the Uncle Bob story."

"I don't want my byline on it."

"I'll make sure it isn't there. It will say 'by *World-Beacon* staff.' They like that anyway. It makes it look like the entire resources of the newspaper are on the story."

"And I just phone up some professors?"

"Right. You've done it before. Remember the Hurricane Edgar story? And they'll tell you that boll weevils never show up around here. Then you ask them about the havoc boll weevils could wreak if they ever did show up here, and then you go with that. Easy. Remember to use the phrase 'wreak havoc.'"

"How much time have I got?"

"Half an hour."

"That's lots."

"Check with me later in my, um, in that office over there. There's something I want to talk to you about."

The deadline rush wouldn't begin for another two hours, so I decided to grab some time in the STF office. I thought about Davis – Shirley: I would have to think of her as Shirley – and tried to figure out what I could find out from Tony that would help my cause. There were interruptions. I fielded three calls from viewers irate about the hockey game being on instead of the news. As usual, I gave them the TV critic's home number. There were several mysterious hang-ups, as well as two muffled messages on the voice mail in what sounded like a foreign language.

It was good to be back on Saturn again.

After forty-five minutes there was a knock. "Hang on," I shouted and took my time getting to the door, banging drawers and filing cabinets shut. I had an idea that this would add to the mystery of what I was doing. And in case it was someone from the task force itself, it sounded like I was exercising proper security.

It was Juanita Eldridge. She was wearing a blanket kind of thing and her hair was up in a bun. "I wonder if perhaps we should have a special knock," she said.

"That would be fun. How about two long and two short?"

"Well, we should discuss it as a group."

"I'll put it on the agenda," I said. "What have you heard?"

"This boll weevils thing is terrible," she said.

"I know."

"I hadn't realized how far they would go."

"The . . . ?" I said.

"Yes," she said.

"I'm not surprised," I said.

"I wondered," she said, "if I should propose an article for tomorrow's paper, to go with the other coverage."

"On the?"

"Yes."

"No, I don't think so," I said, I hoped not too hastily. "That would tip our hand. I think we need to wait until all of the products of your researches are at hand. How are your researches, by the way?"

"It's a rather complicated subject," she said.

"Perhaps that's deliberate," I added.

"Quite."

"And we also need time to digest the professor's paper. You've seen it?"

"Only extracts. But they seem quite brilliant, particularly about the water thing."

There was another knock and I stood up, being careful to glance warily around the room first.

"What shall I do?" she asked.

"Pretend that you're interviewing me for your Ph.D."

"I already have my Ph.D.," she said.

"Nobody has to know that. Coming!" I shouted.

I opened the door, Tony came in as Juanita went out. They nodded at each other.

"Who was that?" he asked.

"Juanita Eldridge. She works here, one of the interns. You've never been introduced?"

"No. She seems nice," he said.

"How'd the story go?"

"Just the way you said. It didn't take too long to find a boll weevil expert. He said they could do terrible things and I quoted him on that."

"You'll get a gold star," I assured him.

"I hope so," he said. He looked around the room at the space art. "What did you want to talk to me about?"

What could I tell him? Suddenly, I was back in high school. I was talking to him because he knew her – Davis, Shirley. Maybe he would let slip some crucial fact. Maybe if I said something brilliant, it would get back to her. Maybe he'd tell me she *liked* me.

"I've been thinking about the fishing story. Maybe the idea is to find something else to investigate, ostensibly, while you're investigating the fishing story. And then, when you have it nailed down, there's no way they can refuse it."

"How would that work?"

"I don't know. I'm just kind of thinking out loud. Maybe there's a business-related thing you could be pretending to look at while you look at this."

"Mmmm."

"How do you organize things over there?"

"In business?"

"Yeah." Now I was getting somewhere.

"Well, we've got the three writers and Davis. She divides it up. We can't really specialize because there aren't enough of us. But I sort of do high-tech stuff when it comes up."

"You like that?"

"I'd prefer straight investigative, but we don't have much of a budget for that."

"I never heard Davis complain about the budget."

"No, she doesn't all that much. I guess she's used to it."

"It's a pretty happy department?"

Any minute, he would catch on that I was prying. But not just yet.

"I think so. Davis is a good boss. Not like the other assholes around here. Everybody likes her and we all get along."

"You're in here all the time. Is that because Davis assigns a lot of overtime?"

"Shit no. I just hang out here when I've got nothing to do. Everybody else has a life."

Ah. A life.

"I don't see Davis in here. So you work unsupervised at night?"

"She used to come in nights when I was working on something hard, now she's too busy with Mr. Hotshot, so I check with her during the days."

Somebody not in high school would have the savoir faire, the sang-froid and everything else you needed to avoid the obvious question. I didn't.

"None of my business," I said, "but who's Mr. Hotshot?"

"You should see the fucking car he drives – sharp little black Audi. They come out of a restaurant he points his key at it and it starts and the lights come on and it does everything but sing the fucking anthem."

"What is he, a lawyer or something?"

"No, he's some kind of broker. A risk analyst, his card says. Talks about the market all the time and leveraging and hedge funds, all that kind of stuff."

I made an effort to yawn. "Anyway," I said, "they spend a lot of time together."

"Yeah. When I started here, Davis and I, we could always go out for a beer and talk about a story. Now she hasn't got time."

I yawned again. "Oh well," I said. "Listen, I'll keep thinking about the fish story and you do that too. Maybe we can work something out."

Alone again, I tossed the golf ball up and caught it. I did this exactly twenty-five times, then I wondered why I was counting. Counting was something you could count on, was the only explanation I could come up with.

Chapter 16

Bowell Park, named after one of our most underrated prime ministers, is beside Watson Lake, the biggest of our three lakes (if you don't count the fourth). Sometimes I would walk down there to think and to get out of my apartment. In a few weeks there would be guys with pickup trucks and trailers, launching bass boats with 200-horsepower motors at the back, sometimes with their names painted on the motor. There would be souvenir stands and loudspeakers, everybody going nuts about fish and Uncle Bob's visit. Right now, it was as it usually was – men in expensive exercising outfits walking fast and talking on the phone. There was a woman sitting on a park bench talking on the phone, a couple of retired people, one of them carrying a plastic bag and chasing after a dog, and there was a drunk passed out on a bench. Parks had changed so much since the invention of cellphones and power walking; I wondered if the drunk had been put there by the Tri-Lakes Tourist Bureau, as a heritage object, a link with the past. These people would stop at nothing.

A fortyish man trotted by, fit and barely puffing. His dog trotted by too. The dog had a holster strapped around his chest, with a phone in it. This was what I was up against. International high-tech tycoons with deep tans, personal trainers, and designer dogs to carry their phones. All I had was the hope of Getting That Story.

I walked and thought. I had a rival. A risk analyst. I would have to defeat him. It was the kind of thing I had to do back in high school, except that I couldn't recall ever defeating anybody.

I can recall wanting to.

In my new high school way I thought, How would a guy like me impress a girl like Davis – Shirley! How would a guy like me win her away from the evil international risk hotshot? He would have a better car, a better face. He would be younger and richer.

What could I do to impress her?

True, there were things I could do that he couldn't. He couldn't write a decent two-line head over three columns. He wouldn't remember to put in the photo credit or use a pull-out quote to make the page fit. But that stuff might not count. I couldn't imagine sitting down with her over a candlelight dinner and saying:

"Look, Davis – I mean, Shirley – I can give you what he never can – an italic precede leading in to a drop-cap, the whole thing ragged right and with two-point column rules."

It wouldn't work. Only Getting That Story would work. It was the thing that Shirley had spent her whole professional life learning to do and to respect others for doing. It was one thing I could do that the risk analyst couldn't. He could assess the story, consider the macro-economic relevance of it and factor in its effects upon currency speculation. He could alert his worldwide contacts to it on five continents. But he couldn't get it, he couldn't Get That Story.

I could see that Uncle Bob Fishing Shocker, as I was beginning to think of it, was important to Shirley. If I could get it, I would be a hero. How would I do that? Without Fred knowing the story, he wouldn't free up the time and resources needed to get it. And if he did know the story, he certainly wouldn't free up the resources and time needed to get it.

Lying would be necessary to get it past Fred, and I wasn't very good at lying, not because of the immorality of it, but because I could never keep a straight face. I would look at the carpet and giggle for no reason. Sometimes I would double-talk, utter the most amazingly convoluted sentences, all in aid of getting the lie across. A dozen years ago, as my marriage was heading into the home stretch, I told a story at dawn about running into an old elementary school teacher and having to take him to the hospital when he sprained his ankle and having to sit for hours in the waiting room until he could be looked at and stopping off for just one beer on the way home, which is why it smelled like I'd been drinking, when actually I hadn't really.

I couldn't pull it off, especially the looking her in the eye aspect. I stared at the floor and giggled, particularly when I got to the part about the hospital waiting room, which I now realize I described in excessive detail.

It's a journalist's thing: If you get the little details right, everybody will think the big details are right too. But she might have recognized I was trying too hard, when I went for the exact shade of green on the walls. The thing is, I tried. And if I couldn't do it drunk, how could I be expected to do it sober?

The memory accompanied me for my first lap around the park, enjoying the exercise and trying not to swing my arms too high, for fear of looking like I was exercising. I needed to talk this over with somebody, but the only person I could think of talking it over with was Shirley, who was the object of the exercise. I would probably try to tell her she wasn't the object of the exercise and I would giggle and not look her in the eye.

Shit.

Beginning my second lap, I passed the park benches and recognized that the woman talking on the phone was Juanita Eldridge. She was both talking and listening intensely and the pronoun "they" sounded frequently. I heard the word "subversion" once and the word "water" and the word "curling." It reminded me that the stakes were high for her – maybe not as high as high school, but pretty high. I tried to pretend I hadn't seen her, but it was too late for both of us. She hung up the phone quickly and shoved it into her purse, giving me a nervous smile.

"Oh, hello," she said.

"Beautiful day," I replied.

"I was just," she said.

"Of course," I said.

"I was meaning to ask you a question about the, uh, thing we're working on."

"Yes?"

"That young man who was in your office the other day."

The other day, the other day. "Oh, Tony Frusculla. He works over in business. He said you'd never met."

"I've seen him around," she said. "Does he have anything, um, to do with?" she went on, and I suddenly remembered that Tony had asked some questions about her as well. Aha! Tony and Juanita. Juanita and Tony in a tree, K-I-S-S-I-N-G. High school was great.

An avenue opened before me. Also a chance to practise my lying. Tony would be great on the task force. Putting him on it would be the perfect cover for his digging into Uncle Bob Fishing Shocker. Why hadn't I thought of that?

Well, actually, I had, but it seemed as if Juanita had first. Which was the beauty of it. Putting him on the task force could be her idea and I wouldn't have to lie about that.

"I certainly did not take the opportunity to inform him of any of the specific details surrounding the particular," I said, slightly horrified at the sound of what was coming out of my mouth, "but I did get a chance to probe him to an extent on the nature of his views relating to such matters. He's quite a serious young chap."

"Not too young, I hope."

"About twenty-four," I said. "Single," I added.

Juanita bit. "Did you get the impression that he would be a valuable addition to?"

"It crossed my mind, I confess. But I'm not certain as to the professor's inclination concerning the possible broadening of the personnel element of the project we are tasked to perform."

"I could talk to him about it," she said.

"Perhaps that's a good idea," I said. "I'll talk to him too. We have to think a bit about the danger of the information being spread too far. Still, Tony would be motivated, without question. He's had quite a difficult life and at least some of it is attributable to."

I looked her in the eye while I said that and didn't giggle even a little.

"That's fascinating," she said. "I'll let you know what the professor says."

She must have worked fast because when I got to my office that afternoon there was a message from the professor in my mailbox. I knew without opening it that it was from the professor because it was a large brown envelope sealed with tape. Inside was a smaller white envelope also sealed with tape. The words TOP SECRET were printed in block capitals on the large envelope. The word CONFIDENTIAL was printed in block capitals on the smaller envelope and underlined twice in red ink. After a few minutes of tearing I got to the inside, where there was a single piece of note paper, with a Grand Valley Inn letterhead.

"NOT TELEVISION," it said. "Call perch."

Something told me that I mustn't seem too eager about this, so I waited a couple of hours, strolled the newsroom, did a bit of work, chatted with Jane Liu, who was working late on a column about "getting your frigging perennials ready for mid-summer," as she put it. But she was fairly cheerful, having just come up with a byline for the stamp column – M. U. Cilage. It was terrible, I told her. Management thought it was very clever, she replied.

She had lots of gossip – new editing horrors, dire statistics from advertising and circulation, a sighting of Mrs. Baxter in Calgary, imminent departures of top managers. As usual, it was the most hated editors who were thought to be on the brink of departure. After years of hearing this stuff, I had learned to discard all but the most promising information. The only item vaguely interesting in Jane's monologue was the news that Fred had been at some kind of management retreat, where the concept of synergy was still in use. I wondered why I hadn't seen him around for a week.

I handled a page that featured a report of several people falling ill from eating poisonous wild mushrooms. The reporter had led the story with the words: "It's that time of year again." I tried to persuade the news desk that the lead was a little over-used and, anyway, would be much better applied to the Santa Claus Parade than to the near death of several of our Tri-Lakes Area mushroom fanciers. But the night news editor liked the lead. Apparently they never had a Santa Claus Parade in Britain.

"OK," I said. "How about we run the lead with a slight modification?"

"Like what?" Hamilton Thistle asked.

"'It's not that time of year again.'"

"Just run it the way it is," he said.

I shrugged and went back to the page, found a picture of some mushrooms and arranged to have a line drawn through it and a circle around it, in the internationally recognized sign for NOT. The circled mushrooms might have been totally edible, for all I knew. But it was better to be on the safe side. No one ever got sick from not eating mushrooms. I finished up the page, and took a proof over to the news desk. Then I went to the STF office, closed the door and phoned the professor.

"Hello," he answered, and suddenly a weakness in our strategy became apparent to us both. Our elaborate password strategy was based on him phoning me. When it worked the other way around, there was no appropriate language.

"It's, uh, me," I said. "Television. That is, not."

"I don't know what to say now," the professor said.

"Well, let's just talk."

"You mean, take a chance?"

"Yes."

"That's too risky," the professor said. "I'll call you back."

He did, immediately, we went flawlessly through the passwords and smoothly into the conversation. He had been talking to Juanita and she had told him of a possibly useful addition to the task force. Did I know the young man?

"I know him," I said. "He's very capable and quite dedicated, seemed to be well informed on the. It's just . . ."

"What?"

Worried that I was outsmarting myself, I moved falteringly ahead.

"Too many people know already," I said.

"They know about?"

"I can't be certain. There have been hang-ups on my home phone. Yesterday, a green car behind me. Green is the colour of the, isn't it?"

"I think so. I'll check."

"It's probably nothing. Yesterday, there was a story in the paper about small planets beyond the solar system, more than thirty of them."

"Well, yes, but."

"Nobody knows how it got in there. I talked to all of my colleagues. And then on the radio this morning. I suppose you heard it. On the CBC? The song. The pan flute."

The professor would never admit to being unaware of a threat. "Of course I heard it," he said.

"A signal."

"Perhaps," he said.

"So maybe too many people know."

The professor thought about it. "The threat could be growing."

"Yes."

"So we need more people on the STF."

"That's a risk," I said.

"It's a risk we have to take."

"This young man," I said. "He is doing valuable work for the paper. They won't want to let him go. I could talk to Fred, but I'm afraid of being."

It took the professor a couple of seconds to catch that one.

"Watched?" he asked.

"I'm not sure," I said.

"I'll talk to your editor myself," he said. "I don't think they're monitoring my movements."

We ended the conversation awkwardly, with wishes for each other's safety and good health. Juanita might have been right: we did need some passwords for saying goodbye.

Chapter 17

I hadn't been in the building in the morning for a few weeks
and the sights were unfamiliar. People walked faster in the
morning. There was less chatting in the newsroom, a more busi-
nesslike atmosphere, a generally unwholesome ambiance, actually. On nights, there was less of a managerial presence. People
did what they had to do but didn't pretend to be working when
they weren't.

Some sights were more unfamiliar than others. One was
Fred, out in the newsroom, talking to people and dressed like a
normal person. Reporters and deskers stared in disbelief as he
strolled about, stopping to chat, showing his teeth and seeming
to be listening to what people, ordinary newsroom stiffs, were
saying.

The other unfamiliar sight was Rand Barry, the tiny but muscular editorial writer. It wasn't that he was doing anything unusual
in the newsroom. It was the fact that he was in the newsroom at
all. There would be months without a sighting as he cloistered
himself in the back with the other editorial writers, doing whatever they did to keep themselves wise, which didn't include spending any time in conversation with newsroom mortals.

Barry was the most reclusive of them all. So when he appeared in the newsroom this time, walking purposefully from one end to the other, stopping to check the bulletin board, everybody just jumped to the logical conclusion, that he was going to kill everybody. That's what Shirley said anyway, after I wandered into the business department for what I hoped would seem like a casual chat. She was staring at him and when I arrived she nodded hello and said, "Be ready to duck behind this partition. I don't see the machine gun, but he could be using something smaller."

I thanked her, then watched Barry for a minute as he walked from the bulletin board to the mailboxes, then over to the library and then back. "We're not in any danger," I said, finally. "Look at him."

"What?"

"He's doing the strut. Machine-gunners don't strut."

Shirley and I were both familiar with the newsroom strut. It's what writers did when they had done something significant, such as being nominated for an award or writing a story the brass deemed important. People from nights would come in on days, people who worked at home would find an excuse to show up. Then they would do the strut and give people the opportunity to congratulate them. Looking at Rand Barry, watching him glance around to see who was looking at him, seeing him seek eye contact with people he'd never spoken to in his life, it was obvious that the strut was what he was doing.

"But what's the strut in honour of?" Shirley asked. "Did you read the editorial page today?"

"Of course not."

She opened the paper and I looked over her shoulder, sniffing her shampoo, which was an ordinary drugstore brand, but nice.

We both saw the cartoon of a St. George, labelled "TRI-LAKES AREA," preparing to do battle with a towering bug, labelled "WEEVIL," and under it, the thing that was making Rand Barry strut.

AN EDITORIAL

Weevil invasion must stop now

Outdated thinkers of the wishy-washy Left must be rubbing their hands in glee today as the Tri-Lakes Area faces the possible onslaught of a vicious attack of unscrupulous insects, possibly imported from so-called Third World nations, known for their deficit financing and reliance on financial support from the neo-Stalinist states of the former Communist Bloc and tolerated far too lightly by helpful intellectuals in the West and at Grand Valley University.

The possible invasion of boll weevils is proof positive that permissive immigration policies carry within them the seeds of their own destruction, not to mention that of the Tri-Lakes Area.

A more steadfast and watchful policy, one that honoured the concept of public health as opposed to mere political correctness, would have kept this threat at a distance from our shores.

The great American patriot and philosopher Thomas Jefferson, now deceased, summed up the matter quite succinctly when he said: *"They are [not] other than the little shrivelled meagre, hopping, though loud and troublesome insects of the hour."*

And though the great philosopher was referring to grasshoppers, his meaning was clear and capable of being extended to all pests of the liberal persuasion.

As students of history well know, the price of freedom from pestilence, not to mention other, more distant forces, is eternal vigilance.

"Wow," I said. "No wonder he's strutting."

"Look at him strut in Fred's direction. He's looking for a pat on the head."

"Fred never pats on the head."

"Don't be so sure," Shirley said. "This is the post–synergy Fred. See how well he's dressed. This is the new guy. Look at his office."

I was thinking about "other, more distant forces," as Barry's editorial put it. What did he know?

"Are you looking?" Shirley asked.

I glanced over there. Fred was not patting Rand Barry on the head, but he was showing his teeth to him and saying something. Fred was wearing a blue blazer, white shirt, and attractive red-patterned tie. His shoes were leather and they were shined. As for the office, there were indeed lights on in it. This really was different. You missed so much being on nights.

"This synergy thing, how does it work?" I asked, as we walked to the back door so we could step outside and Shirley could smoke. She said she would quit when she got her weight down, but when she got her weight down she worried about it going back up if she quit.

It didn't help that I'd quit and gained twenty-five pounds.

"Maybe I'll find out about synergy if they ever think of promoting me," she said, as we walked around the building. "The way I understand it, you go off to a resort somewhere and sit in a conference room and do role-playing. Then everybody tells you what's wrong with you and you get a little chart that shows it graphically."

"Shows what?"

"What's wrong with you."

"Graphically?"

"Yes. They put what's wrong with you on a pie chart."

"And then what?"

"And then you come back to the office and begin working on becoming better."

I wasn't following very well. "A better person?"

"A better manager," Shirley answered. "When you walked by Sheldon this morning did he growl at you?"

Sheldon was the city editor, one of the nicest guys in the world.

"Yeah, he did. What was that about?"

"He was at synergy with Fred. I hear they told him he was too nice."

We rounded a corner and saw Jane Liu sitting on a bench outside the front door, another smokers' haven. She was doing an interview with a man dressed all in green and wearing a baseball cap with a picture of a tree on it. She didn't look happy. On another bench was Alexei Ponomarev, wearing his straw cowboy hat, reading his book and underlining passages in it. When we saw the straw hat and the underlining, it usually meant Alexei was agitated about something. When he was agitated about something, it meant the Grim Pig cartoon was coming soon. The editors would spike it and run a syndicated one in its place. The cartoonist would get the rest of the week off and come back as good as new the next week. That's if they noticed. The Grim Pig had run probably four times since I'd been at the *WB*. Nobody ever complained, except the publisher.

"I had an idea," I said, while she butted her cigarette in an overflowing ashtray.

"Always dangerous," she said.

I was about to make a wisecrack when I remembered that this was my big chance, maybe my only one, to show her what a big mistake she was making hanging out with risk analysts.

"You may not like it," I said.

"Maybe I won't."

"I want to take Tony for the task force."

"The Saturn Task Force?"

"Yeah."

She stopped and turned to face me, looking angry. I hadn't seen that before, not directed at me. It was attractive in an odd way.

"You can't do it," she said. She stared off towards Watson Lake, which was half a mile away, on the other side of six lanes of Michener Road.

"I can. I can go to Fred right now and get him to OK it. I was just hoping you'd agree. I haven't talked to Tony yet."

It was fun to watch her softening as I explained the thing to her, the STF serving as a cover for Tony as he chased Uncle Bob Fishing Shocker, not to mention Juanita Eldridge while she chased him.

"Jeez," she said. "How are you going to keep them from knowing what he's doing?"

"I think I can do it. They love secrecy and if I explain how top secret Tony's mission is, they'll buy it. The other thing is, he'll officially stay in the business department, so it looks to the professor and Juanita like he's working undercover, and they'll like that even better."

You could see the gears turning. "And that means he can do work on Uncle Bob Fishing Shocker posing as a business reporter," she said.

"Right. I was never this clever when I only hung around with earthlings."

"The more I hear of it, the more this task force sounds like it's going to be fun," Shirley said.

Chapter 18

Tony Fusculla was a hard sell at first. He had the suspiciousness and surface hardness of the twenty-four-year-old city kid, didn't trust anything or anybody in this burg. But he tolerated me because he trusted Shirley and she trusted me.

I hated to bring him face-to-face with the necessities of modern journalistic life at his tender age, but there was no other way to explain the story, no point in lying, at least not this time. So I explained the duplicity that would be necessary to get the story. It took a while and he would interrupt me occasionally with comments, a typical one being "holy fuck!" But once he understood the mission, he was an eager puppy dog. Only after he committed to serving on the STF did I mention Juanita Eldridge's position on it. I didn't want him signing on for the wrong reasons.

Tony was canny. "Have I met her?" he asked. But when he walked away, there was a bounce in his step.

That left the matter of getting Fred's approval. With luck, the professor would have softened him up nicely with a panicky reinterpretation of our telephone conversation. The Saturnians were getting closer and a larger task force was needed to counteract it. So that would be OK. It was true that I hadn't actively been keeping Fred informed of our progress, but he wouldn't expect that, given the top-secret nature of our work. Plus, I had made a point of nodding conspiratorially at him whenever we passed in the hall.

Still, how would it be with this new, synergized Fred? Being confronted by an open door was a change and the lights being on was unsettling. "Parker," Fred said, "come in, come in." He shook my hand, seized my elbow, and guided me to a chair.

The room was essentially the same, as far as I could tell with the lights on. The same trophies. The same photograph of Fred and Uncle Bob. The fish looked like they were swimming faster, but that was probably just my imagination. There was no soothing music, which was fine. The soothing music made me nervous.

Fred sat at his desk and picked up what looked like an index card. "How, um, have you, uh, been?" he asked.

"Fine," I said. "You?"

He glanced at the card again, then looked at me and showed his teeth. "Never better," he said.

"About the task force," I said.

"Just a minute," he said, and glanced down at the card again.

"Are you feeling all right?" he asked. "You look a little tired. The weather is nice, although I hear rain is predicted for the weekend."

"That would be too bad," I said.

Fred looked up from his desk. "What?" he asked. He put the card down and leaned back in his chair. "The task force," he said.

Something else occurred to me. "I wanted to ask you about today's editorial on the boll weevil," I began.

"Did you enjoy it?"

"Oh, certainly," I said. "I was just a bit startled by the reference to 'distant forces.' Did the editorial writer know about?"

Fred laughed, showed his teeth and said, "Ha ha."

"Actually," he said. "I inserted that phrase myself. I will brief the editorial board when the research has moved nicely along."

"Right," I said. "I was just wondering."

"So is the research moving nicely along?"

"Quite nicely, I think. I've had several discussions with the professor and read some of his stuff. Juanita is doing her researches. It's just that."

I glanced over my shoulder. That meant I was glancing into the newsroom, where a couple of people were watching. Having the lights on had its disadvantages.

"I understand," Fred said.

"We just need to do our work faster," I said. "There is some urgency."

"Professor Blanchard has spoken to me," he said. "He appears quite worried. In November, Saturn is in conjunction with Jupiter, he informed me."

For a moment I felt a twinge of irritation. The professor hadn't told me anything about Saturn and Jupiter.

"Of course, he'd be worried," I said.

"And I had an interesting note from Dr. Baxter," Fred said.

"Mrs. Baxter?"

"Concerning progress reports. She was out for a walk with her poodle and saw something alarming. That's in strictest confidence, of course. I just wanted to underline."

I leaned forward and lowered my voice. "There is a business side to this – people, quote unquote, for whom it might be in their best interest" – Why was I talking like this? Was it the index cards? Was it the lack of music? Would this sentence never end? – "if elements of sabotage were introduced, relating to commercial activities of importance to the viability of the tourism dimension, not to mention the water dimension."

Fred stared at me. Something like admiration was in his eyes.

"You mean?" he said.

"Yes," I answered.

We both looked at the photograph of him and Uncle Bob.

"Your proposal?" he said.

I took a deep breath and tried to phrase a simple sentence. "The professor and Juanita, they're fine, but we need some speed. There's an energetic kid in business, Frusculla, who likes to dig."

Fred tapped the fingers of his left hand on the desk. He looked at me, then out into the newsroom.

"Done," he said. "Anything else?"

"He needs to keep his official connection with the business department, so as not."

Fred looked down at his desk again, then back at me. "I couldn't agree more," he said. "Anything else?"

"I don't think so," I said, standing up. "Thank you."

Fred stood too, picked up an index card in his left hand and extended his right. "I've enjoyed having the opportunity to chat with you," he said.

Chapter 19

The new Grand Valley Inn has one of the nicest locations in the city. It sits northwest of downtown, beside Baker Lake, the second largest of the Tri-Lakes Area's four lakes. From the revolving restaurant at the top, diners can see across to the beautiful cottages on the north side. Sometimes the restaurant fails to revolve, owing to what the management calls "labour issues," and then diners can see across the parking lot to the bypass.

When it became necessary for the expanded Saturn Task Force to meet with senior editors, I decided it would have to be out of the building, so as not to raise suspicions. When I reported that to the professor, he responded the way I hoped he would: the fact that I was trying to avoid raising suspicions made him more suspicious – of our enemies, not of me. What better location for our meeting, on the last Monday of the month, than this scenic spot, in which we were given a windowless conference room. Fortunately we had all taken the precaution of admiring the view on our way in.

I introduced Tony to the professor and Juanita and introduced the professor to Rick Smithers, the managing editor, who had been sent in by Fred to get an advance look at what we were doing. Fred had begged off, on the grounds that he wasn't a detail man, but Jane Liu gave me the unofficial truth, that Fred had gone back to Toronto for a synergy top-up.

The five of us sat down at an oval table, designed for fifteen, judging by the number of water glasses and bottles of water. I sat near the big pad of paper on the easel, which I was prepared to use in an emergency.

Smithers's presence could have alarmed me, but it didn't. For one thing, he loved being in on a secret so much that he wouldn't blab. For another, he could be persuaded to be deathly afraid of Saturn. For a third thing, he was actively stupid.

Smithers was a husky guy in his late thirties who affected a rough manner, always made a show of loosening his tie and rolling up his sleeves at news meetings, and wore one of the few moustaches remaining in the Tri-Lakes Area at the turn of the century. He was also secretly nice. He liked to appear cynical but was really rather naive.

"As I understand it," he said, leaning back in his chair and resting one foot against the edge of the table, "we're surrounded by Martians, eh?"

"Saturnians," we all said, as one.

"So when will the story be ready? We've got tons of space next week, but it tightens up after that. Then pretty soon people go away on holidays."

The professor and I both shifted uncomfortably. For me, any thought of hurrying the story along was alarming. For the professor, this was his first encounter with the practical side of newspapering, the side that was less concerned with the substance of the story than when it could run.

"Don't you even want to know what the story is about?" he asked.

"Oh sure," Smithers said. "Martians. What do Martians look like. I'm thinking of pictures. Are there, like, Martian babes? Do Martians have hooters?"

"Six," Tony said, from his slouch at the other end of the table. Juanita looked briefly offended, then decided to giggle.

"We'll have to use a wide-angle lens," Smithers said. He may not have been joking.

"We're working on the pictures situation," I said, "but it will take time. One of the problems is that the Saturnians are able to transform themselves so that they look exactly like us."

Smithers played with his moustache for a moment and looked at Tony. "Two hooters," he said, thoughtfully.

The professor brandished his paper bag, which I had returned to him, largely unread.

"I have a rather lengthy research paper that will be of interest to your readers. Perhaps it could be published on accompanying pages," he said.

"Sure," Smithers said. "Research. If you can get it down to thirty inches or so, we can handle it, provided it's not a Wednesday. The paper's crammed with supermarket ads and you won't find an open page anywhere. Plus, we're starting to get some of that electronics advertising too. I thought it wouldn't start till Halloween, but I guess that's the way it goes these days."

Smithers looked at us for confirmation that we all knew the way it went. The professor clearly didn't. I could see where this was going and liked it quite a bit. I walked over to the easel, took the top off a green magic marker and wrote "30 INCHES – RESEARCH."

The professor looked puzzled. "I'm sure that I can – what's thirty inches?" he asked me.

"We can talk about some of the details later," I said, and wrote "DETAILS" beside the "30 INCHES."

"MacVeigh," asked Smithers, "what kind of space do you think you're gonna need?"

"Two facing pages," I said, then thought better of it. "On three consecutive days," I added.

"Jesus, MacVeigh, you know we can't do that. We didn't do that for Diana."

"You've talked to Fred, haven't you, Smithers? You know how important the story is to him."

"Yeah, yeah. But six pages? That's a lot of words. That's going to take a long time."

Yes, I thought. "That's a risk we've got to take," I said.

"OK," Smithers said, getting to his feet. "Gotta run. Good luck with the rest of your meeting. The grub is good here and they say the restaurant is revolving today."

He walked out, and the professor got up and closed the door. "What a rude man," he said.

"Especially for an earthling," I said. Tony smiled a bit, although the professor did not find it amusing. When Juanita saw Tony smiling, she smiled too.

The professor took his seat and pointed at the big pad. "What did he mean, thirty inches?"

"That's column inches, thirty column inches," I said. "A newspaper column is about twenty-two inches deep, when you take out the folio and such. So your research paper would get about a column and a third. I don't know whether that includes picture and headline. That could be negotiable."

"Approximately how many words would that be?" the professor asked.

"A little better than a thousand," I said. "That's quite long for a newspaper."

The professor was not impressed. He told us that his research paper had taken him the better part of his life to complete. There were at least 200,000 words in that paper bag, the vast majority of them of extreme importance. A subject of such significance could not be dismissed in a mere thirty inches. And as for the portfolio –

"Folio," Tony said. "The date and page number." I could see that he was getting into the spirit of it. This was really dragging out nicely. I went to the big pad and wrote "FOLIO" on it, underlining it twice, as I remember having seen Fred do.

"Just to make sure that we're absolutely clear on this," I began, before the professor interrupted.

He cleared his throat and looked over his shoulder. "I think before we go any further, we should hear from Miss Eldridge. She has been doing some serious researches, which are of vital urgency because of the."

I saw Tony looking over the professor's shoulder, in the direction the professor had been looking. Behind the professor was a framed print of a New England scene, barns and dirt roads in the snow, a man on horseback, a frozen pond. Tony looked quizzically at me, which I ignored.

"Well, I really want to go back to the question of column inches," I said, "but I know time is of the essence. Please go ahead, Ms. Eldridge," I said.

"Thank you," she said, reaching into her large purse and withdrawing several folded pieces of paper. She unfolded them, smoothed them down. She looked over her shoulder and began reading.

"*Saturnian Sightings in Toronto*," she began. "*A Case Study*. By Juanita Eldridge, D. Litt."

She still had the severe hairdo, but was dressed rather stylishly today, in black leather pants and a blouse of black silk, open a couple of buttons from the top, at about the level where her reading glasses hung when she wasn't using them. "Jeez," Tony said. "I didn't know you were a Ph.D."

The professor coughed. Juanita gave him a sideways glance, then returned to her reading. I noticed that the page on top carried the logo of an expensive Toronto hotel.

"On Thursday, 20 May, I journeyed to Toronto by motorcar. Entering the city from the north and proceeding southward along the . . ."

"Ms. Eldridge," I said. "I appreciate the thoroughness of your report, but perhaps we could skip over some of the preliminary details."

I had no idea where this was going and I couldn't wait to hear.

"Very well," she said, and began reading again.

"After obtaining a parking space for my motorcar, for which I paid a deposit of ten dollars, I hired a taxicab and proceeded to the residence of the subject I had been assigned to interview."

Someone other than I had been assigning interviews to her. What was going on? I looked at the professor, who did not return my gaze.

"I was greeted at the door of the subject by a functionary of some sort, unnamed, a large man dressed in a black suit. He ushered me in to a well-appointed room that might have been a library, owing to the large number of books that lined . . ."

I cleared my throat. Juanita turned a page.

"The subject, Dr. Thelma Baxter –"

Oh, shit.

". . . proceeded to relate to me the story of an incident that had greatly alarmed her a fortnight previous."

"Mrs. Baxter," I said, "that would be the owner of the *World-Beacon* and other quality international newspapers?"

"Yes," said Juanita, taking off her glasses. I looked over my shoulder. There was a reproduction there of a painting of New England in the summer, barns and dirt roads and trees, a man on horseback and a nice pond.

She resumed reading, neglecting to put her glasses back on. "The subject related to me that she was in the habit of going for walks in her neighbourhood, which she described to me as a quiet and peaceful area, with large trees and free of the usual commercial hustle and bustle. One such walk, on which she was accompanied by her pet poodle, Ronald, and a functionary, unnamed, took place several days previous. She believed it was either the Friday or perhaps the Thursday."

This was going to take some time, which, in the long run, suited my objectives. I glanced at Tony. Instead of the expected look of journalistic indifference, he wore a rapt expression. It could have been the subject matter, about which no one could have warned him in journalism school. Or it could have been where Juanita's reading glasses were resting. Time dragged a bit more for me than for him, but that was OK too. The longer it took for her to complete her report, the longer it would take to deal with it. On the other hand, I really needed to find out what was going on with Mrs. Baxter and how Juanita had wound up talking to her.

I also had to pretend, for the sake of my credibility as STF leader, that none of this was a surprise to me. I experienced a fleeting longing for the simple pleasures of paginating the gardening pages and riding a horse along dirt roads in New England.

"When Mrs. Baxter called you," I began.

"When she called Mr. Morgan," Juanita corrected.

"Of course," I said. "When she called Fred and he contacted you – perhaps you could explain that sequence of events for the benefit of the rest of the group." I looked at Tony.

"Yeah," he said. "How did that work, anyway?"

Juanita gave a little toss of her head. "Mr. Morgan simply said that there had been reports of a sighting in Toronto and he was going to speak to you about it. Right away, I realized there was some urgency in the matter so I asked him for the particulars and went ahead to investigate."

"Fred and I agreed that would be the best way to proceed," I said. "And that's how we got where we are. Everybody clear on that now?"

"My mummy went to school with Mrs. Baxter," Juanita added.

The professor and Tony nodded. "Carry on, Juanita," I said. The little rat.

"On that day," she read, "either a Monday or a Tuesday, their walk took them to a fork in the road and there was a brief discussion between Mrs. Baxter and her functionary as to which direction to take. They determined, eventually, to take the left fork and were proceeding along that street when they heard strange, rather muffled noises."

The professor nodded rapidly several times and leaned forward in his chair.

"Were the noises like voices?" he asked.

"I'm coming to that," Juanita said and resumed her reading.

"The functionary attempted to steer her away from the noises, but the poodle, Ronald, pulled her in their direction. Turning a corner they saw a large, grey lumpish object in the middle of the sidewalk, from which noises were emitting. The lump was not moving in any direction, but there appeared to be movement within it."

"Good God!" said the professor. Tony was transfixed.

"As they neared, the blob's sounds became recognizable as speech. 'Cold,' it said, along with other words that Mrs. Baxter said were rude. The functionary persuaded her to cross the street at this point and walk in the other direction."

"Did Mrs. Baxter have a more detailed description of the blob?" I asked.

"She said its skin appeared to be rough, like a blanket, and that when she asked her functionary if he had ever seen such an object before, he said something along the lines of 'not in this part of town.' She felt that he was trying to shield her from further information, so as not to alarm her."

"And that was what aroused her suspicions?"

"Yes. She remembered that Mr. Morgan had mentioned the task force when she visited the *World-Beacon* and she thought this incident would be of interest to it."

"And it is," I said, as decisively as I could make it sound. "Is that the end of your report?"

"I have further details about the drive back to Grand Valley," Juanita said.

"Were there further sightings?"

"No, not as such," she said.

"Thank you," I said. "Did you make copies for the other members?"

"I decided not to because of the," she said.

"There is no time to make copies," the professor said. "This incident makes it clear that we have to accelerate our timetable. We must publish quickly, so as to warn the population."

"Thank you, Professor," I said, thinking, You lunatic bastard.

I turned to Juanita. "I presume you will need some time to complete your researches," I said.

"I'm not so sure," she said. "I've been talking to Professor Blanchard and we are in agreement that some sort of preliminary publication might aid us in further researches."

"Yeah," said Tony. "Smoke the bastards out."

Uh-oh. I looked over at Tony who was looking at Juanita in an unscholarly way. "That was a very scholarly report," he said to her.

"But a bit early to publish," I said, trying to re-establish a scholarly pace. "We would need other samples in other neighbourhoods, for purposes of comparison and . . ."

But Tony was a journalist. I hadn't counted on that working against me, but I realized too late that it could.

"Jeez, Parker," he interrupted. "You know how it works. We put a story in and then everybody who knows anything calls us and plus the bad guys tip their hand and the next you know, we can nail the whole thing down."

The professor gasped. Juanita jotted something down on her hotel notepaper. I might have gasped too. I would have to talk to Tony, remind him what the story was, show him where Saturn was on a map. I would have to talk to the professor, find a way of making him see the peril of publishing too soon. He was an academic; that shouldn't be too hard. Juanita would be more difficult. She could see the end of the story now; she could see awards, fame, job offers from the *Times of London*, CNN, *The National Post*,

The National Enquirer – and she wanted it all right away. She was twenty-four and there wasn't much time.

Maybe Tony could deal with her. But first I had to deal with Tony.

The meeting ended with a consensus on immediate action. I wrote that on the flip chart, IMMEDIATE ACTION, underlined it twice, and promised that by the time we reconvened in a week, we would have a preliminary timetable. Some of that old Ottawa mindset was coming in handy.

I knew what that timetable would be if I didn't think of something: The Mrs. Baxter sighting goes on page one, Fred commissions Brian Blezard to track down similar sightings, which he does, back to the Old Testament, an unscrupulous rewrite person makes the professor's research intelligible and it is published, a demand to get rid of blobs in the Tri-Lakes Area is carefully orchestrated by the city desk and given a philosophical dimension by the editorial board, letters to the editor pour in, we phone politicians for reaction and they all promise to do something about it, we publish tips for parents on how to blob-proof their children. And the story climaxes in an exclusive interview with Uncle Bob, who promises to investigate the problem personally when he visits the Tri-Lakes Area next month.

That, I predicted, satisfies Fred and his notoriously short attention span, it gets the New Owners off his back and the task force is disbanded before we can even begin to make a dent in Uncle Bob Fishing Shocker story. I miss my chance to be a hero in Shirley's eyes, and I miss a pretty good story too.

When I finally pried Tony away from Juanita, by offering him a ride to the office, I laid out the timetable for him, point by point, minus the point about my needing to be a hero for Shirley. Tony was not seeing as clearly as I had hoped.

"I get what you're saying," he said, "but couldn't we do both stories?"

"What both stories?"

"Mrs. Baxter's Blob and Uncle Bob Fishing Shocker."

I wheeled the car into the *WB* parking lot, turned off the Ella tape, rolled up the windows and turned off the ignition.

"Tony," I said, "Mrs. Baxter sees a homeless guy sleeping under a blanket in her neighbourhood and thinks it's a creature from outer space. Do you want to write that? Do you want your byline on it?"

"Well, no," he said.

"And if you do write it, one of two things happens. Either it becomes a three-day wonder, after which the task force is over and you lose your cover for doing Uncle Bob Fishing Shocker, or the story takes off and it's open season on blobs all across the country. Do you want that?"

"Shit no," Tony said.

"Well, then, you've got to help me drag the thing out."

"How the hell am I going to do that?" he asked.

"Do some research of your own. But it's got to be research that confirms the need for further research, OK?"

"OK."

I didn't like him looking so hangdog, so I suggested that Eldridge might be able to help him with his research. There was a thing she had mentioned, about an irregularity at the mall. Maybe they could work on that together.

"Eldridge," he said, feigning lack of interest. "That's the Yale girl?"

"Princeton."

"Whatever," he said, getting out of the car. "We'll fail to get something on it, and you have my promise on that."

"I knew I could count on you," I said.

Chapter 20

The good thing about all this was that it gave me another excuse to talk to Shirley. The pretence would be to ask her about the care and feeding of Tony. The funny thing was how long it took me to get up the nerve to phone her. When she was Davis, I would phone her at the drop of a hat. Now that we were on a first-name basis, at least in my mind, it was harder. I paced around my apartment after the task force meeting, thinking of things to do that needed my immediate attention, such as cleaning out the medicine cabinet and putting the Ella records in alphabetical order.

When I finally reached her at about 2:30, she said she had to cover a chamber of commerce meeting, but could meet me for a drink afterward. So I waited, around five o'clock, for her in the lobby of the new Prince of Wales Hotel, which was now called the Disney Time Warner Prince of Wales Suites Grand Valley.

I sat there for ten minutes, looking over the *WB*. It was a wonderful paper in ways that most people failed to recognize. A connoisseur, such as myself, could find infinite pleasure in it. Today I was concentrating on the last classified page, where international news briefs were used to fill the spaces that should have been occupied by obituaries. Every few days, when not enough people died, part of the page would have to be filled off the wires at the last minute. Usually, the page was tossed to Hugh Robbins, who was always free at those times.

Although Hugh wasn't that old, his headline writing was a throwback to an earlier, even less glorious journalistic age. He was reliable, quick, and entirely devoid of imagination. Unbeknownst to himself, he had developed a cult following in the newsroom for the heroically literal headlines only he could produce. Once I playfully congratulated him for a particularly good one and he replied in his best journalese.

"Thanks for the kudos," he said.

Examining the last inside page of the D section, I tried to picture him last night, pondering a story about the new president of Taiwan, trying not to anger his billion-plus Communist neighbours next door in China. TAIWANESE LEADER TAKES OFFICE, he wrote.

Hugh's next task would have been the story out of Chicago about the couple who won half of a $363 million lottery, and decided to take $90 million in a lump sum, rather than take $180.5 million in yearly instalments.

He wrote: LOTTERY WINNER CLAIMS PRIZE.

I was just about to see what was under the headline MASSIVE EARTHQUAKE CAUSES DIFFICULTIES, when I heard Shirley's laugh from across the lobby. I looked up and she saw me, waved, then tapped a well-dressed young man gently on the arm before starting in my direction.

I watched her approach as he watched her leave. She was big, husky I might have said in an earlier, less enlightened period of my life, as recently as two weeks ago, fairly tall, good posture, a long stride, a bit dressier than I was used to seeing her and looking quite sharp to my mind. I stood up, then realized she would think something was odd about me standing up. So I sat down.

She only noticed the newspaper. "Some difficulties they're having with that massive earthquake, eh?" she said.

"True," I said, "but at least a new leader has taken office in Taiwan. Want a beer?"

We walked into the new George Drew Room, now called the Disney Time Warner George Drew Salon, which was filling up with Chamber of Commerce guys and girls, greeting each other and loudly trading wisecracks about drinking. James Norwood, our publisher, was there, laughing with the biggest advertisers. We got a table in the corner, an ale and a ginger ale, slice of lemon.

"Well," she said, and smiled sweetly, lighting a cigarette. "Uncle Bob's visit is going to put $47.6 million into the economy of the Tri-Lakes Area."

"Those are official chamber of commerce statistics?"

"Right you are. Actually, it could be closer to $47.7 million, but they are keeping the estimate conservative."

"And the community will be showing him the welcome for which Grand Valley is justly famous?"

"Our very own publisher was urging the community to do exactly that. How on earth did you know?"

I shrugged modestly. She laughed, then stopped laughing. "Do you ever get the feeling we've been in the news business too long?"

"Any business gets to be too long," I said. "At least this one is full of laughs."

I wondered, suddenly, what kind of laughs there were in the risk analyst business. There was no way I could ask it.

I did ask, as offhandedly as I could, "Who was that guy you were talking to?"

"Paine Shaw," Shirley said. "New guy on the chamber of commerce board."

"Sharp dresser."

"Oh, you think so?"

"Sure. Looks like he's got some dough."

"Could be. Risk analysis is a wide open field in this town."

"That's what he does?"

"What?"

"Risk analysis?"

"Yes. He's a risk analyst."

Well, we established that – also, that he was rich, good-looking, relatively young, and she touched him on the arm. What else could I ask?

"He think Uncle Bob's visit is just what Grand Valley needs?"

"We actually haven't talked about that at all."

"What *have* you talked about?" I heard the voice of my old friend the objective observer. What are you doing? it was asking. Shirley gave me a thoughtful look.

"What have we talked about?"

"Yes. You're going out with him, aren't you?"

Shirley sipped her beer and looked at me over the rim of her glass. "Going out is a little strong," she said. "We had dinner a couple of times, a movie once. How come you know this?"

This was a good time to make it light again. "I always get the story. You know that."

"I like him," she said. I waited for her to elaborate and she didn't.

"I can check into him, if you want. Make sure he isn't a Saturnian or a bass fisherman."

She sat back and smiled. "That would be nice," she said.

There was no way to press my advantage. There was no advantage to press. So I went on with pretending to be concerned with the thing I had pretended I wanted to see her about.

"So . . ." I said. "Tony."

"He's doing all right?"

"His concentration is a little off. The college girl –"

"That's beneath you."

"Sorry, Juanita. Juanita has his eye. He actually bought into her story for a little while today and was pushing for us to get it into the paper right away."

"Saturnians?"

"In Rosedale. Looking very much like homeless people, if you didn't know better. I talked some sense into him after the meeting, but it will be a struggle. The thing is, why would he care about impressing me when she's there?"

"But she's a goof," Shirley said.

"Goofs come in all sorts of packages," I said. "Tony likes this one."

I told Shirley about Fred bypassing me to give Juanita the Toronto assignment and got a laugh describing my attempts to make it look like the whole thing was my idea. It seemed like a good, hearty laugh. Maybe risk analysts didn't get laughs like that.

The publisher walked by our table on his way out and gave us the distracted smile he gave people he thought he should know.

"What about the professor?" Shirley asked.

"I'm worried about him bolting. He really is scared about Saturnians. It's more than a story to him. To him, everything adds up. Water levels, wrong numbers."

"I bet you didn't talk him out of it."

"No. I need to keep him interested. But I don't want him to get so panicky he runs to Fred. Then we'd rush something into the paper and everything would be ruined."

"Yikes," Shirley said. "It would be out of control in no time."

"Uh-huh. I don't know what to do," I said, maybe a bit more forlornly than I felt. It occurred to me that vulnerability was reputed to have a certain power with women.

Shirley toyed with her glass. A light like a flashlight darted around the room as a reporter carrying a television camera went from table to table collecting enthusiastic comments from chamber of commerce people on the impending economic boom.

I heard the word "spin-off" and I heard the figure "$57.6 million" and then heard the figure "$67.5 million." It would be into the billions by the time the members went home to dinner.

"You need a better relationship with the professor," she said finally.

"I don't know. It's OK," I said. "We always use the password together and he doesn't know I spilled the mustard and ginger ale on his research."

"Still," she said. "Do you think he trusts you?"

I pondered that. "He believes I'm from this planet. But he may think I'm a little odd."

"That's because you're from the planet News," Shirley said. "You have to convince him you're a regular guy."

"A regular guy? He's a professor?"

"Well, you have to convince him you're a professor's idea of a regular guy."

"Mmmmm," I said.

"Does he play golf?" she asked.

I remembered that he did, actually. Even if he hadn't let it slip to me, I could have guessed it from his research paper. Golf was one game that didn't come under attack for its Saturnian influences.

Then I figured out what she was getting at.

"Wait a second," I said. "I haven't played golf in twelve years. Golf drives me to drink. You expect me to come out of retirement, go through all the grief about my backswing and my slice and all that for some guy who believes Saturnians are running the House of Commons?"

"Not only do I expect you to do that," she said, "I expect you to lose."

She flashed a smile that was both innocent and wicked. I could have kissed her. Of course, I could have kissed her anyway.

Chapter 21

Tri-Lakes area "anxiously awaits" acclaimed evangelist

By Anthony Frusculla

with files from Brian Blezard

Representatives of the Worldwide World of Uncle Bob Wednesday expressed satisfaction with Grand Valley's preparations for the visit of the acclaimed fisherman and evangelist over the Canada Day long weekend.

"The Tri-Lakes Area feels like just a little bit of North Carolina," said a spokesman after touring several of the city's major fishing and convention facilities and previewing accommodation arrangements.

"People are friendly and the business community has got a lot of the old get-up-and-go."

The weekend-long fishing tournament will culminate in a waterborne evangelical service, known as the Mass for Bass, during which Dr. Uncle Bob will bless the fish and those who catch and release them, as well as conduct a harbourfront mass baptism and barbecue.

Mayor Martin Havelock, contacted by telephone during a fact-finding tour of Latin America, said the city anxiously awaits the visit by the celebrated evangelist,which will "add a new dimension to celebrations of Canada's Birthday."

There were twenty-six representatives in all. As far as Tony could break it down, nine of them had responsibilities for media coverage – six electronic and three print. Four concerned themselves with accommodations, four with the marketing of Uncle Bob literature and souvenirs, three with transportation, two with computer installation, three with fishing, and one with spiritual matters.

As they fanned out across the city, the twenty-six communicated by means of cellphones. They recognized each other by the tiny lapel pins they wore, which showed a fish and a loaf, if you got close enough to look. Among their duties were to check the acoustics in Murray Westgate Memorial Arena, to purchase seventy-three fishing licences, to sample the food at five downtown restaurants, to arrange for the rental of nine minivans, two sport utility vehicles, and four personal watercraft, to scout the tops of buildings for camera angles, to examine the positioning of newspaper boxes, to drive along country roads looking for emergency docking points, to test cellphone reception from various points of the city, to buy flares and arrange for the delivery of worms and crayfish, to locate the optimum location for Uncle Bob's satellite dish, to compare pizza delivery times from all of Grand Valley's thirty-eight pizza establishments, to walk all the golf courses in the Tri-Lakes Area, to establish contacts at the radio and TV stations, to test the beds in four hotels, and to test-drive the parade route east along Michener Road from the bypass, then south on King Street to the harbourfront on Watson Lake.

Representatives of the Worldwide World of Uncle Bob visited city hall to pay a courtesy call. Informed that Mayor Havelock was unavailable, they spoke to the roads commissioner. Queen Street was a better parade route than King Street, they said, but Queen Street ran one way from south to north. Would it be possible, given the $47.6, possibly $47.7 million, that Uncle Bob was bringing to Grand Valley, to reverse those directions for three days? And by the way, Uncle Bob himself had made a point of asking if the roads commissioner could sit in his personal number-one backup boat during the Mass for Bass.

The roads commissioner said reversing Queen seemed a perfectly reasonable thing to do and he would check with the mayor when he returned from Europe.

Four representatives of the Worldwide World of Uncle Bob paid a courtesy call on the *World-Beacon*, where they met with the publisher and the advertising manager, who discussed the special edition of the *WB* that would be published in the week before the beginning of the visit and allow advertisers the opportunity to welcome Uncle Bob and honour his presence with special sale prices. The representatives of the Worldwide World of Uncle Bob suggested that two special editions would be especially well received. At the paper, the advance team also met the managing editor, in the absence of Fred, and had a quick word with Dick Rivers, the Tri-Lakes Area's best-loved columnist.

Rivers, in his column the next day, described the tension he felt leading up to his introduction to Uncle Bob's staff, what he had finally decided to wear, and various details of his childhood leading up to this moment.

"I have met many important and world-famous figures in my life, from the premier of Ontario on down," he wrote, "but I was unprepared for the emotion that overtook me when I realized that I was meeting people who were but one step away from the most important person I would ever meet. If there was ever a time to shine my shoes, it was now."

Tony was not allowed full access to any of the meetings. Nor was he allowed to shadow the advance team at close range. But by keeping his distance he was able to get a sense of what was going on. Later, he talked to the people to whom Uncle Bob's people had talked and from those conversations developed a sense of what Uncle Bob's needs would be.

He would need immediate telephone contact with anyone in the world at any time from anywhere. He would need access to any television station from anywhere in North America, particularly those featuring competing fishermen and/or evangelists. He would need pizza at two in the afternoon and 11:30 at night, anchovies, no pepperoni. He would need the entire floor of a large hotel. It would have to be sprayed for mosquitoes. He would need customs clearance and storage facilities for his special supply of holy water. He would demand the right to approve in advance all photographs of him that appeared in newspapers and any videotape that ran on television. He needed a case of a particular brand of diet cat food, for his three cats, which apparently were named for three of the Four Horsemen of the Apocalypse. There was no information on which one had been left out.

Uncle Bob would require an empty store, either in the mall or in a prominent downtown location, for the sale of Worldwide World of Uncle Bob merchandise. And he would need a local speechwriter to help him with the Canadian angle for his July 1 address.

"And that's it?" I asked. "That's all he wants?"

"That's all I know for now," said Tony.

Shirley, Tony, and I were at Score's at four in the afternoon, for a meeting of the BPF, the Bass Protective Force, as Shirley had dubbed it. She was wearing her hair in a ponytail and her University of Manitoba sweatshirt, a look which I thought was an improvement over her smart outfit of the day before. Also I liked the fact that Paine Shaw was nowhere in sight. It was all I could do to keep from pumping her for further details, but we were supposed to be pumping Tony on the details of Uncle Bob Fishing Shocker.

"Do you think you saw anything that will help?" Shirley asked.

"Hard to know," Tony said. "They were all guarded and secretive, but that's like any organization. They all act like they've got something to hide as soon as they see a notebook. Peewee hockey teams act like that."

"What about the stuff they were doing," I asked. "Any clues there?"

This was fun, forming the BPF, talking about clues, hanging out with Shirley in bars, getting that story.

"All I could think of," Tony said, "was when they were out driving around in the country, looking for emergency docking points. That was odd. I mean, if the boat's in trouble, it has flares. Anyway, they're not out after dark and if it's really bad weather, the thing will be postponed anyway. Nobody will let fishing boats out in a big storm."

"So there could be something going on there," Shirley said.

"Yeah," Tony said. "But it could be they're just being cautious. Uncle Bob's a big investment. And it's their ass if anything happens to him."

It was time to strike a heroic attitude, something that would set Shirley to wondering what she could have been thinking when she allowed herself to go out with a risk analyst.

"What are these guys doing for fun?" I asked.

"Far as I can tell, they eat pizza and talk on the phone," Tony said.

"So we're not going to catch them whoring around or drinking to excess or littering or anything like that," Shirley said.

"They're on their best behaviour," Tony said. "It's part of the job. Some of them play golf. That's about as sinful as they get."

"That can be pretty sinful," I said.

"I think a couple of them are playing tomorrow out at Grand Valley Oaks," Tony said.

Shirley had an expression on her face that I wasn't sure I liked. "How do you know that?" she asked.

"Because I've been following them around all frigging day," he said. "And because I talk to the people they talk to. They go into the clubhouse at the Oaks, reserve a 6:30 a.m. tee time. Then they buy a bunch of golf clothes . . ."

"They didn't bring their own golf clothes?" Shirley asked.

"Doesn't look like it, and they didn't bring their clubs either, because they arranged to rent some."

"Weird," I said. "It's the way Saturnians would set up a golf game."

Tony looked startled. Actually, I was a bit startled myself. Was this Earth or Grand Valley? Shirley looked at me, still with that expression, then at Tony. "You said that they walked the golf courses today?"

"Yeah, but I think Grand Valley Oaks is the only place they're actually playing," Tony said.

Shirley looked at me again. "Oh to be a fly on the wall," she said, and I immediately realized what I would have to do to be a hero.

"Six-thirty is really early," I said.

"The professor's up, I bet," she said. "Probably has a couple dozen footnotes done by then."

I took a deep breath. Taking a chance on love, as Ella sang, was one thing; taking a quadruple bogey for love was something else entirely. This time there was no choice. "I don't suppose you play golf," I said to Tony.

"Nope," he said. "Stupid old fart's game."

"Be that as it may, I suddenly feel the urge to feel the click of five iron against ball, hear the satisfying clunk as the ball drops into the cup, feel the gentle breeze blowing through my hair."

"The BPF is in your debt," Shirley said. "This is a noble thing you're doing."

It was too. It wasn't going to be satisfying clinks and clunks and gentle breezes. It was going to be the sting of the shanked five iron, the sickening thud of ball striking tree, the gentle tall grass brushing knees slogging through the rough. Still, it had to be done, for a number of reasons, Shirley being the best of them.

When I got to the paper I went straight to the task force office, closed the door and dialled the professor's number. "This isn't television," I said when he picked up.

"I'm supposed to say that," he said.

"Oh, sorry. I was in a hurry. The perch knows something new, by the way."

After that, the conversation went smoothly. The professor was easily persuaded that only the solitude of the golf course would allow us to converse freely on some rather alarming new developments and the idea of teeing off at 6:33 didn't bother him. We agreed to meet at Grand Valley Oaks.

Now all I had to do was clean the twelve-year-old mud off my clubs and come up with some alarming new developments.

Chapter 22

By the fifth hole it was painfully clear that I'd made a big mistake. We should have taken the 6:27 tee-off instead of the 6:33. That way Uncle Bob's three staffers would have been behind us, indeed, close behind us, waiting for us to make our next bad shots, and we could have kept a good eye on them by looking back.

Initially, it had seemed smarter to be behind. Now we were struggling to keep them in our sights – or at least, I was, since the professor wasn't aware of this extra dimension to our game.

What made it especially difficult was the fact that Professor Blanchard was not a good golfer. He didn't lose balls, but he didn't hit them very far either. He patted the ball gently up the fairway, taking elaborate and time-consuming set-ups, waggles, and warm-up swings before each feeble shot. Even though there were three of Uncle Bob's golfers and only two of us, it was clear early on that we would lose ground on them.

Complicating matters was my determination to lose to the professor to keep his spirits up. That was not going to be as easy as I had assumed. Rusty, out of shape, and inaccurate as I was, I was easily the class of our twosome.

It was a nice, warm, sunny morning, you could say that much for it, and it helped my mood. Desperation would not set in until later. For the professor, the weather was no help. He took his game very seriously, loud, if mild, curses accompanying his failure to make shots that he had no right to expect to make. I had to cheer him up and distract him, otherwise there was no point in this thing.

On the first hole, it was easy. I sliced my tee shot into the woods, declared my ball lost, took the penalty strokes, hit into the sand trap, took two to get out and three-putted – an abysmally played hole, accomplished strictly through my natural ability. But after that, the losing got harder. On the second hole, I also sliced, but made the mistake of blaming it on Saturnians, which seemed like a good idea at the time.

"Damn," I said, as my ball disappeared from view. "I never do that."

"You never slice?" the professor asked.

"Never," I said. "It's as if some force . . ." I quickly looked over my shoulder, then over my other shoulder. The professor teed up his ball and also sliced.

"Good heavens," he said.

"It could be a coincidence," I said, but the professor had bought into the idea. Which was great, except that from then on I stopped slicing for the first time in my golfing life. I tried to slice, but instead of the ball going off to the right, it went straight. I tried aiming it off to the right, and I wound up hooking back into the centre of the fairway. The more badly I tried to hit it, the better it went. Meanwhile the professor was hitting his little baby shots thirty yards up the centre of the fairway. To be sure, that helped us keep Uncle Bob's fairway army in sight for a time, but all of that would be for naught if I won the game.

In desperation, I tried hitting the ball properly, thinking that would get me slicing again, but all it did was cause me to hit the ball properly. The professor, meanwhile, was hitting it his regular thirty yards a crack, and cursing each time.

"Curses," was what he said when he cursed, but he was sincere about it.

I tried chatting him up to take his mind off his troubles. Asking questions in the way that journalists do even in social encounters, I learned quite a few things about him, including how he first encountered Saturnians.

They were on his tenure committee. After he had been an assistant professor for fifteen years, they denied him tenure, he said, because they believed Latin was a dying language and would not attract undergraduates. They would not go so far as to abolish the course, but they would not have a tenured professor teaching it.

Professor Blanchard at once suspected that academic factors alone could not have denied him his goal. Soon after his tenure hearing, he read a story in a newspaper about alien sightings in Arizona. The unearthly creatures were described as speaking a language that bore a strange resemblance to Latin. Alone late at night, he took to watching science fiction movies. He noticed the strange way outer space creatures shook hands. One night, a movie version of *Julius Caesar* replaced the usual science fiction. Professor Blanchard watched it with interest, knowing that Latin was the language of the Senate of Rome. To his amazement, and then horror, he saw that the handshakes of the (Latin-speaking) plotters closely resembled the handshakes of the green Saturnians he had watched just a few nights earlier. It began to add up.

Then he noticed that students were behaving unusually and then members of the UGV support staff, and then dogs, and then traffic lights and then water levels. "Of course, no one would listen to me," the professor said, as I grunted sympathetically at the sixth tee. "I began writing letters to the newspapers, but no one would print them."

"It's often a lonely mission," I said. "But I guess things improved for you when Fred took over the paper."

"Mr. Morgan understands," the professor said. Mildly cheered, he boomed his tee shot fifty yards straight down the centre of the fairway.

I wanted to find out exactly what it was that Fred understood, but Professor Blanchard did not talk about it. Meanwhile, we were in danger of losing sight of Uncle Bob's golfers, who were putting out on seven as we teed off on six. Also, a foursome had caught up to us from behind. Desperate measures were called for.

"I don't know about you," I said, "but this hole looks sort of – well, suspicious." We both looked at it. It had green grass, a fairway trap on the left about two hundred yards out, a grove of spruces to the right, and, near the green, the lone oak tree that gave Grand Valley Oaks its name.

The professor wanted to understand. "I think I see what you're driving at," he said.

"A minute ago, when I looked, there were golfers over by that trap. Now they're gone," I said. "I think we should skip the hole. It's just the perfect set-up for a."

The professor looked over both shoulders. "All right," he said. "Just put down a five for both of us."

We headed off down the fairway pulling our carts and went straight to the seventh tee. Now we were within range. Better yet, the next several fairways adjoined each other. They would be coming down eight as we went up seven and I could get a good look.

That was one problem solved. The problem of winning would not be so easy. After the front nine, I was leading by seven strokes, due to my inability to hit bad shots, and the professor's inability to hit good ones. We stayed in visual range of Uncle Bob's golf squad, mostly due to their constant pauses for telephone conversations and what seemed to be a tendency to hit into water hazards. From my vantage point, they all looked like they could play the game. But there was something unusual about the game they were playing. It seemed to take them longer to play a hole than it should have.

My attention shifted from the professor to the Uncle Bobbers and back, depending upon the emergency of the moment. Occasionally some movement in the distance would catch my eye, but for the most part the professor's crankiness was the first priority. The crankier he got about golf, the crankier he got about life; the crankier he got about life, the crankier he got about Saturnians. And the crankier he got about Saturnians, the more impatient he grew about blowing the whistle on them in the pages of the *Grand Valley World-Beacon*.

To take his mind off it and make myself sound trustworthy, I began talking golf. Trustworthy people usually talked about golf while on the golf course. The article I'd read about chin position seemed a good place to start.

I started on the tenth green. I was there in three, having hit another one of my cursedly straight drives, followed by an only slightly messed-up five iron and a mediocre chip. The professor was on in five strokes, each one straighter and weaker than the one before.

"You know," I said, "I've been reading this article in a golf magazine about how the chin has been neglected by many of the older-style theorists, even Tommy Armour."

"Really," said the professor, visibly brooding.

"Yes," I said. "You remember how instructors used to worry overly about where the eyes were, vis à vis the ball."

"Mmmm," the professor said, taking his putter out of his cart and striding onto the green.

"Of course, later," I said, "there was that whole silly business about establishing the centrality of the nose at the moment of address."

"Curses," said the professor, who had left his twenty-foot putt ten feet short. I had an eighteen-footer and tried to hit it way past the hole. It rolled right in. There was a whole new theory of golf here that could come in handy for me at some point, only not right now.

"Shit," I said, and the professor looked at me. "Shit, I wish I could do that every time," I explained.

We walked to the next tee. "As a researcher, you'd appreciate this golf research," I said. Down the fairway, we could see the three Uncle Bobbers preparing to approach the green in their new golf duds. I gave them names: Shadrach, Meschach, and Abednego. Shadrach was tall and wearing royal blue golf slacks. Meschach was taller and wearing lemon yellow. Abednego was muscular, wearing raspberry and talking on the phone. It seemed to me that at least one was always on the phone and that may be what was keeping them from getting too far ahead of us.

"This article said the chin should be pointed just behind the ball," I went on, as I teed up my ball. I made a show of pointing my chin behind the ball. "The difficulty is that I can't actually see where my chin is, relative to the ball. In fact, I can't see my chin at all."

I took my best swing and, mercifully, sliced it into the woods. There was the beautiful sound of ball hitting tree, then rock, then other tree.

"Curses," I said.

The professor teed up his ball. "Did you notice anything odd about my research?" he asked.

Odd? His research? "Odd?" I asked. "Why do you ask?"

"There were peculiar stains on some of the pages," he said.

Uh-oh. I tried a diversionary tactic. "Did you notice anything about the shape of them?" I asked.

The professor stopped in mid waggle. "No," he said. "But the stains had a distinctive colour."

"A mustard colour?" I asked.

The professor stopped his backswing and nodded.

"Oh dear," I said. "This complicates matters."

The professor was so alarmed that he hit the ball almost seventy-five yards, but sliced it badly. "That's the thing about the chin," I said. "The nose is better because if you look cross-eyed, you can see where your nose is pointing. The chin, though, you can never tell, unless you take a mirror with you out onto the course."

"I don't think it's my chin," the professor said.

"It's true some strange things have been happening," I said. Up at the green, the Uncle Bobbers were holing out, Meschach putting the flag back in the cup, Abednego using what might have been – a fax machine? And Shadrach looking through some sort of instrument.

By the eleventh hole I had a headache from trying to deal with all of this and still keep the ball on the fairway, or off the fairway, actually. I was tired of keeping an eye out for Shadrach, Meschach, and Abednego. I was tired of watching the professor hit the ball thirty yards and yell "Curses!" The more he did it, the more I itched to throw away my plan and just win the game, by lots. But I had to lose. I had to do it for Shirley.

Finally, I figured out a way to do it, a way to lose holes without losing ground on Uncle Bob's golfers. I would stay in the fairway by using my new-found technique of trying not to stay in the fairway and concentrate my bad shots around the green, where they would be less costly in terms of time. A messed-up chip didn't require searching in the woods for a lost ball. A four-putt green took no time at all. I could lose the hole, and quickly too.

Two holes later, now only three strokes up, I had perfected the technique. I would hit my chip clear across the green, putt a twenty-footer twenty feet past the hole, miss the return putt by ten feet, and take two to get down from there. The professor, with his unspectacular and consistently terrible game, was catching up, and humming quietly to himself.

I decided there was no harm in attributing my misfortune to distant forces. On the 14th hole, having taken three putts to get within three feet of the cup, I struck the ball too hard, as if involuntarily, as if guided by the kind of unseen hand I had seen in movies several times. The ball rolled fifteen feet past the hole. I stood where I was for a few extra seconds, looked over my shoulder, looked over to the next hole, where Uncle Bob's men were on the phone again, looked at the putter, looked up to the sky. By the time I finished putting out, the match was tied. I accepted the professor's somewhat cheerful condolences and said: "I didn't know they could do that."

"Do what?" the professor asked and I mimicked the jerky putting motion I had made a few minutes ago.

The professor made an entry in his notepad. "You see what I mean," I said. "There are dimensions to this thing that we are only beginning to understand."

As we proceeded, at the professor's stately pace, down the 15th fairway, Uncle Bob's men were beside us, going the other way on the 16th. They were talking animatedly and I wanted to hear what they were saying. Cleverly, I punched my ball into the rough separating the two fairways.

"You go ahead," I called to the professor. "It won't be hard to find and I'll catch up with you on the green."

In the rough, I found my ball, then a tree to lurk behind. "Better check in," Meschach said and Abednego took out his telephone. After a moment he said: "It looks fine. Here's the last ones: eleven, seven, nine, six. Eleven is on 12." Then he hung up.

That means something, I said to myself, having no idea what. Lining up my shot out of the rough, I was distracted by shouting. It was the professor, waving a club — it looked like a four iron — at Uncle Bob's men and shouting.

"How dare you!" he yelled. "Get away from this place immediately."

"Easy, Professor," said Shadrach.

"There's nothing to be alarmed about," said Meschach.

"Alert," said Abednego, into his telephone.

I trotted over. "What's going on?" I asked the professor.

"You know very well what's going on," he said. "These . . . these 'men' are in the process of disrupting the —"

"Oh, I'm sure there must be a misunderstanding," I said, smiling at the Uncle Bobbers.

"Yeah, absolutely," said Abednego. "We're just out for a game. You have any idea where the green is from here?"

"I don't know," I said. "I'm a stranger here myself."

The professor eyed the three men suspiciously, but was beginning to relax a little. "Do you see the oak tree?" he asked.

"Yeah."

"It's to the left of it, just over the hill."

They thanked us and walked on quickly, leaving the professor in urgent need of reassurance. The last thing we needed was a case of assault on the golf course, with the professor telling anybody who would listen, including reporters, that the threesome in front of us was from outer space. And the last thing we needed after that was the STF getting involved in the fishing derby. At least I think it was the last thing we needed. Maybe it was just the thing we needed.

It was one or the other.

"Those guys," I said. "Can you imagine a nice day out on the golf course and you're spending all your time on the phone to your broker?"

"I'm not sure," the professor said. "There was something suspicious about."

"Anybody wearing lemon yellow tends to look suspicious. I wouldn't worry about it."

"That man called me 'Professor.' How did he know that?"

"Oh, I'm sure it's just because you look professorial," I said, as if I didn't really mean it. The professor shrugged, still worried. But he brightened when he watched me take three to get out of the rough. He could go ahead on this hole.

The espionage opportunity was over. Shadrach, Meschach, and Abednego had been spooked by the professor. I watched them move swiftly and skilfully up the 16th and tee off on the 17th, while we floundered our way up 15. There would be no more landing in water hazards, no more talking on the phone, and no hope of us catching them again. Still, I had learned something. I was sure I had.

I was free now to concentrate on the other important task, which was improving Professor Blanchard's mood and gaining his trust by making sure I didn't beat him on the golf course. By virtue (not his exact word) of hitting into a trap, he gained only one stroke on me on 15, then squandered it on 16, three-putting while I accidentally chipped one right into the hole from twenty feet off the green.

Meanwhile, the professor was annoying me mightily. He complained about our task force meeting room, complained about Tony Frusculla's language, complained about mosquitoes on the course, complained about the *World-Beacon*, complained – although not in so many words – about me, complained about Saturnians, which took in just about everybody, including the foursome waiting patiently behind us at each hole, and complained, most especially, about the length of time it was taking to get the products of his research into print.

We went into the 17th hole all even and emerged from it the same way, when even my most woeful swings could not exceed the woefulness of his. The 18th was the same. Although I did everything I could think of to avoid reaching the green, so, unintentionally, did he. Inevitably, we both arrived there, each of us having expended six swings to get there. I was hot, thirsty, and thoroughly pissed off. There were blisters on my hands and my feet hurt. All that kept me going was the thought that very soon I could give up golf again.

As we approached the green, I tried to jolly the professor along, without actually lying, which he might be able to detect. "I can't believe that I've been able to keep up with you," I said to him. "My game is certainly not in your class."

"No," he said. "You've been quite fortunate to keep the score close. I'm sure you'd be happier against a weaker opponent the next time."

The little pointy-headed puke. Two lucky putts later and he was finished, with a nifty score of 128. All I needed to do was three-putt from thirty-five feet. I'd done that hundreds of times without even trying. I missed the first putt by only four feet, then reminded myself that all I had to do was miss the four-footer and I had won – that is, lost. As I lined it up, the professor walked behind the cup, in my line of sight.

"I doubt if you'll make it with that putting stance," he said. "But don't worry. It's no disgrace to lose."

That did it. My entire plan, my entire day's work went out the window in a blaze of rage and a bonfire of competitiveness. I never wanted to win so badly in my life. I painstakingly lined up the putt, carefully took my backswing, and sent the ball rolling smoothly toward the hole, which it missed by quite a bit.

Mission accomplished. Curses.

Chapter 23

For a guy seeking serenity, trying to avoid cynicism, trauma or hassles of even a minor sort, I wasn't doing too well. Everywhere I turned was greed, stupidity, and delusion. Not to mention editorials. On the other hand, there was a certain excitement about it all, a certain dash, a certain sense of being a double agent. I knew that I didn't really have the clothes for being a double agent, but other than that, things were fine. A beer hadn't looked good to me for weeks.

There were too many meetings, that was for sure. Double agents wouldn't go to a lot of meetings. But then, double agents didn't usually hang out in Grand Valley with the enemies of Saturn, on the eve of a fishing derby.

The Saturn Task Force meetings, now held daily, were going well. The professor and I were getting along. He quite liked me, now that he knew he could beat me at golf. I hated him more every day, but that didn't matter. Tony and Juanita were glad of any excuse to see each other, so the meetings passed quite pleasantly.

I would shift the locations, so as not to arouse suspicions. We met in a bowling alley, in the STF office, and in Bowell Park. At that meeting, a couple of days after our golf game, I even suggested that it might be a good idea to change passwords. It was an inspired idea, creating lengthy and intense discussion, a heightening of suspicions, and, in the end, total failure. We decided to keep our original passwords because, as Tony astutely remarked, "They'd be expecting us to change them."

You could tell that he had been spending at least some of his time with Juanita wisely.

From time to time, either the professor or Juanita would come up with a compelling reason why the story should run now. One time was when an unearthly detergent commercial was glimpsed on television. On another occasion, a mild protest by the university and Unitarian crowd against the impending cruelty to bass, Juanita saw a familiar face in the crowd that she couldn't quite put a finger on but was quite sure she had seen somewhere else. Worse still was the widely reported occurrence of solar flare activity. Such incidents would lend a new urgency to our mission, making it more difficult for me to sidetrack it. Otherwise the story would be done, our mission would be over, and where would I be then?

But there are always ways, particularly when you are dealing with distinguished academics and graduates of some of the world's great universities.

One day, when it looked like the pressure to publish would be irresistible, I introduced the potent notion that we had no business carrying on unless our task force had a mission statement. It was an idea even more powerful than I had hoped. Immediately the professor adopted it and carried it even further: We could not have a mission statement, he said, unless we first had a strategic plan. So we put off our substantive deliberations for several days while we worked on that. Eventually, after a thorough discussion of all the pros and cons, we came up with a strategic plan, which was that we would work collaboratively in order to identify and expose elements of distant forces at play in our society.

With the strategic plan in place, the mission statement took only a couple of days. "Making Earth a better planet," was what we came up with. It took some time, which was good, to reject certain unrelated clauses that the professor and Juanita wanted to append, some of them having to do with such things as abolishing the French language, solar flares, university tenure committees, and inappropriate behaviour by tennis players.

Tony was becoming a valuable member of the group, not to mention a valuable member of the Bass Protective Force. Each day, while ostensibly off investigating the forces of Saturn, he worked the phones, checking other places where Uncle Bob had been, getting the low-down on the key members of his entourage, learning the financial details of the operation as well as a few fishing tips.

The Bass Protective Force meetings were the most fun, even if the shadow of Paine Shaw did loom over them. Shirley laughed at my account of the golf game, gasped in awe at the thought of turning the anti-Saturn faction against the Uncle Bob faction, and just generally seemed to be enjoying herself. Once she touched my arm as we were leaving Score's, which I regarded as significant, although she may have just lost her balance. Just after she did that a shiny black Audi pulled up and she got in. What's that guy got that I haven't got? I asked myself.

A shiny black Audi was one thing.

The only meetings that weren't going well were the ones with the editor. Fred was becoming increasingly jittery, which wasn't like him, especially with all the synergy he had been having. I guessed that he was getting some pressure from head office. That made him nervous and his nervousness fought a constant battle against his synergy courses. He knew he was supposed to be a sensitive and feeling employer, but he had to talk on the phone to Mrs. Baxter every day.

On top of that, he was probably hearing from Professor Blanchard. Although the professor now had a high regard for me, after learning how badly I putted, he was not without vanity. He knew how good his research was and he wanted the public to see it.

With two weeks to go before Uncle Bob's arrival, I was summoned to a morning meeting with Fred. Driving to the *WB* was slow. For the first time since I moved to Grand Valley, the white lines on Michener Road were being painted. Flower boxes were being hung from the lamp posts and small trees in large pots were being strategically arranged. One of them would block the storefront of Mr. Lucky's XXX Underwear Mart from the gaze of anyone on the parade route.

Hitting the red light at Queen and Michener, I looked for my favourite squeegee kid, but she was nowhere in sight. The bus shelter, which usually had the best graffiti in town, was cleaned up. In front of it were new signs, prohibiting spitting, littering, and boom boxes.

On my way across the newsroom to Fred's office, I stopped at Lorne Marshall's desk to alert him to the greening of Queen and Michener. He said he already knew. They were saving that information for the special edition.

I had forgotten about the special edition. Two special editions, actually, forty-eight pages of puff copy about Uncle Bob, with supporting advertising from hopeful local merchants. Saturn had kept me away from it. With all the evil of which it was capable, I still blessed Saturn for that.

The lights were on in Fred's office, but he turned them out as soon as I was seated. He asked me a couple of questions about my health and well-being, consulting his index cards. While I answered – things were fine; I was fine – he opened the top drawer of his desk and put the index cards away.

"I have every specific confidence in your ability to bring this research to a successful conclusion," he said.

We both knew what that meant. It meant he had no confidence at all.

"Of course," I said.

"The owner, in particular, will be delighted when the series is published in the *World-Beacon*."

"She said that to you?"

"Words to that effect, yes."

Fred began one of his silences. Once I would have tried to break it, out of sheer discomfort, but today I had nothing to say. I looked at the newspaper lying beside me. The big headline was about Uncle Bob's visit. Apparently the economic benefits of it had been underestimated, according to new statistics that had been discovered by the chamber of commerce, in cooperation with Uncle Bob's research department. The mayor, just back from a fact-finding tour of South America, welcomed the news. The rest of page one was pretty sketchy. So much of the staff was either following Uncle Bob or Saturnians that there weren't many people left to cover anything else. Most stories were off the wire, barely rewritten: some people in Belgium who had made a cross-word puzzle out of chocolate; an earthquake that might threaten cloth production in Fiji; high winds in Louisiana that would either help or hinder the reproduction of boll weevils. In each case, a half-hearted attempt had been made to localize the story. In each case the member of Parliament, Hon. Winston Booker, was withholding comment until he had a chance to study the matter more fully.

Fred stood up and walked to the fish tank, where the fish seemed to be swimming slower. "The situation is being brought home to Dr. Baxter," he said.

"I heard about the terrifying incident in her neighbourhood," I said.

"Now there has been another one, and it has caused her considerable alarm."

"I hope no one was hurt," I said.

"Fortunately, no," Fred said. "Her chauffeur was there to offer assistance had any been needed."

"What happened?"

"The chauffeur was driving Dr. Baxter from her home to her office when something – it had green hair and was brandishing a club – jumped out at them and splashed a substance all over the windshield of the Jaguar. Dr. Baxter was startled and urged the driver to escape, which he did, slightly injuring a pedestrian who appeared to be an accomplice of the . . . creature that caused the commotion in the first place."

"Poor Mrs. Baxter. Did she call the police?"

"She had her people call the police. They reported that there was nothing that could be done and further, that the driver might even have been in the wrong for driving away after striking the pedestrian."

"Goodness," I said. "Didn't they know it wasn't an ordinary pedestrian?"

"They claimed not to understand that. Dr. Baxter has some strong suspicions about the police and the nature of their relationship with."

"Is this a story for us?" I asked. "Surely the Toronto papers . . ."

"Dr. Baxter has some strong suspicions about the Toronto papers."

I could see what was coming. All my hard work with the professor and the task force, all my inspired stalling, was wasted, because of Mrs. Baxter. Even if I could talk sense into Fred, I couldn't talk sense into Mrs. Baxter. Nobody could talk sense into her. She had too much money to listen to anybody.

An early story was going to be in the *WB*, whether I liked it or not. Once the story was published all would be lost, the task force, the bass force, my chance to be a hero.

"The task force will have to do it, then," I said. "If we can talk to Mrs. Baxter, we should have the whole package ready day after tomorrow."

"Tomorrow would be preferable," Fred said.

A Saturnian version of my life flashed before my eyes. It seemed to have rings around it.

"Mrs. Baxter was impressed by young Eldridge," Fred continued. "She would readily be interviewed by her."

"OK," I said, standing. "I better go. There's work to do."

Fred nodded and didn't shake my hand.

The Bass Protective Force meeting was decidedly gloomy, so gloomy that the hulking Rodney Sullivan came over to our table twice to ask if everything was in order.

We told him it was.

"Shit. I'm getting so close," Tony said. "A week, maybe ten days, I'll have it."

"What have you got?" I asked.

Tony was sly about it. Some hotshot in Investigative Journalism 101 had told him not to entrust editors with too many details. "I'll show it to you when it's done," he said.

Shirley tried to help. "Maybe we can do Uncle Bob Fishing Shocker some other time."

"I don't think so," I said. "The time to do it is when he's here. He won't be back."

"Anyway," Tony said, "I have to go back to business writing, isn't that what they told you?"

"Yeah," Shirley said. "Smithers told me you'd be back in harness on Friday."

"Well," I said. "It's been fun."

"It has been fun," Shirley said, and really did touch my arm.

"I liked working on it," Tony said. "I mean, I didn't know it would be like this coming out of J-school. They never told us you'd have to be so sneaky to get good stuff into the paper. This is fun, you know, but it's weird that we have to do it this way. Did you ever think of that?"

"It used to be much more straightforward," Shirley said. "Maybe it was less interesting, but you knew what you were doing."

"Maybe we can have Bass Protective Force reunions and stuff," I said. Shirley didn't answer. She lit a cigarette and stared off into space for a few moments. Finally, she looked back at me.

"Who's writing the Saturn story?" she asked.

"Well, I'll probably do it. I can't wish it on Tony and the others can't write."

"I think the professor should write it," Shirley said.

"Fuck," Tony said.

"You don't get it," Shirley answered. "If the professor writes it, nobody will understand it. There won't be a big scare and no innocent people will be jailed as suspected Saturnians. And when Fred sees how little impact it has, he'll demand that the task force continue and produce more stories."

Why didn't I think of that? "I'm in awe," I told Shirley. "I thought I understood newspapers, but that's amazing."

"You can buy me a beer," she said. "That's what a real newspaper guy would do."

Chapter 24

If you walked into the newsroom of the *Grand Valley World-Beacon* on the morning of June 20 and wondered where the action was, you would have no way of knowing. There were people standing around and talking, some reporters busy on the phone, some copy editors moving stories around on their big screens. There was no particular noise, no particular buzz, no centre to it. The newsroom looked, as it always looked, as if nothing was going on. You knew something was, but you didn't know where to look for it. There were clumps of desks, clumps of people, but no centre to it, and no definition to the edges. Also, it was very dark.

When I started in the business, when pages were still made up out of hot metal from linotypes and page layouts were dummied in pencil, newsrooms had a centre. It was the news desk, a large horseshoe, around which people sat. The outside of the desk was the rim, the people who sat around it were copy editors. The inside of the desk was the slot. The slot man, usually an assistant news editor, knew what was going in the paper and where it would go. He would hand out pages to the rim. A guy, always a guy, would be handed four stories and a photo for page 16. He would edit them, write headlines and send them to the composing room to be typeset, send the photo off to be engraved. Then he would get another page, complaining all the while about the quality of the material he was handling.

There would be smoking and much yelling around the desk, a sense that this was the centre of the action. Nearby was the city desk, with fewer people, but a clear sense of being at the centre, reporters coming and going, being summoned and dismissed, their stories, on yellowed sheets of copy paper, being passed up the line.

The sports department was over there, all male. The women's pages were on the other side of the room, all female. The important editors sat in glass offices facing into the brightly lit newsroom, brightly lit so that those yellowed sheets of copy paper could be read carefully.

Now newsrooms have to be dark, so that no overhead light interferes with the glow of the computer terminal screens. The big pagination computers used by copy editors take up so much room that it is no longer possible for the copy editors to sit around one desk. They are so spread out that the slot man or woman cannot sit among them. She must walk among them. The city desk is on the other side of the room, a couple of people indistinguishable from any other couple of people. Physical proximity is no longer necessary since stories are passed back and forth electronically.

In the newsroom, the women's section doesn't exist. The sports department is unrecognizable as such. A guy like Lawrie Andrews, wearing his Brooklyn Dodgers baseball cap, shares space with women who look like they should be in the entertainment department, but are covering hockey. There are baseball caps in the entertainment department too, which is recognizable only because it has movie posters. Only the editorial writers keep

up a time-honoured newspaper tradition by staying cloistered in
offices away from everybody else.

Old-line critics say today's newspaper office is indistinguishable from an insurance office. That's not true, because a newspaper
office is much messier. There are today's papers and some of yesterday's. There are old dummy sheets and schedules, folders from
the library, bits of lunch and stray volumes of encyclopaedias.

The sound is like an insurance office, though. There is a relative quiet to the operation now. No one has to raise a voice to
be heard over the clatter of typewriters and teletypes. There are
no typewriters and teletypes. In the early days of computeriza-
tion, a few people used to keep typewriters at their desks for
writing memos and photo orders and love letters. All of that stuff
can go through the computers and come out of high speed print-
ers now. The more careless lovers forget to erase the electronic
traces of their ardour from the system, which provides a momen-
tary thrill for those in the know.

You would have no indication, if you walked into the newsroom of the _Grand Valley World-Beacon_ that morning, that the real
action was at my desk, on my screen. I had the professor's story,
the story that would blow this town wide open, if I wasn't careful.
The first test would be the morning news meeting.

The morning news meeting at the _Grand Valley World-Beacon_ is as
unimpressive-looking as the rest of the operation. A dozen men
and two women carry coffee mugs of all descriptions into a windowless room at ten in the morning. The editor leans back in his
chair and looks at the ceiling. From time to time, he leans forward
in his chair and jots a note down in a notebook. At those moments,
everyone else around the table leans forward too.

Smithers, the managing editor, runs the meeting. He goes
around the table, asking each editor what they have for page one.
They all have something. They all want to be invited back. Davis,

as she was called in the meeting, had a French high-tech firm thinking of locating in the Tri-Lakes Area, bringing four hundred jobs. Everybody looked at Fred. He continued to stare at the ceiling. Lawrie Andrews, the acting sports editor, had a story about a woman golfer in New Zealand. Fred stared at the ceiling. Andrews passed a photo of her around the table. Fred leaned forward in his chair and wrote in his notebook. City had a traffic study about the dangers involved in reversing the directions of King and Queen for Uncle Bob's visit. Fred stared at the ceiling. National had the rumour of a general election. Foreign had violence in Zimbabwe. Entertainment had a preview of a television movie about tropical fish. Fred leaned forward in his chair.

It came to me, specially invited for this occasion only. I outlined the Saturn story as badly as I could, describing it as "interesting academic research." But nothing could stop Fred from being excited. He ordered up a reaction story and photos for the inside spread. We would have the top two-thirds of page one, plus a turn to page five and two full facing pages inside. I told him that the professor wouldn't have his picture taken, for fear of reprisal. "I'll find something," the photo editor said, which meant a still from an old movie.

The bottom of page one would go to the New Zealand golfer and the tropical fish. The main art would be Uncle Bob, for the tenth day in a row. He was with Lech Walesa, for some reason. Walesa appearing very thin beside him.

As the meeting broke up, Fred showed me his teeth and I smiled back. "This will be genuinely big," he said.

I hope not, I thought. I went to my desk, called up Professor Blanchard's story on the big pagination screen, and began editing it. The page-one part needed work. It had to seem intelligible while remaining almost meaningless. It had to have the sense of urgency that all page-one stories have, while at the same time concealing what the urgency was about. The two-page spread inside was easier; it was incoherent enough to run as written. The professor typed quite well too, which was helpful. There weren't many typos to fix. I ran the spell-check and turned it over to the news desk, which I knew would also run the spell-check, before putting it in the paper, unedited.

Chapter 25

Important findings revealed to public

By Dr. H. W. C. Blanchard
Special to the World-Beacon

Countless civilizations ago, perhaps as long nine million years, or perhaps longer, what we know of as the galaxy was a vastly, some would say significantly, different series of chemical, mineral, and biological patterns than would seem to be the case in the present time.

The events leading up to the most recent two million years are only now beginning to be understood by scientists in North America and on other continents. Yet, as a special investigation by a *World-Beacon* task force demonstrates, not everything is as it would appear.

The startling findings are indicative of profound migratory developments that could, according to informed sources, seriously affect relationships among various species currently inhabiting

Please turn to FINDINGS page A5

EDITORIAL

Time to draw the line

A disturbing legacy of liberal cover-up stands revealed to us today, in light of startling findings contained in a special *World-Beacon* investigation.

World Marxism and its friends in the left-wing media and the University of Grand Valley are shown to have conspired in a dangerous silence that threatened peace, free markets, and the appropriate population make-up of our society.

Now that the truth is known, governments fail, at their peril, to take appropriate action. A measured response is called for, not so strong as to alarm the populace or interfere with the workings of the free market, yet not so weak as to give comfort to our enemies.

With courage and steadfastness, we may overcome this conundrum, which was visited upon us in a time of socialist-inspired ignorance.

"God, you're a genius," Shirley said. "They don't understand a word of it."

"I know," I said. "But they wrote the editorial anyway."

"And the cartoon couldn't be better."

"True," I said. Alexei had drawn a long lineup of people waiting to buy the *World-Beacon* from a newspaper box.

"I love the page-one headline too," she said.

"I'm proud of it. I asked Hugh Robbins for help."

"It's really good, and I like how nothing happens in the story before the turn."

"That wasn't hard. The professor was worried that it was too inflammatory as it was."

"The column is fine too."

That was true. Dick Rivers had, without actually knowing what the story meant, written a moving account of how it had affected him, as he moved through his day.

"When I was a boy, I had a puppy called Tige," his column concluded. "I often think about him at times like this and wonder if he is in a better place."

I'd come in early to see how bad the paper looked. Everybody assumed I was doing the strut. We were sitting in the *WB* cafeteria, drinking coffee and looking around. Scattered about the room were employees, mostly from other departments, their newspapers open to the two-page spread that contained the professor's research. It was illustrated with movie stills from science fiction epics. Michael Rennie as Klaatu in *The Day the Earth Stood Still* was on page eight; a four-storey spider from the movie *Tarantula* was on page nine, just below Sigourney Weaver in *Alien*. The employees read the paper the way newspaper people do, glancing here and there over the page, their faces showing little in the way of emotion. I thought I detected more than the usual puzzlement this time, but it might have been wishful thinking on my part.

"I wonder how many of them are going to get twenty-seven paragraphs in," I said.

"Twenty-seven paragraphs?"

"Yup. That's where the first mention of Saturn is."

"I didn't see Mrs. Baxter's squeegee kid in the story at all."

"No, I got the professor to write it cryptically so they wouldn't know we were on to them."

Shirley shook her head. "How does this stuff get by everybody? Didn't somebody look at it and say, 'Hey, you've buried the lead. Get the Saturn stuff up to the top.' Doesn't anybody ask, 'What does this mean?'"

"You know the answer."

"Yeah. It's Fred. They know he likes it so they like it."

"The emperor's new story."

"What about Mrs. Baxter?" Shirley asked. "Is this going to satisfy her?"

"I don't know. It depends on if she actually reads it. If she reads the reaction stories, it will look like something's happening."

Indeed it did. Grand Valley's politicians knew better than to say "I don't understand what you're talking about" when asked by a reporter to react to a crisis. Consequently, the Hon. Winston Booker, MP, allowed himself to be quoted in the page-one sidebar as being "concerned" and blaming the present government for allowing things to reach this sad state. The provincial health minister said she would take a look at it, which allowed the reporter, Brian Blezard, to write that "a full provincial investigation is planned." James Norwood, president of the chamber of commerce and publisher of the *World-Beacon*, said he hoped the news wouldn't detract from the considerable progress the Tri-Lakes Area was making in becoming a hub for tourism and economic development. Matt Foley, coach of the Grand Valley Valleyers, said, on behalf of the hockey club, that he knew all hockey fans would be praying for a peaceful solution. And Mayor Martin Havelock, reached by telephone during a fact-finding tour of New Zealand, said he hoped the community would pull together in this time of trouble.

AREA POLITICIANS REACT TO CRISIS was the effective headline I commissioned from Hugh Robbins for the reaction story.

All of a sudden I was very weary. "I don't know," I said. "At least I tried."

"You've done everything you can, Parker," said Shirley. "It's really incomprehensible and boring."

"Thanks," I said. "But you never know how it's going to play out there. The newspaper boxes are all empty. I checked them on my drive in. It looks like the people are buying it."

"That's because the first Uncle Bob section is in today."

There may have been something in that. It was preprinted and stuffed into the paper, twenty-four pages of photos of Uncle Bob, a map of his itinerary, many photos of glorious events in his past, and a string of highly lucrative advertisements, in which local merchants, including all the funeral homes, five pizza delivery outfits, and Mr. Lucky's XXX Underwear Mart wished Uncle

Bob an enjoyable visit to the Tri-Lakes Area. "Wish 'em" ads, we called them. This would be followed up in a week with another section, a complete fishing derby program, and more wish 'em ads from the local business community.

The section was heavily promoted, with newspaper box cards and a large teaser at the top of page one, right above IMPORTANT FINDINGS REVEALED TO PUBLIC.

"Your complete guide to Faith and Fishing," said the teaser and it seemed to be selling papers.

"So the story is out there," I said. "I just wish there were some guarantees it will fail."

"I'll do some nosing around with my contacts," Shirley said, giving me a puzzled look when she saw me flinch at the word "contacts."

She added: "If I find out anything I'll call you at work tonight."

As I walked through the newsroom on my way out to my car, I was given a thumbs-up by Smithers, and Lorne Marshall yelled "nice story" at me. This wasn't looking good.

That night I hid in the Saturn Task Force office, rolling the golf ball around on the desk top, taking stock and trying not to be cynical. I hadn't succeeded in preventing the story. That was bad. But I had stickhandled it skilfully and prevented it from being of any interest to anybody who tried to read it. That was good. But the *World-Beacon* had played it really big anyway. That was bad. There was at least a small chance that your life wouldn't be worth a plugged nickel in the Tri-Lakes Area if you were a Saturnian, or somebody thought you were.

I was still sober, despite it all. That was good. I'd fallen in love. And that was good too, on balance. It wouldn't be good if Shirley didn't fall in love too, and meanwhile there was the rich guy with the expensive black car. That was bad. And I'd missed my chance to be a hero, which was bad, even though Shirley did seem to admire the effort I'd made, which was good.

Uncle Bob Fishing Shocker was toast, it looked like. That was bad. But there was a chance it could be revived if the Saturn story bombed and needed more work, which would be good.

The phone rang and I jumped for it, thinking it was Shirley with news of the story's impact. "Hello?" I said.

There was an intake of breath, followed by a silence from the other end. Finally, the professor spoke. "We still need passwords," he said. "Our enemies are even more dangerous now that we have exposed their perfidy to the spotlight of public opinion."

"This isn't television," I replied.

"But the perch knows something new," he said.

"So," I said, "there's good buzz in the newsroom about your story."

"My research," he said.

"Yes. Were you pleased with it?"

"I thought the newspaper might have devoted more space to it. One entire section, concerning the misuse of electricity in ballroom dancing, was omitted entirely."

"I notice that," I said. "But it is a daily newspaper, as we say. There are always space problems."

"Also," he said, "I thought the headline was a bit sensationalistic."

We chatted for a few more minutes. I didn't say that our work was probably over. There was no point in alarming him, not that he didn't live in a constant state of alarm anyway. We promised to keep our eyes open and stay in touch.

There were two other phone calls, both concerning television, before the one I was waiting for.

"This isn't television," I said, and heard Shirley's laughing voice.

"But the fish, um, doesn't know its own strength. Is that it?"

"Close enough," I said. "What's up?"

"It's sunk like a stone."

"I can't believe it. Big headlines on page one, two full pages inside, reaction from politicians and the hockey coach, columns, editorials."

"It's true," she said. "The open-line shows didn't have anything. The local TV news didn't pick it up. It didn't go national. It didn't make the wire."

"What about the university?"

"Nobody is taking it seriously. People at UGV know all about Professor Blanchard."

"And what about your, um, contacts?" I asked.

"Nobody in the business community is talking about it," she said. "My contacts say everybody is excited about the fishing derby and Uncle Bob and all that. Most people didn't even notice this."

"That Paine guy, is he one of your business contacts?"

"Yes, one of them," Shirley said.

"And what does he think about all this?"

"Well, he says that people have just got used to weird stories from the *WB* and they don't react to them any more."

"That makes sense," I said.

"Yeah. Some of them used to get excited about the stories, like the boll weevil. Some of them used to get mad. Now they just turn the page."

"People are smart," I said.

"Right. And you know what this means?"

"Yes, the public remains unconvinced. The STF's mighty mission must continue."

"Do you want me to tell Tony?"

"He's here in the newsroom," I said. "I'll tell him myself."

Tony was indeed in the newsroom, leaning over Juanita Eldridge's desk, pretending to be examining a document. Heading over there I encountered muted expressions of congratulations from some colleagues and puzzled stares from others. As I walked past the news desk, Hamilton Thistle intercepted me.

"Old chap," he said. "On the important findings story, I've been meaning to speak to you about – what do you call them in Canada: followings?"

"Follows," I said. "Only we don't do much following in Grand Valley."

"Well, I saw the editor looking for you just a moment ago. Perhaps that's what he wants to talk to you about."

"Perhaps," I said, and changed direction, heading now for Fred's office, which was dark.

Folos would be good. They would keep the task force together, maybe long enough for Tony to come up with something on Uncle Bob Fishing Shocker. On the other hand, what kinds of folos could we do? All the people who could react had already reacted. We could try some analytical stories, some what-does-it-mean stuff, but if we did it too well, people would know what it meant. Our only hope was the professor. He probably had more research that he hadn't shown us yet. Maybe on the water levels. We could crank out some stuff about that, get a headline about More Important Findings, get some reaction to them, the promise of more government investigations. Maybe someone would promise a royal commission this time.

I knocked on Fred's office door. I heard the hiss of the wind blowing through pine branches, then the call of a loon, then Fred saying: "Come in."

I went in and felt my way to the chesterfield. The fish were still swimming quickly. I confidently awaited Fred's disappointment.

"I think our project was effectively done, MacVeigh," Fred said.

Effectively? "Thanks," I said. "I'm concerned about the reaction, though."

"Excellent reaction," Fred said.

"The way I hear it, nobody is reacting at all."

"Nonsense," Fred said. "Dr. Baxter has already phoned and she is delighted."

"But nobody else is running with it."

"I know," said Fred, smiling. "We have it all to ourselves."

I had forgotten. Fred would be the last to worry about anybody else.

"That's great," I said. "I've got some interesting plans for folo stories."

"Folo stories?" Fred said.

"Well, sure. We can really push this thing ahead now. The task force is just hitting its stride."

A wolf howled.

Fred entered into one of his silences. I waited, counting six laps around the tank by the blue fish and four by the orange one before Fred spoke.

"MacVeigh, your work is done," he said.

"Done?"

"The task force has done exactly what it set out to do. The story is first-rate. Mission accomplished."

"Thanks, but, you know, there were some holes in the story, as you are aware, and with some more time we can fill in the gaps and push it forward."

"The story couldn't be better," Fred said.

It occurred to me then for the first time: *He hasn't read it. He won't ever read it.*

"Thank you, but . . ."

"It's time to move on," Fred said. "They need you back on the day desk. I want to thank you for all you have done. Take a couple of days off and come in Monday morning."

On other planets they may know how to react to news of this sort. None of my earthly training had prepared me for it. Weeks of important work, including some that was very difficult for me, such as scheming and lying, had led to this moment. And this moment was awful. My only hope of getting the girl, never mind the story, depended on the task force and Fred was shutting it down, all because he couldn't be bothered to find out how bad the story he had commissioned really was.

There was no reasoning with him, no persuading, no changing his mind. For a moment I lost my head and decided to risk everything by being honest. Maybe being devious wasn't the way to do this story. Maybe the direct route would work.

"Fred," I said, "we've known each other a long time. I've really enjoyed working on this story and now there's another story I want to do, but I can't do it without your OK because it involves a friend of yours."

Without mentioning the Saturn connection, without mentioning how far we had gone in investigating the matter, I outlined Uncle Bob Fishing Shocker in general terms. The acclaimed evangelist owed a lot of his appeal to his skill as a fisherman, but that skill was a myth. He won his fishing derbies by cheating.

Fred listened quietly, without moving, without taking a note. Finally, he said, "Have you got good sources on this?" he asked.

"Very good," I said. "Now that the Saturn story is over, I'd have the time to go ahead. It's a great story. It would put the *World-Beacon* on the map. Do I have your permission to pursue it?"

Fred stood up. "It's not a story," he said.

"But . . ."

"When you disband the task force, please convey to the members my heartiest congratulations."

Chapter 26

When I called Shirley for consolation after my conversation with Fred, I got her answering machine. That was eleven o'clock at night, which I did not consider a good sign. I pictured her out, rocketing around in a shiny black Audi, listening intently to thoughts on risk avoidance or risk management or whatever it was. Meanwhile, there I was, sitting in a tiny office with space posters on the wall, having failed at failing. *I try my best to create a story no one will read and the editor thinks it's great. What kind of newspaperman am I, anyway?*

Two hours of brooding later, I concluded objectively, as I removed Venus and Mercury from the STF office wall, that this would be the ideal time for me to have some Scotch whisky. Nothing was working out. I wasn't getting the girl. I had tried my best to get some real journalism done and succeeded only in getting some unreal journalism done. Which the editor really liked. I should just drown my sorrows and pack it in. Everybody would understand. The only thing was, it was late. The liquor store was closed; so were the bars. I realized that I didn't want to get drunk badly enough to go hunting up a bootlegger at this hour of the night.

That insight would have been a good start on the road to sobriety, if I wasn't already there.

My gloom wasn't lightened the next morning by Professor Blanchard, who was exuberant. "I'd like twenty extra copies of yesterday's paper, please," he said, when we met at the Tim Hortons on the bypass.

"Call circulation," I said, the best I could come up with on four hours' sleep. I needed something crueller to say. This fucker beat me at golf. I finally settled on, "You getting lots of slaps on the back over at UGV?"

That worked. "I'm afraid most of my colleagues only read *The Economist*," the professor said.

"Do you think we'll get a nomination?" Juanita asked, chewing delicately on a muffin that had healthy ingredients.

Newspaper awards were a mystery to me, but they were at the front of Juanita's mind. "I think we've got as good a chance as anybody," I said, meaning it.

When I finally delivered the news that our mighty mission was over, it got a mixed reception. The professor looked angry and glanced over his shoulder, forgetting that he'd seated himself with his back to the wall. Tony looked sadly at Juanita. Only Juanita seemed cheerful, made so by my mention that Fred liked our work.

"Did he mention me by name?" she asked.

"Of course," I lied.

The professor had been watching people come and go, apparently without seeing anything suspicious. He had told me more than once that Saturnians were unlikely to be attracted to dough-nut shops.

"There's something that doesn't ring true about this," he said.

"In what way, Professor?" I asked.

"Why would they discontinue our work, just when we're getting close, unless . . . ?"

This was good. Sentences were beginning not to end. Some of that old Saturn Task Force spirit endured.

I comforted myself with feeding his paranoia. "I'm not sure you're on the right track," I said. "There's probably a perfectly reasonable."

"The more you look at it," he said, "the more."

"Well, that's usually the case," I said, "but in this case, the people making the decision have the best of."

"They often do," he sneered.

"Listen," I said, "if Mrs. Baxter herself is contented with."

"Dr. Baxter!" the professor snorted. "What does she know? For all we know she might be."

Tony glanced at me. "She'd be really pissed off if you ever accused her of that to her face," he said.

"Anyway," I said, "you'd never get through to her at her office and nobody gives out her home number."

The professor liked a challenge. "I'll find a way," he said.

When I got home, there was a message from Shirley. She'd got my message, was sorry and would meet me at Score's later on. I must have looked terrible when she arrived because she gave me a light hug. I made a mental note to look terrible more often.

She didn't ask what the beer was doing on the table in front of me. In fact, I hadn't touched it. Ordering it had been enough of an accomplishment. I wanted to see how it looked there for a while before actually drinking any of it. And actually I didn't want it all that badly. But I felt like the central figure in a tragedy and something tragic was called for. Ordering a beer seemed safer than falling on a sword.

I didn't ask Shirley where she'd been the night before and she didn't volunteer the information. I did tell her about my conversation with Fred, and my shocked realization that he hadn't read the story.

"That story was his idea," I said. "We worked on it for weeks, he cleared a huge amount of space for it, he knew Mrs. Baxter was big on it. Why wouldn't he read it?"

"He never reads stories," Shirley answered. "I'm surprised you didn't know that. He dreams them up. That's what he does. He's too busy dreaming the next one up to read the last one."

"That means they're all great stories to him."

"Exactly," she said. "He never has to read how shitty they turn out."

It was an interesting thing to know but it didn't help. If Fred didn't read, we could never convince him that our story was inadequate. All my efforts at making it inadequate were in vain. Furthermore, he would be convinced that the Saturnian dragon had been slain and we didn't need to do any more.

I told Shirley about my direct approach to Fred on Uncle Bob Fishing Shocker. "It's all over," I said. "My last chance to do something useful and he says it's not a story. I'm back on the day desk tomorrow, writing stupid headlines on stupid stories, editing the coin column and the chess column, eating the luncheon special in the cafeteria. This was exciting. Now what?"

Shirley looked at me and then at the beer and then at me again.

"How nice of you to order that beer for me," she said.

I looked at her with what I hoped showed as gratitude. "I'm nothing if not considerate," I said.

She took the bottle and drank from it. I felt relieved. Drinking had seemed like the dramatic thing to do. But there were still limits on how much drama I could stand.

"Where is Mrs. Baxter on this?" Shirley asked.

"She loves the story too, according to Fred. The professor is blaming her personally now. I did my part to encourage that, although I don't know where it can possibly lead. There's no way he's going to get through to her."

Shirley looked up and laughed. "I bet I know where we can get her home phone number." She waved her arm and in a moment Rodney Sullivan loomed over us.

"Is there a need impinging upon either of you?" he asked.

"We just wanted to alert you to the fact that we know someone who has it in mind to irritate and annoy your former employer," Shirley said.

Rodney smiled. "Oh dear," he said.

"Fortunately," Shirley said, "this person who wants to do the irritating and annoying doesn't have Mrs. Baxter's home phone number."

"I see," Rodney said. He scribbled on a coaster and handed it to Shirley. "I'd better entrust this to you," he said. "Otherwise it might fall into the wrong hands."

"That will help a little," I told Shirley, as Rodney lumbered away and she slipped the coaster into my shirt pocket. "If I tell the professor not to bother Mrs. Baxter, he will, and Mrs. Baxter is sure to think the professor is a Saturnian. But it may not be enough. We need to figure out a way to tip her over the edge."

"We'll do it," she said, then added. "I've got to dash." I saw something shiny and black flash by the window. She stood, she touched my arm, said "Ginger ale," then dashed.

For a moment, I stared around the room. Off-season, the place was uncrowded. The TV sets were showing archival curling footage of men in thick matching sweaters and toe-rubbers. As they curled, they smoked cigarettes.

Rodney reappeared, bearing a ginger ale for me which he described as "gratuitous."

He sat down: "This person who wants to be vexatious to my erstwhile employer," he said.

"Yes?"

"What manner of person is he or she?"

"He's really annoying," I said, "but harmless."

"I see," he said.

"Do you know quite a bit about her?" I asked.

"I pride myself on being a scrupulous observer," he said.

"If I wanted to change her mind about something, how would I do that?"

"It is not a viable option to change her mind," he said. "Not by reasoning. The more you attempt reason with her, the more stubborn she becomes. If you wanted to bring about a modification in her thoughts, you'd have to scare her."

I could picture myself throwing a big scare into the owner of the *Grand Valley World-Beacon* and other internationally respected newspapers.

"How would you do that?" I asked.

"Oh, you know, rough her up a little."

"Seriously."

"Objects hurled at her limousine could be effective. Crude left-wing slogans painted upon the side of the house. A threat to kidnap her Ronald."

"Ronald?"

"The poodle."

"Rodney, all of those things involve breaking the law. What is she afraid of that could be exploited through more conventional means?"

Rodney looked at the ceiling. "Fear is not a word that I would customarily associate with Mrs. Baxter," he said. "I would say that there are things for which she has a profound revulsion. I would not say that there are things for which she has fear."

"What would she have a profound revulsion to?"

"People," Rodney said.

"People?"

"Yes. Ordinary people. People who don't work for her. People who wouldn't be at the meetings she attends, people who wouldn't be at the dinners she goes to."

"Where would she encounter such people?"

"She rarely does," Rodney said. "She doesn't walk on the public streets outside of her neighbourhood, and never without a bodyguard. She doesn't attend movies or sporting events. She never goes to a mall."

"So how do you know she's revolted by people, if she never sees them?"

"She observes them through the window of the limousine and she speaks of it, how revolting people are, how loud and boorish and ill-dressed, and how we must use our – I mean, her – newspapers to educate them and make them less revolting."

"That must have been fun for you, to work for her," I said.

"I wasn't included in the general odiousness, because I was in her employ, I wore the black suit. And the pay was quite acceptable."

There was a commotion at the back of the bar, a fierce argument over draw weight, it appeared. Rodney stood up. "Please excuse me," he said. "I have some exit consulting to effectuate."

I was left alone with my thoughts, which was not a good place to be left. The thoughts wavered between total despair and faint hope. The hope was worse than faint. It was premised on the notion that a lunatic Latin professor could frighten the proprietor of an international chain of newspapers into doing something that would help me win the affections of a woman even though I did not own a black Audi. I didn't like my chances.

Chapter 27

Tri-Lakes area man resumes normal life

"It's that time of year again," quipped Parker MacVeigh, 49, as he returned with mixed feelings to his job on the day news desk of the *Grand Valley World-Beacon.*

MacVeigh had spent the last several weeks involved in top-secret journalistic research into the possibility of Saturnian influences on life in the Tri-Lakes Area and the possibility of a rigged fishing derby.

"It was an exciting time," said MacVeigh. "However all things must come to an end."

MacVeigh was interviewed in the midst of intense preparations for the annual Tri-Lakes Area Bass Classic, which he said he wants no fucking part of.

MacVeigh said he intends to spend his days doing as little work as possible and his nights trying to figure out a way to make himself an attractive potential companion for Shirley Davis, 41, business editor of the *World-Beacon.*

"I'm not sure this is possible," said MacVeigh, "but I sure as heck am going to try.

"She's way too good for a high-tech shithead like that."

As it turned out, my new quiet, undevious life lasted only partway through the weekend. It was difficult at first to get used to a life without intrigue. When I walked in Bowell Park on Friday, I saw people plotting. I saw children plotting. I saw squirrels plotting. When I went to the Loblaws on Friday night, I took a complicated circuitous route to the milk, so as to throw pursuers off the trail.

By Saturday, I was beginning to come out of it. I walked again, and this time saw nothing suspicious and did almost no lurking. The golf game on television seemed normal enough. One or two of the commercials could have been suspect, but I gave them the benefit of the doubt. Later in the afternoon I walked beside the lake, examining it carefully for signs that any of its water had been disturbed. Eventually I ended up downtown, watching workmen – some of the jobs created by Uncle Bob's visit, some of the millions of dollars brought to the Tri-Lakes Area – put up the foundations upon which the giant tents would rest. In the tents, spectators could watch the fish being weighed as the contestants returned from their day on the lake.

A television camera was pointed at someone and I stopped to see who. I should have known. It was the Hon. Winston Booker, MP, standing by the platform, in front of a sign proclaiming the fishing derby and Uncle Bob's imminent presence. Booker was shaking hands with somebody who looked like a member of his constituency executive. The message for the TV audience was clear: Hon. Winston Booker, MP, was owed at least part of the credit for this wonderful event. The message for me was clear too: If the hon. member was leaping to the front of the parade, the parade was probably pretty successful.

On Main Street, some of the stores were already displaying their Mass for Bass specials, as advertised in the *WB*'s first special edition. Robinson's Funeral Home and Furniture Store had a sign in the window welcoming visitors in English, French, German, Japanese, and Esperanto. For a moment, I thought the Esperanto was Saturnian, but only for a moment.

Workmen were also busy where Queen met Main and where King met Main. New signs had been put up, then covered over with material that looked like green garbage bags. These would be for the change of direction on the day of the parade.

Somebody hailed me. It was Dick Rivers. We exchanged observations on the weather and then he said, "I'm just out looking for something for The Column. All this," he said, gesturing in a general way at everything, "reminds me of something from my childhood, but I'm damned if I can think of what it is." I grunted something and he looked around.

"You know," he said, "it really *is* that time of year again, isn't it?"

He scribbled something in his notebook, then bounced off. I walked on. The weather was warm and pleasant and I was beginning to think that real life wasn't so bad. Especially if you didn't have to write a column about it. Watching people indulge in real life was something like rediscovering home after a long trip overseas. You appreciated it more when you had been away.

The blinking light on my answering machine made me realize my recovery was not quite complete. Immediately, I was overcome with thoughts of intrigue and romance. Amazing that a simple red light on a machine could do that. It would be Shirley, calling to tell me that she had ditched the risk manager and had suddenly realized that I was the guy for her, maybe when I bought the beer and didn't drink it and it made her realize how sensitive and vulnerable I was and why hadn't she thought of this before.

Or it would be Fred, calling to say that I had made him realize that he had been running the newspaper the wrong way ever since he came to Grand Valley and now he had decided to change everything and put me in charge and we would start by going big on Uncle Bob Fishing Shocker.

Or it could be both of them, one after the other, the combination offering me a chance to live happily ever after, maybe beside a golf course.

When I rewound the tape, I heard Professor Blanchard's voice. He began by criticizing me for not having a password on the answering machine. Then he told me that he had to talk to me. Then he ended by criticizing me for not having a password on the answering machine. "Anybody could be listening," he said.

How could anybody be listening to my answering machine? I knew the answer already. If you were from Saturn, you could listen to anything you damn well pleased.

"Well," the professor said, when I reached him and we had gone through the passwords, codes, and other niceties, "I've talked to her and I think everything is going to be all right."

"You what?"

"I obtained Dr. Baxter's home telephone number, I won't say how, other than to say that I have my methods, and I called her and alerted her to the continuing danger."

I guessed my plan was working, but the thought of it made me shudder anyway. The professor and Mrs. Baxter. Together.

"Was she receptive?" I asked.

"Oh yes. Of course, she had to pretend to disagree with me on account of the."

Of course.

But," he continued, "I know I was able to make her aware of the continuing presence and the need for more research and more publicity."

"Did you tell her who you were?"

"I thought it would be more prudent if I didn't," he said. "Anyone could have been. Eventually, when she looks at the evidence, I'm sure that she will be able to make the connection."

"We'll just have to hope for the best," I said. I wondered what the best was.

EDITORIAL

What planet are they from?

Property-respecting Canadians are outraged today at the spectacle that presented itself on the grounds of Ontario's legislature Thursday. Millions of protesters, some from far away, armed to the teeth with bricks, clubs, and teeth, senselessly attacked police in a pitched battle that had something to do with one of their usual grievances. Grass was trampled and many shrubs damaged.

Members of the government rightly stayed far from the scene, not wanting to be implicated in any unpleasantness that might arise.

As for the so-called protesters, they seem to have forgotten that they have the right in a democracy to advance their cause in the traditional way – by hiring a battery of lawyers and taking the matter to court. Failing that, they should quickly make the return journey to outer space, where they belong.

"Nice editorial," I said, after Fred and I had gone through the usual lack of niceties. This included me starting to sit down and Fred motioning for me to remain standing.

He had summoned me just minutes after I arrived at work Monday morning. "It was very persuasive," Fred said, "particularly to Dr. Baxter. She happened to be going past the legislature in her limousine and saw the uprising. She wondered what it was about. When she saw our editorial this morning, she realized that the Saturnians had increased their level of activity."

"I tried to warn you," I said.

Fred looked at me, as if he had forgotten which side I was on.

"She had an upsetting phone call, from a man who claimed to be an ally but was probably one of them. He pretended to be alerting her to the dangers, but he sounded rather threatening, she said. Now, the events at the legislature have brought it all into perspective."

"I see," I said, not quite seeing.

"She is very upset," Fred said, "and rather frightened. She said it is only a short drive from the legislature to her neighbourhood, and maybe less if they use one of those space vehicles."

"And?"

"She thinks the full power of the law should come down on these people, particularly the greener ones."

"I see," I said, still not seeing.

"However, she is aware that the public needs educating before it will fully support such action," Fred said.

"Those were her exact words?"

"I'm paraphrasing slightly."

"So we need more stories," I said.

"Yes."

"The Saturn Task Force?"

"Yes."

I tried to be coy. "I'm quite busy," I said. "There's a lot going on at the day desk. I'm in the middle of a section front on Uncle Bob's drapes . . ."

Fred nodded understandingly. "The task force is even more important," he said.

He stood up and we solemnly shook hands. Then I went back to the STF office, took the Mars and Venus posters out of the recycle, and put them back on the wall.

C harlie McPartland had a gleam in his eye that probably hadn't been there since the October Crisis.

"When a newspaper really cranks it up, it's something to see," he said.

It used to happen all the time when Charlie was breaking in, but the practice went out of fashion when notions like fairness and objectivity began to take hold. But now it looked like they wouldn't last either.

For ten days the *World-Beacon* filled its front pages with diatribes against foreign elements who controlled the opposition to everything the *WB* held dear, such as globalization, clean streets, and cloth. These diatribes were called "news analysis." Editorials then cited the news analyses as fact, using them as the basis for passionate, metaphor-laden calls for action, including deportation, against those who would take the world and the Tri-Lakes Area back to the Dark Ages.

Oddly, or so it seemed at the time, the public largely ignored it. Either the public had better sense, or the public had other things on its mind. Or Other Forces were at work, which was Professor Blanchard's take on it. Public indifference was all the proof he needed. But, as I was finding out with the professor, just about anything was all the proof he needed.

The *WB* cranked it up on the other front as well, offering page after page of enthusiastic welcome to Uncle Bob, his arrival mere days away, his daily progress measured as an elementary school principal announces the approach of Santa Claus during the Christmas pageant.

ACCLAIMED FISHERMAN–EVANGELIST CLOSING IN ON TRI-LAKES AREA was the way Hugh Robbins summed it up in a headline that ran unaltered for several days until someone noticed and changed "fisherman" to "fisher."

In truth, there wasn't much to report that hadn't been exhaustively reported in our special editions but such distinctions don't matter much when a newspaper is really cranking it up. Almost the entire city staff was kept busy putting new spin on old stories about the parade route, the special scales that were being brought in to weigh the fish, the menu for the giant outdoor fish barbecue, mass baptism, and Canada Day celebration that was to highlight Saturday's activities at the Harbourfront. Each was reported as if it had just been learned. In fact, the phrase "the *World-Beacon* has learned" appeared in half a dozen stories a day.

The Worldwide World of Uncle Bob organization helped by contributing press releases on various aspects of the upcoming event, including attendance predictions, testimonials from various world figures, all deceased but quite distinguished, and statistical information of interest, such as the fact that Uncle Bob's sermons, if printed out in twelve-point Corona and laid end to end, would stretch from Grand Valley to Berlin, Germany.

Local dignitaries were a reliable source of things the *World-Beacon* could learn. The office of the Hon. Winston Booker, MP, phoned twice daily to alert our city desk to new contributions our elected representative was making to ensure the success of this important venture. The president of the chamber of commerce, of course, was just down the hall in the publisher's office. And His

Worship, Martin Havelock, frequently phoned in messages of encouragement and support from his latest fact-finding mission, in a remote part of the Amazon.

When a newspaper is really cranking it up, certain topics that are not on the cranking agenda tend to be overlooked. This was the case with the *World-Beacon*, whose readers were spared details of Mideast peace talks, the leadership race in a major Canadian political party, a water pollution scandal in Ontario, and many items of local interest, such as a fire at a local high school, an allegation from one of the city councillors that the mayor was not really in the Amazon, and a suggestion from the assistant roads commissioner that changing the directions of Queen and King streets might pose a safety hazard.

There was not the staff to report these developments, nor the space to display it. The *WB* was marshalling all its forces and directing them to the target. Dick Rivers wrote eloquently on his feelings each day as Uncle Bob's arrival neared. Brian Blezard, now a constant presence in the newsroom despite his freelancer status, learned, in an exclusive, of the same four people at UGV who always protested everything. He infiltrated their meeting at the Unitarian church in which they voted for a motion that money spent on fishing licences should be spent instead on making a giant quilt celebrating the International Year of the Whale. Blezard's news analysis of the threat this posed occupied a corner of page one for two consecutive days. Rand Barry wrote editorials condemning the protesters, linking them, in a bold stroke, with the anarchists and people from distant places who had nearly brought civilization as we know it to a standstill the other day outside the legislature.

The food pages reran Uncle Bob's barbecue sauce recipe, by popular demand, and the food editor (Jane Liu, the stamp columnist, chess columnist, and pet columnist, using yet another name – Al Dente) contributed a rare opinion column pointing out that none of the critics of Uncle Bob had ever contributed a recipe worth mentioning. A day later, Jane, writing as Rod Gunn, the outdoors columnist, made the point that catch-and-release was how they fish on other planets, and cited several recent movies as evidence. Even the stamp columnist, M. U. Cilage, weighed in, with a condemnation of countries – all of them, as it turned out – that had failed to issue Uncle Bob commemorative stamps.

I bumped into Cilage/Gunn/Dente one morning as I was on the way in and she was on the way out. Jane looked exhausted, but happy. "You wouldn't believe the freelance money I'm making," she said.

The television critic, Chet Edgemar, was given a section front to do an analytical comparison of several top-rated fishing shows and came to the conclusion, "which some would lack the courage to state," that Uncle Bob's was far and away the best.

A newspaper really cranking it up is quite a spectacle, such a spectacle that I kept the Saturn Task Force door open so I could watch. Fred was a constant and active presence in the newsroom, walking from terminal to terminal, consulting with senior editors, looking over the shoulder of the headline writers, frequently revising their work, as I discovered from monitoring the computer system.

Having recently done that kind of work myself, it was hard not to admire some of it, seeing wire stories from obscure world capitals rewritten to highlight a positive fishing angle, then given headlines such as EARTH'S NATIONAL SPORT, seeing health advice columns slightly altered to replace words such as "exercise" with words such as "fishing." The headline would now read FISHING IS GOOD FOR YOU, subtlety not being among the priorities of a newspaper really cranking it up.

At the same time, it was a bit demoralizing for the Bass Protective Force, which I was causing to meet frequently, partly because of the increasing urgency of the situation, mostly so I could spend time with Shirley. Reading the paper each day, we could see what we were up against, sense how remote the chances were of doing anything to counteract it. Shirley was in a particularly crappy mood, since her department was in the thick of business community boosterism. Each day's business pages featured an exclusive interview with James Norwood, in his capacity as chamber of commerce president, rather than *World-Beacon* publisher, in which he would laud some different aspect of the "eagerly anticipated events we eagerly anticipate," as he described them. To make matters worse, Shirley had to invent the publisher's remarks each day, because he was too busy to be interviewed.

At my suggestion, she gained what comfort she could in the strategic placement of typographical errors in the interviews, so that Norwood would appear to be saying he "welcomed the dawn of a new bra in Grand Valley" or saluting "the increased awareness of spirits" in the Tri-Lakes Area. To our shock and horror, some of the senior editors, including Fred, were actually reading what went into the paper and we were forced to abandon that tactic, reverting to the more conventional and considerably easier practice of making sure that each story contained nothing that would be of interest to the average reader.

A race against time was what it was – our noble little band against the Saturnians and the powerful machine that was the Worldwide World of Uncle Bob, plus its allies in the mass media, which unfortunately included the newspaper that paid our salaries. The idea of a race against time sort of appealed to me, since I couldn't recall ever having been in one in my life, with the possible exception of trying to get home from a schoolyard baseball game in time for supper.

But I didn't like the odds of this particular race against time and something else was beginning to worry me that should have occurred to me weeks ago. Shirley raised the question at one of our meetings: What if we won the race against time, nailed down Uncle Bob Fishing Shocker, and then couldn't get it published?

We were at Score's, Rodney Sullivan hovering protectively nearby in case any of the clientele got out of hand. The place was crowded, though curling season was well over, and even the Norwegian all-sports channel, picked up on satellite, was showing reruns. Score's was running a happy hour special, two free beers for every twenty dollars lost on the video lottery terminals, and you could feel the excitement in the crowd. Rodney seemed to like us, for some reason. I wasn't clear on which one of us he liked the best and, given his size and potential for violence, I wasn't going to ask. For the moment, I liked having him around. Nobody, green or otherwise, was going to push him around.

"Of course they'll publish it," I said. "They have to publish it."

"Why?" Shirley said.

"Because it's a story," I said.

"You're being really old-school," she said. I winced. "I mean that as a compliment," she said. I unwinced.

"I don't see what old-school has to do with it," I said.

"It means that you think that just because a story is a story somebody is going to publish it."

"Right."

"What did Fred say when you told him about the story?"

"He said it's not a story."

Shirley raised an eyebrow in an irritatingly fetching way. "I rest my case," she said.

"Look," I said, "He was preoccupied or something. He was just off the phone with Mrs. Baxter."

"He's preoccupied all the time," Shirley said. "From the time he set foot inside the *World-Beacon* building, he's been preoccupied."

Tony didn't get all the old-school/new-school stuff. He fiddled with a coaster, took his phone out of his pocket and toyed with it in various ways.

"It's a great story," he said. "A couple more people return my calls and I've got it."

"Right," I said. "How can it not be a story. It's got all the ingredients – greed, corruption, sports, the outdoors, the dirty vicar. The dirty vicar is the best newspaper story there is."

"He's not dirty, that we know of," Shirley said.

"Well, he's corrupt. He cheats at fishing. That's almost dirty," I said. "They see that story, they see the way Tony has it all nailed down, there's no way they won't print it."

"Yeah," Tony said.

"I hope so," Shirley said. "But I think they don't define a story the way we do. We think a story is little guy getting screwed by big guy, or big guy getting caught cheating. They think a story is big guy getting screwed by government, or little guy cheating on welfare. This one doesn't fit in."

"We'll see," I said. "I think if we get the story, everything works out."

To be pessimistic would be unheroic and I didn't want to appear that way. Still, I could see what Shirley was getting at. If these guys didn't play by the rules, the story was a non-starter.

The good thing was that Tony was making progress. He had some potential eyewitnesses in North Carolina and some leads at other fishing derbies in Canada. He was working hard, ostensibly chasing Saturnians, and helped by the fact that Juanita Eldridge, a possible distraction, was in Toronto chasing Saturnians herself. This consisted mainly of sitting by Mrs. Baxter's side and listening to her complaints about the way the world is today, many of which could be, when you thought about it, attributed to the actions of people who were either green or cleverly disguised to conceal the fact that they were.

Professor Blanchard was making progress too. He was always making progress. Every day since I had known him he had made progress. He made progress by reading the newspapers and watching TV, cataloguing the day's events, recording them in longhand, transferring them to his computer, putting in the appropriate fonts and colours, printing out the results and placing them carefully in the paper bag.

Occasionally, he would let me have a look. What I saw didn't alarm me. After years of refinement, the professor's theory had become completely self-contained. Each new development, every bit of world or national news was self-evident proof that each new development was the result of an extra-celestial conspiracy launched from you-know-where. The professor's "research" now consisted in listing the day's events, without comment, other than the odd exclamation point, or the word "aha!" placed in parentheses.

"IBM shares continued their decline (!)," the professor wrote, in a typical entry. "On the same day, note that Europe was battered by heavy winds and rains. As if that were not bad enough, heavy publicity continued in advance of the publication of a book (?) about someone called Harry Potter! Where is *he* from?"

Even Fred would have a difficult time seeing it as publishable. So of course I encouraged the professor, telling him he was on the right track and we would have one hell, pardon my language, of an exposé in just a short time. I made sure we met at least twice a week, and when Juanita Eldridge was in Toronto, I arranged for a speaker phone to be installed in the STF office so she could participate and we could be kept up on Mrs. Baxter's thinking. The speaker phone sparked a new discussion of security and passwords that ate up an entire hour, to my great satisfaction.

I was feeling energized, enjoying this double game and the race against time, and looking forward each day to my Bass Protective Force meetings with Shirley. I was even enjoying ginger ale with a slice of lemon. Life was good, if a little weird.

Chapter 29

Giggling was the absolute worst thing we could do, but it was unavoidable. Here we were, two adults, well into middle age, hiding behind trees just off the twelfth fairway of the Grand Valley Oaks Golf and Country Club. We weren't sure why we were there. All we knew was that we were supposed to keep an eye on the water hazard and be very still.

This was proving to be difficult. It was dusk, mosquito time. Each time one of us slapped, the other one would put a finger to the lips. Then we would giggle again.

It was Thursday, June 29. Uncle Bob and his entourage had arrived in town without ceremony a couple of hours ago. The big parade in his honour was the next day. The day after that would be the fishing derby. The race against time was racing ahead.

And here we were, Shirley Davis and I, in the rough on 12, for reasons known mostly to Tony Frusculla who had sent us there with precise instructions. He was otherwise occupied, staking out Uncle Bob's hotel; somebody had to watch the twelfth fairway, Tony said, from a particular spot in the rough. Shirley volunteered. Then I volunteered to go along, as muscle.

We began laughing about that, about me being muscle, as we dodged across fairways on our way to 12. We also laughed at the way we were equipped.

"If the pioneers had been sent out to watch the twelfth fairway," Shirley said, "they wouldn't be carrying bottles of mineral water, blankets, binoculars, cellphones, and bananas for you to snack on."

"You can have one of my bananas if you want," I said. "At least we don't have to carry long rifles, salt pork, and canoes."

Tony had said to be ready for action just after dark, although he would not say what kind. A grove of pine trees provided cover and a nice covering of needles. We each took turns darting out into the fairway, in the lull between foursomes, to make sure that our hiding place couldn't be spotted. Then we settled in to watch.

We waited. The hiding place was small and we had to huddle close together. We slapped. We giggled. Nothing happened. The last foursome went by. It got darker. Nothing happened. The moon began to appear, not much of one. "Not a very romantic moon," I whispered, for the sake of whispering something. Shirley looked at me in an odd way. Why did I say that? I thought, at the same time as I realized the moon was actually romantic as hell and I turned my head to kiss her and she turned her head to kiss me and we bumped heads and giggled. Then we sat there for a minute. I thought about pretending this hadn't happened and then I thought the hell with it and we got our heads right this time and were enjoying a very nice kiss when we were illuminated by spotlights.

"Oh shit," I said, meaning several things. The lights swept over us then moved on. We manoeuvred ourselves quietly over the pine needles into deeper cover, glancing at each other but unable to see much in the shallow moonlight and deep shadow of the rough off the twelfth fairway.

A mosquito bit me and I didn't slap. The lights – they were headlights and they had swept over us as the sport utility vehicle turned – now trained on the water hazard. Three men got out of the vehicle. Its motor continued to run, drowning out their murmured words, except when one of the men stumbled and said "sheeit," in what could have been, to my thoroughly befuddled senses, a North Carolina accent.

They lifted something heavy out of the van. We couldn't see what it was, but knew it was heavy by the awkward way they carried it and grunts we heard. I slapped and Shirley giggled and we ducked. A flashlight beam swept the rough just over our heads. We kept down and when we heard the large splash we didn't see what made it. Then doors slammed and we looked up in time to see the van drive off, turning onto the road behind the thirteenth tee and disappearing into the night.

"Wow," I said, meaning several things.

"What was that?" she asked, probably meaning several things as well.

"We'd better get back and report this to Tony," I said, not getting to my feet.

"I like it here," Shirley said.

By the time we got to Score's, looking for all the world like a couple of people who had experienced just a small pine needle shower, we had sorted most of it out. The risk analyst was only a friend. "I think he might have been gay," Shirley said. "He certainly wasn't taking any risks."

She confessed that she had made the friendship a bit more public than she might have otherwise, once she saw the effect it was having on me. I threw a pine needle at her.

I confessed that most of my involvement in Uncle Bob Fishing Shocker was to make an impression on her. She said she thought that was cute. We both confessed that we were enjoying the hell out of the story, and we both confessed that we didn't think we were too old for this sort of thing, meaning several things. We rubbed each other's mosquito bites.

In the old days, I might have said that things could only get worse from here, but I didn't feel that way this time. In the old days, I might have thought that this called for a drink to celebrate, but I didn't this time. Wasn't love grand?

What we hadn't sorted out was what we had seen – or heard – on the twelfth fairway. Tony was eager to tell us. He had been eager to tell us for an hour, as Rodney Sullivan informed us on our way in. "Your youthful colleague has been appearing a trifle dolorous this evening," the beefy bouncer said. "I hope it was not due to any indiscretion on my part."

I assured him it was not and we hurried to Tony's table, noting the number of empties in front of him and the way his fingers drummed on the tabletop.

"How's tricks?" I asked, making a point not to grin like an idiot.

"Stupid fucker," Tony said. "Just sits in his fucking room and orders pizza. With anchovies."

On the big screen behind him the local news was playing, showing a long line of black minivans driving down Michener Boulevard, then a cut to the reporter with a camera on her shoulder, pointing it up at a hotel window. Why was she carrying the camera when somebody else had to be there carrying a camera to take a picture of her carrying the camera? I would never understand television.

"Did anybody visit him, that you could tell?" Shirley asked.

"Bunch of guys get out of an SUV about 9:30 and go into the hotel. They looked like his boys."

"Three?"

"Yeah."

"Those would be the guys we saw at Grand Valley Oaks," I said.

"What were they doing there, did you see?"

Shirley began explaining what we saw and didn't see. I thought I saw her blush a bit while she explained it.

"There was a splash," Tony said. "What kind of splash – like a log being thrown in or a rock?"

"Not a log," I said, "because after we – because we checked the water hazard before we left and there was nothing floating in it."

"It was a watery kind of splash," Shirley said. I looked at her like she'd just said the smartest thing, but I had no idea what she was talking about.

Tony did, though. "Fuck, that's it!" he said. "We gotta go."

We dropped some money on the table and hurried out the door. Moments later we were in the parking lot of the Disney Time Warner Prince of Wales Suites Grand Valley.

"I've got to check this," Tony said. "You wait in the car and watch my back."

We were awfully glad to wait in the car and found it very difficult to concentrate on Tony's back. He trotted quietly over to a parked SUV with mud on the wheels and peered in the back window. Then he trotted back, reached into the car, and grabbed a small camera.

"Come look," he said.

We tiptoed over, giggling, and peered in. In the back of the SUV was a large metal container, like a milk can. Tony shone the flashlight on the label.

"CAUTION: HOLY WATER," it said. "® WORLDWIDE WORLD OF UNCLE BOB. (BEST BEFORE 4/5/04)"

Tony took a photograph and we ran back to the car and quietly rolled out of the parking lot. As we drove down Main Street, past the Welcome Uncle Bob signs and the plastic fish in the baskets hanging from the lamp posts, Tony banged his hand on the dash board in excitement.

"So?" I said.

"So that's it," Tony said. "We've nailed the bastards."

I wasn't concentrating. I had the rear view mirror adjusted so that I could see Shirley in the back seat and was making googoo eyes at her. I thought I was being ironic about it, but it was so long since I'd made googoo eyes at anybody that I couldn't be sure. She was trying not to laugh and trying to concentrate on what Tony was saying, since it was important.

"I don't understand," Shirley said. "They dump some holy water into the water hazard."

"Not just holy water," Tony said, "a holy fish."

"A fish."

"Don't you get it?" Tony said. "It's the fish that's going to win the fishing derby. They catch it down South. The bass go up to twelve pounds down there, but six or seven pounds would do it without arousing suspicions. They carry it across the border in the holy water —"

"Anything to declare?" I said.

"Just this holy water," Shirley said. "Best before 4/5/04."

We realized Tony wasn't laughing.

"Sorry," I said. "They bring it across the border in the holy water, which nobody ever checks. Then what?"

"Then," Tony said, "they dump it somewhere for safekeeping, like into the water hazard."

"On 12."

"The water hazard on 12. Then they haul it out, stick in Uncle Bob's live tank and it wins."

"Why don't they just keep it in the holy water?" Shirley asked.

"Because they need it."

"The fish?"

"No, the water."

"And it's had a fish in it?" Shirley asked.

"I guess so."

"Yuck. They don't *drink* holy water do they?"

"I don't know what they do with fucking holy water down there," Tony said.

Shirley started laughing so I thought I should too. It really was hard to concentrate. There could have been a better night, journalistically speaking, for Cupid to shoot his arrow into the rough on 12.

"We've got to stop them," Tony said.

"How are we going to do that?" I asked.

"We have to take the fish," he said.

That part was easy enough to agree on. The question was what to do after that. We could take the fish and keep it, so that Uncle Bob had to win the fishing derby fair and square, which he probably wouldn't do. And we could take a picture of Uncle Bob's men trying to find the fish in the water hazard on 12. But the picture wouldn't prove anything and Uncle Bob losing the fishing derby wouldn't prove that he'd been cheating.

This was a lot to think about and I figured it was time for more googoo eyes but traffic was heavy and I had to adjust the mirror for driving. For a moment I was in danger of concentrating on the task at hand, but Shirley squeezed my hand, which had been resting between the seats. I pretended to be thinking for the few minutes it took to return to Score's parking lot.

Back at our table, Tony peered at me, then at Shirley. "Something's going on," he said. "Are you guys laughing at me?"

"No," I said. "Nothing's going on."

"We're just laughing," Shirley said. "You've got to admit there's something sort of ludicrous about trying to figure out how to get a fish out of a water hazard."

The humour wasn't there for Tony. It almost never is for a reporter closing in on a big story.

"How big is that water hazard?" he asked. "Could we net the fish?"

"What?" I said.

"The water hazard," Shirley said. "How big is it?"

"It's pretty big," I said.

"Could we net the fucking fish, is what I asked," Tony said.

"The fish," I said.

"I don't think so," Shirley said. "I think it's pretty deep, too. We wouldn't be able to see the fish to net it, especially if it's after dark. And it would have to be after dark, right?"

I realized they were both looking at me.

"Right," I said. "The fish after dark."

"What about we get scuba gear and we swim around and catch it that way?" Tony asked.

I tried to concentrate, looking away from Shirley, who was signalling for a waiter.

"That could work," I said. "If we got caught we'd just say we were hunting for golf balls. People do that all the time. It's a lucrative operation selling old golf balls."

Shirley frowned. "Three people who work for the *Grand Valley World-Beacon*, swimming in a water hazard looking for golf balls to sell."

"That's a point," Tony said.

"Besides that," Shirley said. "The water's too muddy. We'd never see anything."

"I guess dynamite's out," I said.

Tony didn't laugh. Didn't he ever laugh? "We want this fish alive," he said.

"So," I said, wanting to contribute something.

"So we have to catch it," Shirley said.

"Catch it?"

"Yes, with a fishing rod and a barbless hook so we don't hurt it."

"And then what?"

"I've got it," Tony said, "we tag it! Then we take a picture of it, put it back in the water hazard, Uncle Bob brings the tagged fish in to the weigh-in, he claims the prize, we take a picture of the ceremony, run the two pictures the next day with our story and we've got the fucker!"

"I'm not good at that," I said. "I haven't tagged a fish in years."

"That's a point," Shirley said. "How can we tag the fish so that Uncle Bob doesn't know it's been tagged?"

Tony stood up and took out the cellphone I had supplied him strictly for Saturn Task Force business.

"I know somebody," he said, as he walked toward the exit.

Chapter 30

Accidents mar hero's welcome

By Brian Blezard

Under a clear blue sky, the acc-laimed evangelist and celebrated sportsman known to millions as Uncle Bob, paraded through Grand Valley streets yesterday before an adoring throng thought to be in the dozens.

Making his first visit to the Tri-Lakes Area, the noted phi-lanthropist waved to crowds as his motorcade made its way along the flag-laden route to the Harbourfront.

"This is one of the most thrilling moments in my entire life," said Griffin Richards, 3, as the beaming evangelist seemed to single her out for a personal wave.

Marion Stark, grandmother of six, had lined up since 5 a.m. to secure her place along the parade route at Michener and Queen. "It was lonely for the first four hours before anybody else came," the 85-year-old quipped, "but it was all worth it when those cars went by and I knew that he must have been in one of them."

The much-honoured fisherman-statesman will be in the Tri-Lakes Area for three days participating in the annual Tri-Lakes Fishing Derby and taking part in other events, such as tomorrow's Mass for Bass, a combined mass baptism barbe-cue, coupled with .

Yesterday's celebrations were delayed for several hours when police and emergency workers were forced to clean up wreckage from a number of motor vehicle accidents on Queen and King Streets, which some officials claim was the result of an overnight change in direction on the one-way streets.

The number of people taken to Tri-Lakes Memorial Hospital was unavailable. James Norwood, president of the Grand Valley Chamber of Commerce, described reports of multiple fatalities as "exaggerated."

Extremists from the University of Grand Valley planned to picket tomorrow's barbecue with signs calling for a reversal of the one-way streets and a ban on fishing. But Mayor Martin Havelock, contacted while on a fact-finding tour of New Zealand, said the city had nothing to be ashamed of.

"We're proud to have a noted fisherman-statesman of Uncle Bob's magnitude in our city," the mayor said. "As for one-way streets, they simply have to move with the times."

Shirley looked absolutely fetching in her hip waders as she wielded her father's fly rod while standing in the water hazard on 12. I stood on the shore with the Popeil Pocket Fisherman (As Seen on TV) that my ex-wife gave me back in the seventies. I was using a yellow and black Go-Deeper River Runt. Tony had a stick with a piece of string tied around it and a worm on a hook. Annabella Alston, his friend from the biology department at UGV, waited patiently. In the small case she carried was the equipment that would give our prize bass an almost invisible tag, should we be able to land it.

So far we had not had much luck. Shirley had caught a five-iron. I had brought in a golf glove, a Nike baseball cap, and a shopping cart.

Tony had not caught anything and he was edgy.

"I should be back in town, trailing that sonofabitch," he said.

"Relax," I said. "You told me he turned in at nine."

Tony tried to relax. It was after nine. The mosquitoes were out and the sun was down. There was a tiny bit of light left but the last foursome had gone by half an hour ago.

Rodney Sullivan paced up and down the edge of the rough. He didn't know exactly what was going on – having never seen three people fishing in a water hazard before – but was content with the explanation I had given him, which was that we would be doing something Mrs. Baxter really wouldn't like. Shirley and Tony had needed some convincing to bring Rodney on board, but I persuaded them that we needed muscle on this job, in case some of Uncle Bob's guys showed up and I was tired of being muscle all the time. Besides, we would need my angling ability.

In the first hour, despite repeated casts with my Pocket Fisherman (As Seen on TV), my angling ability was not looking good. Shirley tied on a new fly, replacing a turkey tail with an elk hair, she said. Tony checked his worm. The biologist from UGV just watched, seeming a lot less astounded than I would have been. But she had probably seen stranger things at the university.

It got darker. I got bored. Shirley and I had been exchanging glances, which could actually be quite fun, I discovered. But now it was too dark for that. To pretend I knew what I was doing, I changed plugs and put on a Heddon Sonic, a popular lure in the fifties. It used to be thought that fish could hear it. My experience as a child fisherman was that if the fish could hear the sound, it probably drove them away. Still I knew they couldn't *see* anything, so it was worth a try.

It must have been after ten when I felt a strong tug on my line. "Got one!" I said. I set the hook and began reeling in. "Weighs a ton," I said. I reeled some more but it was putting up a terrific fight.

After ten more minutes of battling, it became clear why it weighed a ton. It was a pair of men's trousers, lime green.

Shirley made the mistake of laughing. "A lot of people couldn't have brought that in," I said. "At least, not in that shade."

She stopped laughing. "Wait a second," she said, through gritted teeth. There was a splash, like the sound of a fish jumping.

"Whoee, it's a big one," she said. "Look at that baby jump. I'll just bring her over to the side of the boat. Get the gaff out. Boy this baby's really something. Just goes to show what I said about the turkey tail and the shallow water this time of year. Whooee!"

Tony gave me a puzzled look. I gave him one back. Shirley played the fish skilfully, keeping up a running commentary on what a great fighter it was and she couldn't believe it would bite so hard in this cloud cover. The fish jumped twice more but stayed hooked. After a while, Shirley called for a flashlight, then a net. Annabella produced the flashlight.

"We have to do it without a net," she said.

The fish had stopped jumping. "I'm getting it closer," Shirley said. "Whooee!" I waded into the water to help, and was just reaching for the fish when I slipped on a golf ball and slid under. When I emerged, it was to the sight of a very large bass being held gently by Shirley, while Tony patted her on the back and Annabella Alston reached into her case.

"It's a beauty," I said. Somehow I remember everybody saying that when I was eight years old.

"It has to be at least six pounds," Annabella said.

"Elk hair does it every time," Shirley said modestly.

It was 10:45 and we were just taking the fish's picture when Rodney came running over from the trees. "Somebody is approaching on foot," he said. "What should I do?"

I had no idea. This only happened in movies. And actually, what we were doing didn't even happen in movies. What would they say in movies? "Hogtie 'em," I said.

"Good idea," said Shirley. "What does that mean, hogtie?"

"I don't know," I said. "Let's wait and see."

We stood quietly, making only the smallest ripples in the water hazard, while Rodney ducked behind a tree and waited for the intruder. Then there were the sounds of scuffling, a muffled cry, and an odd metallic sound.

"I've got him," Rodney said and we all emerged from the water hazard to look.

"Professor," I said, "I'm glad you've come. And I see you've brought your scuba outfit."

Professor Blanchard said something, which was difficult to understand, since his mouth was covered by Rodney Sullivan's hand.

"It's OK, Rodney. You can let him up," I said.

Rodney let go of him and returned to his observation point. The professor struggled to his feet, his oxygen tank threatening to topple him over. "I'd like you to meet some of my associates," I said. I introduced him to the group. The professor looked nervous. He nodded at Tony, then looked away, as if he wasn't sure he was supposed to know him.

"These people," I told him, "have been helping me in my research, the research that you are, um, aware of."

"Quite," the professor said.

"Did you come out tonight to assist?" I asked.

"Yes, certainly," the professor said.

"We've been examining this water hazard for evidence," I said. "We have had reason to suspect —"

"Ah, yes," the professor said. "Actually, I've been examining other water hazards. Checking on the, um, water."

"Of course," I said.

It was then that Rodney's flashlight picked up the string bag of wet golf balls hanging from the professor's belt.

"And have you turned up anything?" I asked.

"I'm afraid not," the professor said, less nervous now. He looked around and appeared to be noticing for the first time that Tony was holding a stick with a worm on the end of string, that Shirley was wearing hip waders, that I was carrying a Popeil Pocket Fisherman (As Seen on TV), and that Annabella Alston was holding something behind her back that seemed to be twitching.

"Could I ask —," he began, but I interrupted him.

"Obviously, I don't need to tell you that we go to great pains not to discuss the exact nature of."

"Obviously."

"I will bring you up to date at our next meeting," I said. "But of course you're well aware of the."

"Of course."

"And the necessity of."

"Certainly."

"Car coming!" Rodney hissed.

The white SUV was coming slowly down the road, about to turn onto the track by the thirteenth green. We raced for the trees, Tony dragging the professor and his oxygen tank, and threw ourselves down on the pine needles just in time.

"What is it?" the professor asked.

This had to be good.

"Remember when we were playing golf here a few weeks ago and you got into that argument with the three Saturnians on the next hole?"

The professor took a deep breath. "I remember," he whispered.

"It's them. They must be coming for you. You'd better run. Leave your tank here. We'll create a diversion."

The professor got up and began running and, helpfully, yelling what must have been anti-Saturnian phrases at the top of his lungs. He crossed 12, heading for 10, just as the SUV's head-lights swung onto the fairway. We created no diversion at all, just lay quietly in the rough watching the professor, running very well for an academic. The SUV turned and began, slowly, to follow him, its lights illuminating the pine trees and occasionally shining up into the dark sky.

"Fuck, let's go," Tony said.

"How's the fish?" Shirley asked.

"He's ready," the biologist said. "Actually, *she's* ready."

"No time for bass sexing," I said. "Let's get out of here."

The biologist gently placed the bass back into the water hazard and we quietly trotted to the point down the road where we had stashed the biologist's truck.

"I hope the professor got away," Shirley said.

"It doesn't really matter," I said. "Even if they force a confession out of him, they'll never believe a word of it. And even if they tell him who they are, he'll never believe a word of it either."

"That's true."

"Shirley?"

"Yes?"

"What was all that whooee stuff when you were bringing in the fish?"

"What stuff?"

"You were chattering away like a good old boy."

"I – I don't know," she said. "It just came over me. I guess I never told you I watch fishing shows on TV."

Chapter 31

Business leader makes statement

By Juanita Eldridge
World-Beacon staff

TORONTO – One of Canada's most respected business leaders has issued a dire warning about the effects of interplanetary immigration.

"If this is allowed to continue," said Thelma Baxter, proprietor of a newspaper group that owns the *World-Beacon* and other international publications, "the style of life that we have worked so hard to achieve will vanish in a puff of green smoke."

In an exclusive interview in her lavish yet tasteful downtown mansion, Dr. Baxter, 39, said there are many signs that the threat is expanding.

"They are walking on our streets, carrying signs, pretending to be homeless and unemployed. We can no longer ignore . . ."

"Good God," I said.

"What?" Shirley asked. We were puttering around my apartment, drinking tea and thinking about lunch.

"This story."

"Yeah, no way she's 39."

"I didn't mean that."

"What, then?"

"The way we played it."

Which was a surprise. It ran back on page eight, below the fold. Buried. Above the fold was a map showing the positioning of boats for this morning's Blessing of the Boats, along with safety tips.

We were just back from witnessing the event, where the safety tips had proven inadequate. Fish derby officials had simply underestimated the difficulty of organizing fishermen to drive up to a floating altar in their boats to receive communion, one at a time. Devout boaters had jumped the queue, and the situation was complicated by the appearance of two would-be communicants on water skis. In addition to a general commotion, a fearsome swell had resulted, the waves causing much spilling of wine and communion wafers. The wafers had turned out to be attractive to fish, who rose to receive them. The fish had turned out to be attractive to seagulls, who dived to feed on them.

In the end, hundreds of unblessed boaters scrambled for shore, grateful for their lives. This was not reflected in the television interviews we had just watched, in which fish derby organizers and spokesmen for the Worldwide World of Uncle Bob declared the event an unprecedented success.

"It's just Fred's short attention span," Shirley said. "A couple of days ago he was hell bent for Martians –"

"Saturnians."

"Now even Mrs. Baxter is lucky to make the paper."

It was true. Page eight was the eighth of nine pages devoted to Uncle Bob, fishing, and related topics. Alexei Ponomarev had drawn a cartoon showing a long lineup of fish, waiting for hooks. Al Dente, writing as Foote Luce, the travel editor, was urging all his readers not to travel anywhere outside the Tri-Lakes Area.

"The Communist cabal at UGV" was tangentially attacked in an editorial for its opposition to fishing and all it was bringing to the economy of the region. The main focus of the editorial was to applaud the long-overdue cleanup of graffiti and the "relocation" of squeegee kids. Dick Rivers, on page one, was declaring himself to have been personally moved by an advance copy he had been privileged to read of today's Canada Day address by Uncle Bob. It was not clear from Dick's column what was actually in the address, but it reminded Dick of many wonderful trips he had taken to the United States as a boy, and also some joyous Dominion Day outings with his father who, although he pretended to hate fishing, probably really didn't.

There were three pages of photos from yesterday's parade, none of any accidents. There was a large picture of the Hon. Winston Booker, MP, holding an American flag, in preparation for Canada Day celebrations. The horoscope had been rewritten to include advice about spinners, jigs, and plastic worms: "Think twice before casting near submerged logs, Scorpio." Mrs. Baxter would surely understand why her exclusive interview had received less attention than it would normally get.

The early sun was warm through the open windows of the apartment. Shirley and I were thinking about getting back to the Harbourfront to catch Uncle Bob's address and maybe grab something to eat at the barbecue and see how the mass baptism went. But we had to wait around for Tony's call. He was in a bass boat, shadowing Uncle Bob, and said he would give us a progress report and let us know if he needed any help.

None of this seemed to matter very much to us. It was an intrusion on the more important story of what was going on in our lives, making us paw each other in the kitchen like a couple of teenagers, when we weren't throwing tea bags at each other.

The phone had rung once, but it was Professor Blanchard, announcing that he knew I had been worried about him and wanted to let me know that he'd made good his escape from the Saturnians, who had not been aware of a particularly deep sand trap on 10, in which their vehicle had become embedded.

"That's great," I told him, "because if they'd captured you, there is no telling what."

"Were you able to complete your project?" he asked.

"Results are inconclusive," I said. "But I'm cautiously optimistic."

He asked why Mrs. Baxter's revelations were not on page one.

"I'm afraid I don't make those decisions," I said. "Clearly, her views are of great significance."

"Sometimes I think the media are purposely doing everything they can to," he said.

"Don't be too sure," I said. "Sometimes what seems like underplaying a story is really a tactic aimed at lulling the."

He grunted appreciatively and we agreed to talk soon, after all this fishing silliness was over.

Tony's call came just after three, interrupting some rather high-schoolish activity on our part.

"What the fuck are you puffing for?" he asked.

"Vacuuming," I gasped.

"Better hurry up and finish it," he said. "They're on the way in. I think they've got the winner in the boat. They keep opening the live well and looking in."

"What was it like following them around?"

"Piece of cake. They never moved. They didn't do anything, just sat in the boat talking, not even dragging a line."

"Don't they need to catch another fish to weigh this one with?"

"Aah, they did that earlier," Tony said. "Nothing of any size. Nothing like the pants you caught yesterday."

Our paper was right about the graffiti. It was all gone. What the paper didn't say was that it had not been so much erased as replaced, by slogans more in keeping with the spirit of the times.

As Shirley and I strolled downtown to take in the barbecue and mass baptism, we took turns pointing out new graffiti, each example neatly printed.

"Which do you like better," Shirley asked, "ANGLING RULES or WELFARE SUCKS?"

"They're both good, but I think I like this one better," I said, pointing to FUCK TAXATION.

Harbourfront Boulevard, as the former alley behind Main Street was now called, smelled like grease. A crowd had gathered, lining up in an orderly way for fishburgers and hot dogs served up by men in aprons bearing the logo of the Worldwide World of Uncle Bob. I saw several *WB* staffers in the crowd, including Alexei Ponomarev, who stood at a distance from the lineup, sketching excitedly, and Jane Liu, who was taking notes.

"Hi, Jane," I said. "Who are you this time?"

"Restaurant reviewer," she said. "E. P. Cure."

"Yuck. Who thought up that name?" Shirley asked.

"I did," Jane said. "They love it."

"What are you reviewing?" I asked.

"E. P. has been told that these people make the best fishburgers in North America," Jane said.

"Who told E. P. Cure that?" Shirley asked.

"A senior news executive who had just come out of Fred's office."

"It must be true, then," I said.

"It is," Jane answered. "Read the paper tomorrow. I hope it is."

We were interrupted by the sound of enthusiastic applause from one of the big tents. Shirley and I hurried over, arriving just in time to see Uncle Bob holding up the biggest bass anyone had ever seen, except for the two of us who had seen it the night before. Uncle Bob's other arm was being held aloft by a pale and rather shaky-looking older man.

"Who's that?" asked Dick Rivers as he arrived at my side, puffing.

"That's the mayor himself, Martin Havelock," Shirley said. "Only an event of this magnitude would take him away from his important fact-finding duties around the world."

"I like the way you put that," Dick said. "Do you mind if I use it?"

"Feel free," Shirley said.

"Nice fish," I said, as we walked from the tent.

"You bet," said Dick. "I think it's all over."

Shirley smiled at me. "It's all over," she said.

We wandered over to the main dock, where there was another crowd. A take-a-number machine had been installed to facilitate the mass baptisms. As the digital screen displayed the number, its holder, often a tourist, from the look of it, would step forward and be assisted into the water by a member of Uncle Bob's staff, dunked, then emerge to stand beside a life-sized cutout of Uncle Bob, for a Polaroid photograph. There were some delays. One mother insisted that her child, holding number 74, should not be immersed in the water until the fishburger he had just eaten had digested for two hours. An argument ensued, with another mother insisting that one hour was sufficient, and the holder of number 75 urging number 74 to get on with it because he had to feed the parking meter.

A further cause of disagreement was the fact that the baptism site was appearing on electronic fish-finders as a likely spot for bass. Fast-moving boats appeared at regular intervals, forcing Worldwide World of Uncle Bob officials to use a loud-hailer to urge fishermen not to cast in the direction of the initiates.

Dick Rivers surveyed the scene. "Nothing for me here," he said, as we approached the holy water booth.

"None for me, thanks," Shirley said.

"What?" Dick asked.

"Holy water," I said. "It's an acquired taste."

"Absolutely," he said, turning towards the parking lot. "I've got to go file my fish impressions column. Have fun."

"He does fish impressions?" Shirley said.

"I can't believe he didn't recognize the mayor," I said.

"When was the last time *you* saw the mayor?" she asked.

That was a point. We walked some more. Everybody seemed to be having a good time. The crowds were mostly orderly. The breeze off Watson Lake was fresh and warm, the boardwalk was full of children, and I was doing well at not being cynical. What the hell: there were worse things in the world than mass baptisms and barbecues.

And tomorrow, if everything worked out right, there would be one hell of a story on the front page of the *Grand Valley World-Beacon*.

"I wonder how Tony's doing," Shirley said, as we sat on a bench, watching the beginnings of the sunset put some nice colours on the lake while the crowd gathered for Uncle Bob's acceptance speech and Canada Day address.

"He'll be doing fine," I said. "The story's written already. He just dumps in the winning weight, the quote from Uncle Bob about the divine guidance of his casting arm, and Bob's your uncle. The hard part will be getting the official responses and denials."

"Shouldn't we be out there helping with that?"

"No," I said. "Uncle Bob won't know anything until he finishes his Canada Day speech. We'll stay here and grab a quote or two out of it for Tony. Then we'll have a quick meeting and figure out how to get a denial from him. Probably at the hotel later on."

"You sure it will be a denial?"

"Aren't you?"

The boats had begun to crowd into the harbour in anticipation of the speech and the fireworks to follow. Uncle Bob's security people in monogrammed wetsuits dashed to and fro on "personal watercraft," as the noisy gadgets were generically known, making sure that the boats were not too close to the floating platform from which Uncle Bob would make his speech.

The beach area was filling up, largely with tourists, many of them carrying video cameras, some sipping trademarked Worldwide World of Uncle Bob Holy Water out of plastic bottles. A constant buzz of conversation hovered over the harbourfront, sometimes hushed, as if the talkers were not sure whether they were at the beach or in church.

At precisely nine p.m., a sudden combination of music and thunder roared out of the huge speakers placed around the dock. A cloud of pink smoke released from somewhere settled on the beach and out of it, wading into the water, came Uncle Bob.

He wore gigantic bathing trunks and a gigantic T-shirt from which his own face smiled out. Around his neck hung a thick chain from which dangled a shiny medal. Waving to the crowd, he waded into the water while the thunderous music played on. On the floating dock, beside the poles flying the Canadian and American flags, two officials wearing a similar T-shirt, but in black, clapped their hands over their heads, a signal followed by the crowd.

The floating dock was only fifty yards from the shore but it took Uncle Bob about three minutes to reach it, wading slowly, creating a small wake. When he reached the platform, the two officials helped him up the ladder out of the water. He turned then, facing first the beach, then the boats, holding his medal out from his neck.

"I wonder how big his bass was," said a man behind our bench wearing a fishing hat.

"I hear it was pretty big," Shirley said.

Uncle Bob was handed a towel and a cordless microphone. "Friends," he said, fingering his medal, "you can't believe the wonderful humility that overwhelms me when I think that Someone has made it possible again for me to win this coveted honour, emblematic of bass fishing supremacy, by sending down a bountiful harvest of large fish."

The officials applauded, the people on the beach applauded, and some of the people in boats honked their horns.

"Hugh Robbins," I said to Shirley.

"What?"

"Remember how Uncle Bob was going to hire a local speechwriter?"

"Yes?"

"And did you hear 'emblematic of bass fishing supremacy'?"

"Ohmigod. It *is*!"

"Without the vaunted love that exists across our longest undefended border in the world," Uncle Bob continued, as we listened raptly, "I could not have racked up this signal accomplishment. Meanwhile, my unprecedented victory is especially momentous because it happens on this historic day, when Canada marks a birthday and only three days before the birthday of the powerful neighbour to the South."

Some boat horns honked again. "I liked 'meanwhile,'" Shirley said, looking at her watch. Uncle Bob, now mostly dry, saluted corporate sponsors, then embarked on a lengthy discussion of the number of philosophies and products his country had been pleased to share with ours. Shirley squeezed my hand and my attention wandered. I think he mentioned post office box numbers, Web site addresses, and toll-free lines.

"If he doesn't finish soon and get back to the hotel," she said, "we're going to have a hard time getting that reaction from him."

"Maybe nobody told him that Saturday night is early deadlines," I said.

"We must stretch hands across the border," Uncle Bob was saying, his voice rising, the fishing derby medal glinting in the fading light. "We must make the border invisible, so that God can move easily across it. We must not be afraid of cooperation. Cooperation is a warm bath, a beautiful lake, like this wonderful one here. Why would we stay out of a beautiful lake? Lakes are for swimming. I invite you here today to join me in this beautiful lake of cooperation and friendship. I invite you, right now, to just take off your watch and jump in."

Shouting these last few words, Uncle Bob handed his watch to one of his assistants and leaped off the platform into the chest-deep water.

Later, it would become known that a tourist on a rented personal watercraft simply wanted to have his picture taken with Uncle Bob. The tourist, as he cruised toward the platform, was talking to his wife on a cellphone, giving her directions. She was on the beach with the video camera. One of Uncle Bob's security people on the dock saw the personal watercraft moving and telephoned one of his cohorts on the water, who moved quickly to intercept. The two personal watercraft operators, both talking on cellphones, both driving with one hand, converged at high speed, right at the spot where, Uncle Bob, overcome with enthusiasm for fishing, religion, our two great nations, and the love shown to him by the people of the Tri-Lakes Area, had leapt into the water.

There was a horrible noise, the water around the platform turned red, and the air filled with screams.

"Oh my God," said Shirley.

"What a story," I said.

Chapter 32

World, Tri-Lakes Area mourn minced evangelist

By World-Beacon staff

It's that time of year again. Seasonal thoughts of water safety soared to the front yesterday as a bizarre personal watercraft mishap took the life of the world-acclaimed evangelist known the world over as Uncle Bov.

The world-acclaimed evangelist was standing in waist-deep water, conducting the first-ever mass baptism and barbecue in the Tri-Lakes Area, when two personal watercraft, travelling at high speed, collided with him.

Mass confusion ensued, as some bathers scrambled out of the water at the same time as others scrambled in, in an attempt to rescue the world-acclaimed evangelist.

No traces of him could be found, leading experts to fear for his survival.

"There was mass confusion," said, Marion Stark, 85, grandmother of six. "I was very confused. It's terrible."

"I was standing right over there," said, Griffin Richards, 3, pointing to a spot on the beach, "and I saw it all."

Grief counsellors are being flown in from all neighbouring provinces and states, to help residents cope with the immensitu of the horror.

Meanwhile, hundreds of lawyers have descended upon

Please turn to HORROR, page A 5

My first ascension

By Dick Rivers

Nothing in my previous experiences, which have been many and varied, including having the Pope wave at me from his window in Rome, Italy, prepared me for my reaction when I saw the horrendous horror of that moment when the two personal watercraft crashed into each other, at precisely the point at which my personal hero, Dr. Uncle Bob, happened to be standing, in water that came up to his waist, although it would not come up so high on me, as I am considerably taller.

It's difficult for me to analyse my feelings, as I reflect upon my thoughts concerning my reaction to seeing a man actually ascend to Heaven, in front of my very eyes.

There was an horrendous sound, the likes of which I had never heard before, but something like a cross between a chainsaw and a meat grinder in operation.

Then, nothing. Oh, some red in the water, which has been well-publicized, but other than that, nothing. No sign of Dr. Uncle Bob. No sign of the man who had so inspired me and influenced my thinking, particularly in the last couple of days.

The only possible explanation, and I have examined all the possibilities, in consultation with my wonderful family, is that Uncle Bob, this exemplary fisherman and orator, this man who changed my life, simply ascended.

Ascended. What do I think about when I think about the word *Please turn to RIVERS, page A 5*

Community leaders deplore Uncle Bob death

By Brian Blezard
Special to the World-Beacon

The world should not think unfavorably of the Tri-Lakes Area because of the tragic death Sa-turday of the world-acclaimed evangelist, Uncle Bib, in a bizarre accident during a mass baptism on beautiful Watson Lake, community leaders said yesterday.

"A person getting sandwiched

between two personal watercraft travelling at high speed during a mass baptism could happen anywhere," said James Norwood, president of the Grand Valley Chamber of Commerce and publisher of the *World-Beacon*.

Similar sentiments were expressed by Grand Valley Mayor Martin Havelock, in a telephone interview from Paris, France, where he is on a fact-finding mission.

"This will really put Grand Valley on the map," the mayor said, adding that he was personally appalled by the tragedy, "as were all the citizens of the city, plus many people in Paris, France."

Winston Booker, member of Parliament for Grand Valley-and-the-Lakes, told the *World-Beacon* that he intends to introduce a private member's bill to mark the world-acclaimed evangelist's pissing.

"I am going to recommend that the government issue a new stamp or something," Mr. Booker said.

Matt Foley, coach of the Grand Valley Valleyers, was pleased to *Please turn to WORLD, page A5*

RELATED STORIES

Cloth industry unaffected – Business, B1

Foote Luce: challenge to Tri-Lakes Area tourism industru – Travel Section, B2

Crossword – D7

Rod Gunn: personal watercraft don't kill people; people kill people – Sports, C3

Editorial: On balance, another successful fishing derby – A8

Tony, Shirley, and I silently pored over our copies of the paper spread out over the table in the food court. Occasionally there would be an exclamation or muttered curse from one of us, or simply a sharp intake of breath, as when I came to the editorial page with its cartoon of the Grim Pig, a single tear running down its ugly cheek.

The food court was where we went on Sundays when Score's wasn't open yet. The Grand Valley Mall was as usual, except for a noon-hour karaoke and kick-boxing demonstration drawing a crowd of about two dozen people over by the water slide.

We were all exhausted from working through the night on the coverage of the Uncle Bob tragedy. All hands had been called in. Even Saturn had been put aside. Tony was more exhausted than that, having simultaneously put in his calls on Uncle Bob Fishing Shocker. The pictures had turned out, the story was nailed down, but to make the story complete the comments had to be pulled in, particularly from the Worldwide World of Uncle Bob and other points, including officials at other fishing derbies in which Uncle Bob had emerged victorious.

It was not easy work, or quick. At Cary, North Carolina, Uncle Bob's people were not answering their phones. They had to be convinced that the story was going to run with or without their comments. Since most of the convincing had to take place over voice mail, it was a drawn-out process. It took until nine Sunday morning for Tony to come up with a quote.

The quote, when it finally came, was: "You print anything about this and we'll sue your ass off, sonny."

"That's good," I said. "We can use it."

"Well," said Shirley, "if."

"If" was the word. In fact, "if" was optimistic. The Sunday paper had sent Uncle Bob right up to heaven. More was ready for Monday, as tributes too late for Sunday poured in and more eye-witnesses were produced.

"This hasn't worked out well for us," I said, to break a long silence.

"It hasn't worked out too well for Uncle Bob either," said Shirley.

"Fucking personal watercraft," said Tony. "Just when we had the story."

"Well," I said, "what can you do when they ascend into heaven on you?"

"Ascend my ass," Tony said. "What about that thumb they found over on the beach?"

"Could have been anybody's thumb," I said. "They probably find lots of thumbs on the beach." I was really tired, punchy tired.

"Not thumbs bigger than your big toe," said Tony. "Only huge lardass guys like Uncle Bob could have thumbs that fat."

Shirley was punchy too. "Are you saying that everything but his thumb ascended to heaven?"

Tony wasn't listening. "They found a toe too. You wouldn't believe how fat it was."

He turned to me. "You're going to see Fred, right?"

"I hope so," I said, "but only if he asks."

As a desperation measure, I had slipped Tony's story under Fred's door early the morning in a brown envelope marked TOP SECRET. Fred never read e-mail and, besides, I had kept the thing out of the computer system as a precaution. No one but senior editors were getting in to see Fred while ascension coverage roared ahead. Tempers were frayed. There had been a near fist-fight on the desk over whether Uncle Bob ascended into heaven or unto it. Hugh Robbins and Charlie McPartland had been using "into," saying it was *World-Beacon* style. Hamilton Thistle said "unto" was the way they did it on Fleet Street and that should be good enough for this provincial town.

Keeping everyone working together – a compromise was arranged on "up to" – had taken up much of Fred's time. Then there were the visiting hordes of international press to deal with. I knew there was only the slimmest chance that he would take a look at a brown envelope appearing mysteriously. But if he didn't, he'd never see the story and his seeing it was our only hope. The odds were heavily against us, but they were more heavily against us if he didn't see the story at all.

I was explaining this when I noticed Tony looking over my shoulder with a puzzled expression on his face. I stopped talking and turned, expecting to see another another singer get kicked. Instead, I saw Juanita Eldridge.

"Hi," I said. "What are you doing here?"

"I thought I could find you here," she said, glancing at Tony, who quickly looked away. "There are some strange things going on at the paper and I think you had all better come in."

"Strange like what?" Shirley asked.

"The police tape is up in the parking lot again," Juanita said, "and there are guard persons around. Mr. Morgan – Fred – has turned on all the lights in his office and strangers have been in there all morning talking to him."

"That's not so fucking weird," Tony said.

"But I think they're people from the government," Juanita said.

"How do you know?" I asked.

"It's just something about them. There are three of them, they have suits on and they look worried and everywhere they go they go together."

"Could be government," Shirley said.

"Also," Juanita said, "Uncle Warren is here."

"Who?" I asked. There were too many uncles.

"Warren Eldridge," Shirley said. "He was here with Mrs. Baxter when she did her tour, remember?"

"I remember," I said. "What's he doing here today, counting the chairs?"

"Yes," Juanita said.

We rushed to the paper, parked on the street, showed enough I.D. to get past the guards, and entered the newsroom just as three men in dark suits stalked angrily out of Fred's office. Fred saw me.

"MacVeigh," he said. "Get into my office. You too," he said, motioning to Tony.

A coyote wailed. Fred turned his back on us and shuffled through a stack of telephone message slips on his desk.

"Department of Foreign Affairs," he said. "Governor of North Carolina. President of the Canadian Chamber of Commerce.

CNN. CIA. CBC. CP. U.S. Department of Wildlife. Archbishop of Canterbury. Oprah. Ducks Unlimited. And," he said, turning to us and holding up a pink slip, "the president of the United States. Do you know what they all want to talk to me about?"

I took a guess. "Uncle Bob's unfortunate demise?"

"Wrong," Fred said. "They want to talk about the phone calls your young friend here has been making about certain allegations concerning a world-acclaimed evangelist and sportsman."

"Oh," I said.

"Jesus," Tony said. "The Archbishop of fucking Canterbury."

"I read your story," Fred said. "I had to when my phone started ringing and the police and government people started arriving."

He paced, accompanied by the sounds of a burbling brook with a woodpecker in the background.

Tony brightened. "How'd you like it?" he asked.

Fred stared at him for a moment. "I want you to appreciate the full impact of what has been happening here in recent hours," he said. "As a result of questions you have been asking in the last day or two, the supporters of the late world-acclaimed evangelist and sportsman have contacted certain organizations, who in turn have turned for support to the governor of North Carolina, who, deciding it is a federal matter, has referred the matter to Washington."

"Holy shit," Tony said.

Fred raised a hand. "In Washington, they decided that the desecration of the memory of a beloved and respected world statesman by a news organization in a foreign country was properly the jurisdiction of the State Department. Consequently, their diplomats contacted our diplomats, to warn them that a publication in this country was in danger of doing severe damage to the warm and friendly relations that have historically characterized our two countries."

"And they came down on you," I said.

Fred picked up the sheaf of phone messages and waved it at us. "They came down on me, as you put it. They even called the police."

Fred had not asked us to sit down and Tony was fidgeting. "What the fuck could the police do?" he asked.

"I'm not sure," Fred said. "My surmise is that it was a weekend shift at Foreign Affairs and somebody decided to call in the police just to be on the safe side. Now we have the police in our parking lot and the television cameras of the world taking pictures of the police in our parking lot. Look out at the newsroom."

I looked. Every television set had a knot of staffers around it. They were watching our parking lot, live on CNN.

I took a deep breath. "Fred, I'm sorry if . . ." I began, but he waved me off.

"The foreign minister calls me and asks me if I know what we're doing. I have to reassure him, even though I don't really truly know myself."

I tried to think of something helpful to say. "Is it true that Warren Eldridge is counting the chairs?"

Fred nodded. "Someone contacted him," he said.

"Well," I said, and then couldn't think of what to say after that. An eagle shrieked, or maybe it was a seagull.

"And now," Fred said, "and now. Just this minute, I get off the phone with the president of the United States. He yells at me. Says what kind of pissant operation am I running here, blackening the name of a great American and citizen of the world and risking the historic trust and cooperation between our nations and he has a good mind to put the squeeze on our softwood lumber and our steel and our oil and some other things as well."

"But," I said, "all we've done is ask questions. We haven't even printed the story."

"That's true," Fred said. "And now we're going to print it."

I nodded, then suddenly realized what he had said. "Print the story?" I asked.

"Of course," Fred said.

"Holy shit," Tony said.

"Um . . ." I said. "Might I ask why?"

Fred smiled. I don't think I'd actually seen him smile before. "Nobody else has it," he said.

"That's a fact," I said.

"Besides," Fred said, "I think the president of the United States may be a Saturnian."

"Fred, thank you," I said.

"Call me C. Frederick."

Epilogue

Bribing the disc jockey, a kid from classified, was easy. "I've got two tickets to the next Valleyers game if you'll play some Ella," I said.

"Valleyers are cool," he said. Then a look of cunning came over his face. "How much Ella?" he asked.

"Fifteen minutes will do it," I said.

Moments later, Shirley and I were gliding over the floor of Salon A in the Disney Time Warner Prince of Wales Suites Grand Valley to Ella singing "My Romance." Maybe gliding wasn't the word. I just like to think of it that way. I was sort of fox-trotting, occasionally adding in a little jitterbug thing I vaguely remembered from high school. This involved giving Shirley a twirl which sometimes made it hard for me to hear what she was saying. But she handled it well, conveying the impression that she was dancing with someone who knew what he was doing.

"I like this," she said, at one point between twirls.

"Me too," I said. "I dance every five years or so if I can find the right partner."

"Clearly you have," she said.

"Clearly."

Around us were other, younger dancers, coping a bit less well with the unfamiliar rhythms. Tony and Juanita were barely moving. But then, they had barely moved all night. They clung, and every once in a while one or the other would move a foot or two. The relationship had ripened nicely since the tragic events of Canada Day. Tony was spending the occasional night not working and was talking of getting a master's degree somewhere. Juanita was learning to swear.

From the look of it, they were the only ones in the room not buzzing over the rumours of a new editor. All eyes were on the table beside the bar where James Norwood, who was still our publisher, was greeting every staffer who went to fetch a drink, although not by name. "Compliments of the season," he would say, and then begin a rather lengthy dissertation on how bad next year would be, what with the impact of convergence, new technology, new owners, political uncertainty, and an anticipated hike in the price of paper. He was not even cheered by the rumours that the Pulitzer people were taking a serious look at our Saturn series. After a time, people stopped going to the bar, which made for an uncharacteristically sedate Christmas party.

Of course, there was always hope. Jane Liu told me that the entertainment department table had timed the publisher's trips to the bathroom. When one was imminent, they would loiter in the general vicinity of the bar, just out of the publisher's range, then make a mad dash for it when he vacated his post.

Never being in much of a rush for ginger ale, I was unaffected by this, but kept an eye on him, just as everyone else was doing. Someone in circulation who knew the publisher's secretary well said the new editor announcement was imminent and it might be someone from inside.

This could mean nothing at all. Two weeks ago, someone in classified who knew the publisher's secretary well said the new owners, who had made their money in software and breakfast cereals, were going to wait until February because the guy they wanted from the States wouldn't be available until then.

This buzz felt stronger, though. You can walk into the newsroom some days and just know, without talking to anyone, that something is going on. That same quality was all over this newsroom Christmas party.

"Can you feel it?" I asked Shirley.

"Feel what?" she said, leering in that way I had grown to like.

"Something's going on."

"I know," she said. "About time too."

Smithers had been doing an OK job in the months following Fred's dismissal. The paper got out on time, made a little money, and didn't get into trouble. But something was missing. Now there were rumours that the new owners wanted someone completely unconnected with Fred's regime. The memory of Mrs. Baxter's unfortunate collapse had begun to fade, helped by the sale of all her assets and her subsequent move to that Latin American country where the generalissimo had named her chancellor of the university, the same one that had awarded her honorary doctorate. Still it made sense for the new owners to bring in someone fresh.

None of the candidates mentioned at the party so far sounded promising. The internal ones were particularly scary – Lorne Marshall, for example, whose ability to demonstrate absolute loyalty to whoever sat at the head of the table made him a strong contender. Dick Rivers's name also came up. His big local reputation would make him a useful figurehead, while the new owners did whatever had to be done. I thought I knew what that was. They would cut budgets and squeeze every cent of revenue they could out of the *World-Beacon*. It would become a dull and stingy place to work, but still profitable because people had to buy it to find out who was dead and what was on TV.

"I heard your name," I said to Shirley. Ella was now singing "Where or When."

"I heard it too," she said.

"You'd be great."

"I know," she said. "But it's not going to happen. They just want a token woman in the running. No way I'd get it. Not with the way things are going."

"I know," I said, giving her a little twirl, which unfortunately crashed her into Tony and Juanita who had picked that very moment to move from the spot they had been enjoying for the last forty-five minutes.

"Sorry," I said.

"No fucking problem," Juanita answered.

We all stopped to chat.

"Nice party," I said.

Tony was still all business. "You see that story about the congressman?" he asked.

I hadn't seen it yet, but Shirley had seen tomorrow's sked. "The guy who wants to send the statue of Uncle Bob up here," she said.

"Yeah," Tony said.

"There goes his fucking National Newspaper Award right out the window," Juanita said.

It had taken less than six months for our story to fade. Now Uncle Bob's reputation was slowly being rehabilitated. Congressmen were speaking up. Journalists, mostly sportswriters, were writing pieces that stressed the world-acclaimed evangelist's contributions to fishing and humanity. Uncle Bob, like Pete Rose, was getting a bad rap. The year-end review articles were beginning to appear, Uncle Bob's unfortunate death listed with all the other notable unfortunate deaths of the year, the account of it unmodified by references to his unsavoury angling practices.

I didn't care. "You know what?" I said to Tony.

"What?"

"We got the story," I said, giving Shirley a squeeze. "They can't take that away from us."

Shirley squeezed back and we danced away.

"You know what day it is?" I asked.

"December 17," she said.

"Saturnalia," I said. "Slaves get freed, I think. Wars stop and some other good stuff happens, which I forget right now."

"Happy Saturnalia," she said. Ella sang "Little Girl Blue." The disc jockey looked at me pleadingly. I made a little ticket-rubbing motion behind Shirley's back and he shrugged.

"Something else," she said.

"What?"

"I know where Fred is."

"Wow. Where?"

Fred's disappearances were always as mythical as his appearances. We had been hearing everything. He was a poet in Penticton. He was playing the saxophone on the street in Ottawa. He was writing editorials for the *National Post*. He was working in a zoo in Winnipeg.

"St. John's, Newfoundland."

"Fishing?"

"Editing."

"Wow. A newspaper?"

"Yup," Shirley said. "And he's hiring."

"How do you know that?"

"Because he . . ."

Her answer got lost in a twirl. Twirling myself, I caught sight of Lorne Marshall at the bar, engaged in an intense conversation with the publisher. Jane Liu was tiptoeing behind their backs toward the bar, empty glass in hand. Behind her, Alexei Ponomarev sat by himself at a table, looking unhappy and sketching.

I twirled back to Shirley, stumbling only slightly. "He what?" I asked.

"I said he called me. He offered me a job."

"Which?"

"Managing editor."

"Wow," I said. I knew I was saying "wow" more than I should, but there was a lot of reason to do it. Besides, it was Saturnalia.

"I think I'm going to take it," Shirley said.

"That's crazy," I said.

"I know," she said. "Will you come with me, Parker?"

We danced some more in silence. I smelled her shampoo, an ordinary drugstore brand, but nice, and watched the DJ search through his collection of rap music. This was a race against time.

"How many lakes do they have around there?" I asked.

"Just one little one," she said. "And an ocean."

"Mmmm," I said. "What about Saturnians?"

"I hear it's lousy with them," Shirley said.

"Let's go," I said.

OTHER TITLES FROM
DOUGLAS GIBSON BOOKS

PUBLISHED BY McCLELLAND & STEWART LTD.

AT THE COTTAGE: A Fearless Look at Canada's Summer Obsession *by* Charles Gordon *illustrated by* Graham Pilsworth
This perennial best-selling book of gentle humour is "a delightful reminder of why none of us addicted to cottage life will ever give it up." *Hamilton SpectatorHumour, 6 × 9, 224 pages, illustrations, trade paperback*

THE CANADA TRIP *by* Charles Gordon
Charles Gordon and his wife drove from Ottawa to St. John's to Victoria and back. The result is "a very human, warm, funny book" (*Victoria Times Colonist*) that will set you planning your own trip.
Travel/Humour, 6 × 9, 364 pages, 22 maps, trade paperback

RAVEN'S END: A novel of the Canadian Rockies *by* Ben Gadd
This astonishing book, snapped up by publishers around the world, is like a *Watership Down* set among a flock of ravens managing to survive in the Rockies. "A real classic." Andy Russell
Fiction, 6 × 9, map, 5 drawings, 336 pages, trade paperback

LIVES OF MOTHERS AND DAUGHTERS: Growing Up With Alice Munro *by* Sheila Munro
Part biography of her famous mother, part family memoir (with snapshots), part autobiography, this affectionate memoir will fascinate all of Alice Munro's legions of admirers.
Biography/Memoir, 6 × 9, 60 snapshots, 240 pages, trade paperback

CONFESSIONS OF AN IGLOO DWELLER *by* James Houston
The famous novelist and superb storyteller who brought Inuit art to the outside world recounts his Arctic adventures between 1948 and 1962. "Sheer entertainment, as fascinating as it is charming." *Kirkus Reviews*
Autobiography, 6 × 9, 320 pages, maps, drawings, trade paperback

ZIGZAG: A Life on the Move *by* James Houston
This "remarkable account" (*Books in Canada*) ranges from the Arctic to New York and beyond and tells of Presidents, hunters, glass factory gaffers, leopards, walrus, movies, bestselling books and 10,000-year-old meatballs.
Memoir/Travel, 6 × 9, 288 pages, drawings, trade paperback

HIDEAWAY: Life on the Queen Charlotte Islands *by* James Houston
This gentle book is a song of praise to the rainforest magic of Haida Gwaii, its history, its people, and the little green cottage the author loves. "James Houston finally writes about his own backyard." *National Post*
Memoir/Travel, 6 × 9, 272 pages, 40 b&w illustrations, map, trade paperback

A PASSION FOR NARRATIVE: A Guide for Writing Fiction *by* Jack Hodgins
"One excellent path from original to marketable manuscript. . . . It would take a beginning writer years to work her way through all the goodies Hodgins offers." *Globe and Mail*
Non-fiction/Writing guide, 5¼ × 8½, 216 pages, updated with a new Afterword, trade paperback

OVER FORTY IN BROKEN HILL: Unusual Encounters in the Australian Outback *by* Jack Hodgins
"Australia described with wit, wonder and affection by a bemused visitor with Canadian sensibilities." *Canadian Press* "Damned fine writing." *Books in Canada*   *Travel, 5½ × 8½, 216 pages, trade paperback*

INNOCENT CITIES: A novel *by* Jack Hodgins
Victorian in time and place, this delightful new novel by the author of *The Invention of the World* proves once again that "as a writer, Hodgins is unique among his Canadian contemporaries." *Globe and Mail*
Fiction, 5⅜ × 8⅜, 432 pages, paperback

THE MACKEN CHARM: A novel *by* Jack Hodgins
When the rowdy Mackens gather for a family funeral on Vancouver Island in the 1950s, the result is "fine, funny, sad and readable, a great yarn, the kind only an expert storyteller can produce." *Ottawa Citizen*
Fiction, 5⅜ × 8⅜, 320 pages, trade paperback

BROKEN GROUND: A novel *by* Jack Hodgins
It's 1922 and the shadow of the First World War hangs over a struggling Soldier's Settlement on Vancouver Island. This powerful novel with its flashbacks to the trenches is "a richly, deeply human book – a joy to read." W.J. Keith   *Fiction, 5⅜ × 8⅜, 368 pages, trade paperback*

RED BLOOD: One (Mostly) White Guy's Encounter With the Native World *by* Robert Hunter
The founder of Greenpeace looks back on a wild, hell-raising career. "Hunter acts. He does things. . . . In all his adventures humour is a companion, but he can also write angry political commentary." *Globe and Mail*
Non-fiction, 6 × 9, 280 pages, trade paperback

THE ICE MASTER: A Novel of the Arctic *by* James Houston
Part sea-story (involving a mutiny and a hurricane), part Arctic saga that tells of Inuit and Yankee whalers in the North in 1876, this rousing historical novel is "a straight-away adventure." *Winnipeg Free Press*
Fiction, 6 × 9, 368 pages, 40 drawings, trade paperback

PADDLE TO THE ARCTIC *by* Don Starkell
The author of *Paddle to the Amazon* "has produced another remarkable book" *Quill & Quire*. His 5,000-kilometre trek across the Arctic by kayak or dragging a sled is a "fabulous adventure story." *Halifax Daily News*
Adventure, 6 × 9, 320 pages, maps, photos, trade paperback

PADDLE TO THE AMAZON: The Ultimate 12,000-Mile Canoe Adventure *by* Don Starkell *edited by* Charles Wilkins
From Winnipeg to the mouth of the Amazon by canoe! "This real-life adventure book . . . must be ranked among the classics of the literature of survival." *Montreal Gazette* "Fantastic." Bill Mason
Adventure, 6 × 9, 320 pages, maps, photos, trade paperback

SELECTED STORIES *by* Alice Munro
"The collection of the year," said *Kirkus Reviews* of these 28 superb stories representing Alice Munro's best. "The whole volume makes one believe anew in fiction's power to transfigure." *Washington Post*
Fiction, 6¼ × 9¼, 560 pages, hardcover

THE SELECTED STORIES OF MAVIS GALLANT *by* Mavis Gallant
"A volume to hold and to treasure" said the *Globe and Mail* of the 52 marvellous stories selected from Mavis Gallant's life's work. "It should be in every reader's library." *Fiction, 6⅛ × 9¼ , 900 pages, trade paperback*

THE MERRY HEART: Selections 1980-1995 *by* Robertson Davies
"A marvellous array of Davies' speeches and reviews, interspersed with bits of his personal diaries." *Hamilton Spectator* "It's a happy thing that the voice from the attic is still being heard." *Montreal Gazette*
Non-fiction, 6 × 9, 400 pages, hardcover

HAPPY ALCHEMY: Writings on the Theatre and Other Lively Arts *by* Robertson Davies
"Far more personal than anything published under Davies's name, and all the more enjoyable for it" (*Edmonton Sun*), this collection shows the full range of his wit and wisdom. *Non-fiction, 6 × 9, 400 pages, hardcover*